What People Are Saying About

Journey of a Forsaken Rose

A lively and at times hard-hitting story, where hardly any folk are what they first appear to be.
Piers Anthony, *New York Times* bestselling author of the Xanth series

T0343535

Journey of a Forsaken Rose

A Novel

To my Jack Bentele. Your help was indispensable.
Also for Granny, Nanny and Papa. I couldn't have asked for better
grandparents. You won't be forgotten.

Journey of a Forsaken Rose

A Novel

Kenneth Kelly

ROUNDFIRE
BOOKS

London, UK
Washington, DC, USA

CollectiveInk

First published by Roundfire Books, 2025
Roundfire Books is an imprint of Collective Ink Ltd.,
Unit 11, Shepperton House, 89 Shepperton Road, London, N1 3DF
office@collectiveinkbooks.com
www.collectiveinkbooks.com
www.roundfire-books.com

For distributor details and how to order please visit the 'Ordering' section on our website.

Text copyright: Kenneth Kelly 2024

ISBN: 978 1 80341 752 3
978 1 80341 762 2 (ebook)
Library of Congress Control Number: 2023952676

A CIP catalogue record for this book is available from the British Library.

Design: Lapiz Digital Services

UK: Printed and bound by CPI Group (UK) Ltd, Croydon, CR0 4YY
Printed in North America by CPI GPS partners

We operate a distinctive and ethical publishing philosophy in all areas of our business, from our global network of authors to production and worldwide distribution.

Contents

Prelude Worth the Rose

Graf tapped his finger against his ax handle and watched the tavern across the street. He clamped down on the urge to barrel through the door with the discipline born of a lifetime of training dogs, and four years in the military of Eastern Rising. Much as he wanted to barge in and take care of matters, it wouldn't serve him.

Besides, he respected a tavern owner as well as any man did, and this one had been good to him not long ago. Back when he'd been drowning his sorrows rather than chasing their maker. No gratitude in trashing the man's business or getting him caught up in Graf's. And he'd been raised better than that sort of behavior. He did not want to disappoint the woman who'd raised him.

The door opened and two bodies stumbled out into the street: a man and a woman. The woman looked disheveled and tired, wearing the uniform of a serving girl and an expression of resigned unhappiness. She looked sober and disgusted and very much wished to be back inside if Graf was any judge.

The man, on the other hand, was red-faced, stumbling with drink, and with worse vices on his mind, given the drunken leer he directed at his unwilling companion -. not that it would be a surprise, to Graf or the woman. Every able body in Eastern Rising knew this man, and if asked to speak honestly, well... he doubted very much that there was anyone who liked this man, not even for his coin.

He was drunk and stupid, but he wouldn't stay that way for long if Graf had his way. He checked the lines of his uniform - never mind that he wasn't supposed to wear it any longer - and stepped out of the alley he'd been watching from, approaching with a stoic, confident expression. "Heir Gregor."

The man looked up. So did the woman. Her expression held relief. His held confusion, and the beginnings of a sneer. "What?"

"I've come to collect you. Keeplord's orders." Nothing of the sort, but Gregor wouldn't know that. Graf doubted he was sober enough even to recognize anything beyond the army uniform.

"I'm busy." Gregor threw a sloppy arm around the serving maid's shoulders, with a much more pronounced leer. "Unless you want to watch..."

"No time." No interest either. He knew enough about the kinds of things Gregor did, more than he'd ever wanted to know. As soon as he could get the maid away, Gregor would learn exactly how much Graf knew.

Gregor scowled at him through petulant, wine-bleared eyes, belligerent and uncooperative. Graf decided to move things along.

He took Gregor's arm from around the girl's shoulders, paying no heed to her gasp. It was disrespectful in the extreme, given the difference in their stations, but considering his plans... Graf gave the girl a slow, stoic look. "Back to work - unless you want to take responsibility for him - and get him back to the Keep."

She couldn't back away fast enough after that, disgust and involuntary horror crossing her features as she shook her head frantically. As she staggered back toward the relative safety of the tavern, Graf hid a grim smile.

No sooner had the girl vanished inside than Graf dragged his burden into the alley from which he'd emerged and threw him against the wall. Gregor yelped as his head cracked the wall. "You...!"

"You don't know who I am... yet." Graf considered his ax, but... not yet. "Don't worry. You will."

Gregor did exactly as Graf expected and lurched forward with a wild swipe of clumsy fists. It was easy to deal with after his time in the army, never mind the reflexes he'd developed before that, working with his father. He ignored the incoherent, wine-sotted snarls from the other man as he ducked and dodged. Then, when the cretin was getting tired, he ducked in and planted a solid right fist into Gregor's gut.

The result was as predictable as everything else. Gregor doubled over and heaved, coughing out wine and bile. Graf waited until he was done. "Head a bit clearer yet?"

"I'll have you whipped..." Graf didn't find the words very threatening, given the heaving gasps that came with them. Then again...

"Reckon so. But not before I've had *my* satisfaction out of you." Graf smirked.

Gregor struggled upright, blood and fury starting to chase away the booze-formed haze. "Do you know who I am?!"

"Better than most... Heir Gregor." Graf sneered the title with contempt. "But more important, I know what you did." He punched Gregor square on the jaw, eliciting a yelp and a ringing crack as his teeth snapped together and three of them broke under the onslaught.

The last haze of booze induced stupidity was gone now. Graf grinned as Gregor backed up, wild-eyed and panting, with blood dripping down his chin. He wasn't at all surprised when Gregor drew the ornate short sword at his hip and swiped in his direction.

It was all the reason he needed to draw his ax, parrying the blows with a lazy skill he'd picked up during his service. He'd been a well-respected soldier in Eastern Rising before he'd been dismissed for his temper, and one too many brawls. If Gregor had ever paid any attention to anything beyond his perverted pleasures, he might have known that.

But he never had. He'd never had eyes for anything other than food and drink and his increasingly unsavory desires. Graf's eyes darkened, his blocks turning a bit sharper with the unwanted memories.

Everyone in Eastern Rising knew Gregor and his appetites. And everyone knew his father wouldn't do a thing. He was too concerned with family reputation, never mind that putting a firm hand on Gregor would have done more for his family's honor than the blind eye he turned.

Anger replaced the lazy anticipation. Graf dodged the next sword swing and brought the ax around to cut a relatively shallow line in Gregor's sword arm. A real soldier wouldn't have cared, but Gregor shrieked and dropped his weapon.

Graf feinted to send him back against the nearest wall, then brought the ax forward in a stabbing motion that pinned one shoulder of Gregor's fancy, though stained, tunic against the wall. A quick motion scooped up the sword Gregor had dropped and pinned the other shoulder.

Gregor yelped and cowered back. Graf might have given him points for not sniveling, in other circumstances. "Remember me, yet?"

He might have saved his breath. The wide, bloodshot eyes showed no sign of recognition. He hadn't really expected it, though he'd hoped Gregor wasn't quite as stupid as he seemed. "Let me help you."

He drew the last weapon on his person, a blue-fire opal decorated dagger his mother had gifted him with when he'd been accepted into the ranks. Gregor's eyes followed it. "You might recognize this. It belonged to a woman who showed distinction in the territory wars a few years back. Before my time. Or yours, I suppose. But she was wounded, sent out. Fell in love. Married the Kennel Master here."

Now there was comprehension in Gregor's eyes. Graf smiled grimly. "I see you do know her. Know she died recently?"

He hadn't needed to ask. But he did rather like the terror dawning in Gregor's eyes. "She... she... she..."

"She was killed. In her own home. With her daughter." Graf folded his arms, deliberately keeping the knife where Gregor could see it, see the sun glinting off the edge. "After other things. Guess the killer thought no one would care much, seeing as her husband died years ago." He watched the flicker of relief, and confusion, on Gregor's face.

The feral expression of a wild dog slipped over his own. "Guess the bastard forgot she had a son. Or thought he'd never know, since he was out guarding a merchant train."

Graf lurched forward, slamming his hand against the rough wood and earning a yelping cringe in return. "Or maybe... maybe you just thought no one would talk, being who you are. Or maybe you thought no one would come for you."

Fear and arrogance chased themselves over Gregor's ugly, bloodstained face. "If you kill me..."

"Thought about it." Graf shook his head. "But death's easy. Final. You die, everyone will make up the stories and swallow them down, no matter how rotten they are. Death's simple."

He held the knife up. Gregor flinched back.

"I want you to hurt. To live with your lesson. To have no choice about it. So, I thought of something else."

Graf smiled, a feral, ugly smile that he'd learned from vicious dogs and vicious people alike. His free hand shot out, grabbing Gregor's belt, pausing as he savored the sudden whitening of Gregor's face.

"When Stablemasters get a wild stallion, they geld him. We do it too, with dogs not meant for breeding. Best way to tame a beast down." He flicked a finger against the belt-knot, watching Gregor tremble and try to cower closer to the wall.

"I wonder... geld a man, does it work the same?" Gregor actually whimpered.

Graf tightened the grip on his knife. "I wonder, Heir Gregor..." He leaned in, right next to the quivering man's ear.

"Ever thought about what life would be like, if you lost *your* balls?"

Gregor whimpered again.

Graf smirked.

Chapter 1

Exile

The whole thing was a farce. Graf knew that. The Historian working on his arm knew that. Everyone in Eastern Rising would have known that... if they'd known what was happening. But then, that was likely the reason this whole thing was taking place at dusk, without witnesses, contrary to tradition. Maybe the Keeplord knew the truth, maybe he just didn't want the possible outcry, if Eastern Rising had known what was happening.

Graf shook his head, bemused. Of course, the Keeplord wouldn't want any disruption of his iron rule. He let his mind wander, distracting himself from the prickling sensation shooting up and down his forearm.

Eastern Rising was - as the name implied - a far eastern community. It was fairly isolated, almost estranged from other civilized bastions. Travelers and merchants were rare, and strangers were almost unheard of and almost never welcomed with open arms. Eastern Rising was a community dependent on farming and livestock, with supplemental game provided by the surrounding forest, and mostly self-sufficient.

The community as a whole was ruled with an iron fist by the Keeplords, lords by lineage; their word deemed infallible law. Punishments against the laws laid down by the Keeplord were numerous: servitude, slavery, manual labor, fines, and - the worst of all - branding with the Black Rose, and banishment.

Graf and his family had always been near the bottom of the hierarchy. According to tradition, the hierarchy started with the Keeplord, Keeplord's family, followed by Historians, Merchants, Shopkeepers, the Guard, and the Serfs - working

1

class - in that order. Graf's family had been low on the ladder, just above convicted slaves and indentured servants.

Graf's family had been charged, generations prior, with the breeding, training, and housing of the dogs who served with the city's watchmen, patrolling the city's borders and accompanying the rare trade caravans. The dogs weren't actually any distinct breed; they were mutts descending from centuries of interbreeding until the inevitable result - medium sized dogs with long, coarse fur in a range of colors. Loyal dogs, physically strong and quick to act if threatened.

After taking over the role of Dog Keeper upon his father's death, Graf had learned why his father had held animals in such high esteem over his fellow townsmen. Dogs responded to love with love, whereas townsmen often responded to love with betrayal, superstition, and animosity. And richer men with contempt for the poverty they themselves often caused.

Graf, like all the peasants - indeed, all save the elite merchants and tradesmen - earned almost nothing for his life's work. The majority of gold, silver, or copper earned went to the Keeplord, who dispensed it among the serfs as he pleased - which wasn't often.

That was why Graf had followed his mother's footsteps into the Guard as soon as he came of age. Working with his father had kept him active and fit, and he'd done well enough. The instincts and reflexes honed by working with guard dogs served him well and earned him the respect his sullen nature and quick temper might have denied him otherwise. Those skills, along with the ones he'd honed on the training fields and in rare combats and hunting trips had been why he'd been selected to accompany the trading caravan the last time they'd gone. It had been a great honor, but one he hadn't appreciated much, seeing how it took him from home, from his dogs, his mother, and his sister.

He wouldn't have gone if the guard captain hadn't told him he could be discharged and slapped with servitude for refusing, or go and come back to a dismissal for his tendency to get into brawls at little-to-no provocation. Dismissal for his temper wasn't great, but it was better than the alternative.

Or so he'd thought at the time. But then, he hadn't known...

The pricking had stopped. Graf shook his head to clear his thoughts. He couldn't afford to be too inattentive now.

Graf was a young man in his twenties, whose work had kept him lean, fit, and sharp of mind. Like most townsmen, he was well-built, with curly brown hair and a mustache that fell over his upper lip and the corners of his mouth like a fall of raw honey. He could have easily merged into any crowd in the host of villagers, except for the small scar just under one eye - a reminder of careless horseplay with his father's dogs as a boy. Until the Guard, he'd been virtually unknown among his fellow inhabitants of Eastern Rising, given that he'd never spoken to anyone much outside his family, his dogs, and the guards who came to test and collect the fully trained animals once they were grown.

He wasn't unknown now. Graf fought back the grim smile that wanted to escape him. Not unknown, not with his time in the Guard and the incident for which he'd been arrested. Not unknown, and not the social pariah most in his position would be.

A rose by any other name might smell as sweet - but the Black Rose of Eastern Rising was meant to be the sign of an outcast, of the unwelcome, of those doomed to eternally roam the Wanwood, never to see their friends and family again.

Most times, the whole town would turn out to see a branding and a banishment. To see, to jeer, to show their scorn. That was why, traditionally, the whole thing was done at midday, so everyone could see.

But not with Graf, and he'd bet every one of his recently confiscated possessions that he knew why.

Graf was hauled to his feet, arm stinging and smarting with the newly branded Black Rose. The Keeplord faced him, the ominous bulk of the East Gate rising as a darker outline against the dark sky. "Greetings, people of Eastern Rising!"

Graf snorted and received a rough prod in the ribs in response. There was no one there. No one but the Keeplord, the Historian... and the guards, who were probably nursing a grudge for what Graf had managed to do to their charge. Never mind that they'd been the ones to take their eyes off of him. Or that the cockroach had deserved it, and more.

The Keeplord kept speaking, following the rote words, despite the irregularity of everything else. "It is according to tradition that the Black Rose be cast into the Wanwood."

Silence, though why anyone would expect anything else, Graf had no idea. They were holding this whole empty pageant of tradition in the dead of night, far from the protests that might have come.

It could have been - would have been - argued that Graf had performed a community service. Done what needed to be done and eliminated a parasite and a pervert from further infecting their city. In other circumstances, Graf might even have received a reward for saving the guard and the Keeplord the trouble.

In any other circumstances.

"Historian." The Keeplord turned his pompous gaze to the elder woman in hooded white robes beside him. "State the reason for his expulsion."

A shrill voice echoed from the hood. "Assault and Maiming of the First Heir of Eastern Rising... without provocation and in cold blood."

Graf snorted, listening to that shrill, whispering voice. It was just like most of what made up the way of life in Eastern Rising - empty. The 'farewell' ceremony was just a formality; a mask

4

to extend the propaganda of a harmonious utopia. Everyone knew the Keeplord's son - Heir Gregor Firstborn - was a pervert and a wart on the collective existence of the town. There were witnesses to his many perversions. But the Keeplord's word was law.

And the Keeplord's word was that his family and their exploits should be immortalized in the record halls. Accordingly, the legacy of Graf's family would wither like dog turds in the sun.

The Keeplord continued with his useless, pointless, speech. "May this be a warning to all! To become a Black Rose is a fate worse than death! In death, there is remembrance... a legacy to pass on to future generations. But the Black Rose will have none of that... for he is... omitted."

It was meant to sound ominous. It sounded ridiculous to Graf. He didn't bother trying to contain his sneer as he was shoved roughly forward. Say what he liked, but he doubted the Keeplord would be *omitting* him from the memories of Eastern Rising. They could end his family's records with the 'disgrace' of his banishment, but the guards who'd served with him and the many people who'd known what Gregor was and what he'd done... well, they wouldn't forget him in a hurry.

Especially Gregor.

He wondered how they were going to 'immortalize' Gregor's 'tragic' circumstances, without his name.

The guards shoved him forward again. It was custom, as he'd learned in the little childhood schooling he'd had, for the Keeplord to escort the Black Rose through the gate to the Boundary line - the enchanted border that decided who could enter and who could leave Eastern Rising, and ensured no Black Rose ever returned. There he would be given a knapsack with dried fruit and meat, a fire-starting kit, and a flask of water. He'd also have returned to him one personal item, aside from the clothing on his back. In his case, it was the blue fire opal blade, with its handle of bone, formed from the jaw of a coyote.

Graf's grandfather had killed that coyote up north many years ago on a hunting trip. Currently, the sacred family possession was in the fat, oily hands of the Keeplord.

The Keeplord stopped just inside the gate and tossed the dagger at Graf's feet. "You know, it won't be hard to replace your sorry ass."

"Stuff you. Your son was a bastard, a vagrant, and a pervert. And I didn't do *anything* in cold blood." Graf's voice dripped with all the contempt he could muster. It wasn't like he needed to hold back anymore.

The Keeplord laughed and raised a hand to study his nails with nonchalant arrogance. "Oh, well, either way... I do suppose I should thank you. After all, my eldest *was* doing a wonderful job of destroying my family's reputation. Quite honestly, I was getting sick of sweeping his little... exploits... under the rug."

Fury ignited in Graf. "Then... you knew. You knew all along what he did, why I acted...!" He saw the guards shift uneasily and felt savage satisfaction. They'd look for answers, for all they were angry that he'd caused trouble on their watch. Another dagger in the Keeplord's chances of sweeping *this* under the rug.

The Keeplord scowled. "I don't care." He moved forward until his rank, rotten breath was blowing directly in Graf's face. "I don't care what he did, or why you chose to act. I don't care if he murdered your family, had his way with the women, served them up for dinner, or anything else."

He sneered. "You just don't seem to understand. My life's work, and that of my children and their children, will be written down by the Historians and entered into the Hall of Records for all time. How would it look if future generations were to read of a man with royal blood doing... such things? And then getting punished by a common dogs-boy, of all things. It would be a travesty, a disgrace. But you..."

He laughed, low and ugly. "Nobody cares about your family's legacy Graf. Nobody cares about your mother, your sister... their unhappy passing... or you. So, in the end... well, it's unfortunate, but it's better you than me and mine that takes the fall."

Graf saw red. He ducked back, grabbing the knapsack and his dagger. The Keeplord flinched back, trying to keep his composure even as his body language displayed his fear, easy for Graf to read after so many years working with dogs and men alike.

His pride was his undoing. Graf had been forced to take a half-step forward to reach the flint and opal dagger, and he used the momentum to his advantage. A sharp jerk upward made the Keeplord flinch back, opening himself up. Graf moved sideways, already anticipating the next move he'd have to make, and slid the sharp blade across the Keeplord's fat throat. He shoved off the stone wall, changing direction and bounding forward, head down as he dove across the warding line. His last glimpse as he crossed the Boundary was of the Keeplord's tubby body falling in a shower of crimson, and the guards just raising their bows to fire the first volley of arrows.

Graf stepped back into the concealing foliage, anger draining to grim satisfaction. Just let them try to erase him and his legacy from the Histories now.

Yet all things considered, he would miss the dogs.

***

There was a big difference between forced solitude and chosen solitude.

Graf never had been very sociable. He'd never been talkative with his neighbors or distant relatives. He'd only ever really spoken with those he was obligated to during his day-to-day tasks. Most of the people in Eastern Rising were paranoid and often a bit shifty, performing good deeds to suit their own needs or merely to save face. You couldn't tell which was which, either. Trust had never been high on Graf's list of options.

But now it was different. Now he no longer had the option of speaking to anyone, even if he wanted to. There wasn't a soul around.

He'd barely entered the outskirts of the forest when the magic had kicked in. He'd looked back to see if there was any pursuit, only to be greeted by an endless wall of trees as far as he could see. The path he'd thought he was on was gone, and he was surrounded by knotted oak limbs, stickler bushes and thorny, tangled vines. Mixed among the drifts of underbrush and old leaves were saplings, reaching from the ground like thousands of haggard fingers and swiping against his leg with every step he took.

North, south, east, west… it no longer mattered much which direction he took. Directions didn't mean much in the Wanwood.

Graf stared around for a moment. "Charming place. Wonder if the inn has fresh sheets."

He shook his head at the unaccustomed whimsy. *They say it's okay to talk to yourself, as long as you don't answer back. Still, I wouldn't want the creatures of the Wanwood writing me off as noodle-brained on my first day here.*

Except there didn't seem to be many creatures. There was very little wildlife at all to be found as Graf trudged on. Even bugs, worms and grubs were scarce. Graf kept going, using his knife sparingly to cut through the vegetation.

Minutes turned to hours, and Graf lost all sense of time. The temperature began to drop as the light dimmed, and the shadowy forest quickly became black as tar. Graf hadn't bothered scavenging for food, deciding to use his pre-packed rations. They wouldn't last forever though. He put that from his mind. *I'll cross that bridge when I reach it.* Hopefully, he'd have found more food by then.

As cold as it was getting, Graf knew he'd have to start a fire to keep from catching a chill. Within the knapsack, he found the expected flint and steel fire starters. He gathered some tinder, and larger branches to build a nest on the ground between two large oak tree roots before the last rays of the sunset faded. It only took a few strikes to light the char cloth and a second to slide it into the pocket under the tinder, and soon Graf had a modest fire going.

He ate some jerky and nuts while staring at the fire, following the traditions of ancient human pastimes long forgotten, until the smoldering fire, burning low, sent him into a light doze.

It wasn't long before sounds roused him.

He couldn't make out the features in the dark, not even now that his vision had adjusted, but by the smell, it was canine. Graf had assumed his food bag might attract animals, and he'd hung it from the limb of a nearby tree, but he had been rather careless with his munching. In the moonlight, he saw the outline of the mongrel sniffing around. Graf kept still, knowing any sudden movements or sounds could surprise the dog and cause its defense mechanisms to kick in. He didn't feel like getting bitten.

The dog finally gave up its foraging, and Graf saw it wander to the other side of the small clearing and lay down. Soon it was snoring, and not long after that, Graf felt himself follow it into slumber.

When daylight arrived the following morning, Graf was surprised to find the dog still nestled in the crook of the adjacent tree root. It was a large, white dog, a female who'd recently given birth, to judge by the flabby looking teats. His movements woke her, and she started to rise, tensing to flee when she saw him.

Graf called out to her, using a phrase his father had taught him. To his surprise, she stopped. He got to his knees and reached out his hand for her to sniff. She was receptive enough to his affectionate gestures, and she was soon in his lap sniffing at and licking his face.

Graf grinned. "We understand each other, don't we?" She whimpered in excitement and, he thought, agreement.

Connecting with animals, especially dogs, had always come naturally for Graf. People were too often lying, hypocritical and conniving, at least in his experience. Many would sell out their own mothers for quick coin, and even those that helped you usually did so with some stipulation to benefit them. Animals, on the other hand, were honest and loved without conditions.

"What should I call you?" He didn't expect an answer from the dog, his own mind working on the question.

Up close in the morning light, her coat was an off-white color, similar to the ivory a trader had brought back to Eastern Rising once when he was a boy. Such a luxury had been far beyond his family's means, but he'd been fascinated by the tales of the creatures from which it came.

"How about Ivory?" The dog responded by slobbering all over his face. Graf chuckled. "Well, I guess that settles it. Ivory."

Chapter 2

Encounter

Ivory turned out to be quite efficient in hunting and retrieving small game. Graf wasn't fond of rabbit and was often still hungry after splitting the meager meals with his companion. She deserved as much as he could spare though. Without her, Graf imagined his hunger would have been a lot worse.

A few uneventful days passed. The terrain of the forest changed the further in they went. The oak and maple trees were still incredibly dense, but they thinned out enough that Graf could cover more distance each day. Eventually, they found the head of a small stream emerging from an outcropping of rocks at the base of a hill. The minute stream grew larger and larger until they found themselves in a small clearing containing a sizable pond.

Ivory tore off into the pond, splashing and doggy paddling about in the center. Graf took a sniff of himself under his wool tunic and cringed. "No wonder I don't see much wildlife. Even the dung flies are avoiding me."

Graf dropped his bag and took off his clothing. The sun was at its zenith over the pond. Shattered light refracted off the water as if through diamond, creating a bright kaleidoscope of color that blinded Graf. He rinsed the worst of the sweat and grime of his journey from his clothes and hung them in a nearby tree to dry. Then he dove in.

The water was crystal clear throughout, not murky and algae-filled like the lake back home. He submerged his entire body underwater and swam to the bottom. Vegetation covered the floor like a blanket made of ferns, mosses, and narrow-leafed plants that shot up like swords. Something shot by his head, and Graf nearly choked and inhaled water before he saw it was just a catfish. Looking up, he could see Ivory's underbelly - she seemed mesmerized by the purple flowers of the lily pads. The air chilled his skin as he resurfaced, despite the warmth of the sun. After calling Ivory back to dry land, he sat down to relax on a slab of granite perched on the edge of the pond. For the first time in a while, he felt content, happy even. He was no longer enslaved by the rules of the Keeplord, and he could live his life as he saw fit. "I could get used to this."

His peaceful frame of mind didn't last long.

Ivory came bounding up to Graf clutching a stick in her mouth. *Smart dog.* As he took the stick, he realized something alarming that destroyed his peaceful frame of mind; the stick was actually the bone of a human arm.

"Where'd you get this, girl?" As if understanding, Ivory began tracking, sniffing back and forth along the bank of the pond. She stopped, pawed the dirt a bit, and barked at Graf, tail wagging a mile a minute. Walking up to stand beside her, Graf looked down at a cracked human skull. Now that he was looking, he could see other human remains scattered around in his peripheral vision, half-buried in the grass and vegetation.

"This isn't an oasis... it's a graveyard." Graf gripped Ivory's fur tight.

The ground began to shake, and Graf could hear a strange gurgling noise as bubbles began to appear on the surface of the water. The bubbles intensified as they began moving toward the shore where they were standing. Ivory hunched down in attack mode, her hackles raised and her tail rigid as she began barking and snapping her teeth in the direction of the disturbed water.

"Ivory! Get away from the..." Graf's warning cut off as a loud blast drowned all sound and water exploded into the air.

Things seemed eerily calm as the water settled, until Graf noticed something strange about the air hovering just above the water. Like fumes above a flame, the air seemed to ripple and quiver. Seconds later, several tentacles appeared as the water sluiced off them. By the time Graf recognized them for what they were, it was too late.

A translucent tentacle shot forward to ensnare him. As more water dripped from the rubbery flesh of the beast, Graf was horrified to see the underside of the tentacle was covered in fist-sized suckers, each of which in turn contained dozens of razor-sharp teeth. Another tentacle shot forward, wrapping around his legs, arms, and torso, lifting him into the air. Searing pain shot through him as the suckers gripped him, and he could see blood oozing from the connections made by the slurping attachments.

He heard Ivory's relentless barking and caught a glimpse of her on the shore. "No, Ivory! Get away!" She didn't heed his warning.

Loyal to her new master, Ivory continued her war dance as another now-visible tentacle approached her. She dove fearlessly at the appendage and sank her teeth deep into its flesh. Merely annoyed, the tentacle smacked the dog aside and sent her flying into a nearby tree. Graf heard her yelp upon impact. He was relieved to see her hobble away into the forest, battered but not dead. Then the water roared to life beneath him and he was turned upside down above the water, held by the tentacle around his ankle. Graf looked down and gasped at what he saw.

"Oh God!"

A hideous face seemed to form out of the water itself, curiously human-like except for the snake-like slits that formed its nose. As water streamed off the face, it became more visible, and Graf could see that the flesh was of a burgundy color, while the eight tentacles surging around him were a rich sapphire blue. Its eyes shone a blinding red, and a voice that sounded oddly female issued from its gaping mouth.

"For centuries this pond has been my sanctuary. And for centuries you wretched creatures have continued to come and defile my waters. Now you dare bring a mangy beast to defecate, drool, and clot my home with its mangy fur?" The beast shook Graf's body, causing a rush of blood to his head that made him dizzy.

"I didn't know this pond was spoken for." Graf knew that screaming or making threats wouldn't help his situation, and did his best to remain calm.

"Ignorance is no excuse! If I barged into your village your men would cut me down in seconds. They'd feast on my flesh and consider it a delicacy, while your king used my skin as battle attire."

Graf doubted that. Eastern Rising was full of superstitious louts, and they didn't even have a king now. But he couldn't deny they'd have probably killed the creature.

Nonetheless, being dangled upside down for useless debate was getting old. "If you're going to eat me, then shut up and do it! I hate loud mouths."

The beast laughed. "And what fun would that be? No... I think not. You came to my home to pollute it with your rank secretions and torture me with your stink. I'll flap my gums as much as I want."

Graf snorted. "Flap your gums? I'd expect a creature of your age and power to have a more sophisticated vocabulary."

The beast let out a shriek that threatened to blow out Graf's eardrums. Covering his ears did little to shield them from the noise, but as he raised his arms, the beast stopped suddenly.

"Black Jade! I've seen that mark before... where are you from, man creature?"

The creature dropped Graf into the shallow water. It wasn't deep enough to stop his fall, and his head smacked into the rocks on the bottom. He surfaced quickly to face the creature, blood dripping from the several sucker-caused wounds.

His pack, his knife… even his clothes were several yards away. At that, he wasn't sure what good his knife would do against a being of her magnitude. He might have been an accomplished soldier, but his opponents had only ever been humans and dumb wild beasts like wolves and deer, not a creature like this. He knew no magic, like the spoken incantations the Historians possessed. In this moment, he felt dull and pitiful, a weak and useless creature.

He swallowed the feeling and answered the question in the simplest terms possible. "Eastern Rising."

"Bernholt…" Her voice seemed distant.

"Huh?"

The creature's body began to shrink and her tentacles retracted, transforming into a smaller, more humanoid form. Though her color and facial features remained the same, her body was now very much like a human female. It was a startling transformation. She must have noticed his bewilderment and spoke with a gentle tone.

"My name is Syncletica, but you can call me Syncie. I've assumed a form more pleasing to you. I apologize for my aggression, but I'm the last of my kind, and I can't afford to be welcoming to strangers."

She began to walk toward Graf, displaying her shapely new body. He'd be lying if he denied being… interested… in her, but after experiencing her true power he was more inclined to panic as she reached out to touch a wound on his chest. He gasped and fell back into the water.

"Fear not. I mean to heal your wounds. If you'll allow me." Syncie extended her arm once more.

Graf calmed and allowed her to touch him. His body shuddered with an ecstasy that both excited and disturbed him. If he hadn't been aroused before, he definitely was now.

The pain in his body was gone, and the wounds created by the suckers had been healed. Looking down, he noticed that healing him wasn't all her touch had done.

"Oh!" Graf covered himself with his hands. "I'm sorry... I didn't..." He flushed.

"Don't be embarrassed, man creature."

"Call me Graf, since it seems we're on a first name basis."

"That we are," Syncie giggled. "That we are. As I was saying, it's only a side effect of the healing process. The same thing happened to Bernholt."

Graf's discomfort was replaced by curiosity. "You've mentioned that name twice now. Who was this Bernholt?"

"He also hailed from Eastern Rising. He rescued my pond from being defiled by wolves that used to swarm this part of the wood. That tattoo was on his arm as well... though that was nearly a thousand years ago..."

"I've never heard of him."

Syncie smiled. "He went by a different name, at our first meeting. Briar... I've forgotten the rest.

He spoke words of sweetness and honey, and I was lonely. I was not used to being so alone. So, I listened, despite the falsehoods in his voice. He was a rogue, words like a rose with hidden thorns, but he behaved well enough with me."

Graf didn't doubt that. He was rather hoping he managed to 'behave well enough' for the remainder of their interactions.

Syncie continued. "When the wolves came, he fought them and drove them away with tricks and clever traps and words and weapons. Drove them away and followed them on so they would never return. He came back once, to tell me the wolves were gone for good. But he was known as Bernholt by then, and he left once more and never returned."

He sounded like an interesting fellow. Although, the Black Rose implied something different than Syncie's fond memories. "The Black Rose isn't exactly a beauty mark where I'm from. It's what they give those who are exiled for murder and the like. I don't know his crime, but…"

"He never said, though he was a rascal." Syncie eyed Graf with her ruby gaze. "And what was yours?"

"I won't deny it. I maimed a man, in vengeance for the loved ones he stole from me. He took my family, defiled my sister, and killed my kin. I made sure he'd never do so much to anyone else. The rest is history, and I don't regret it."

Syncie smiled, and Graf relaxed. "I can hear the truth in your words, Graf." She blew a soft breath. "Bernholt saved my life and my home, and I vowed that whenever he or others like him came to my waters, they would find refuge. I only wish I'd spotted your mark sooner."

Graf heard growling and turned to see Ivory limping back into the clearing, obviously hurt but still eager to defend him.

"Easy girl." Graf signaled her to stand down.

"I can heal her too, if she'll allow me."

Graf nodded and waded toward Ivory. He knelt in the shallow water and held out his hand, calling to her. Ivory calmed but kept her guard up, walking to Graf's side and no further.

"It's okay." Graf stroked her back. The dog relaxed as Syncie reached out her hand and placed it on her head.

There was a blast of blinding light, and a giggle from Syncie. "Oh, I see. And you didn't wish to…"

A low noise from Ivory. Another high, watery sound of amusement from Syncie. "In your own time then. I'll not spoil your fun. He is quite a good match."

The spots cleared from Graf's eyes and he looked down to see Ivory on her back, rolling around in the mud. She shot up like a lightning bolt and tore off again into the water, and Graf could have sworn she looked smug, for a dog.

Syncie giggled again. It was a weird sound and, unlike her speech, didn't sound human. "Now that I know you as a friend instead of an interloper or an enemy, you have my permission to swim in my water any time you'd like. It'd be nice to have company stay for a while. And who knows... maybe the better we get to know each other..." She smirked and placed a hand on Graf's face. It transformed back into a tentacle and began to sensuously wrap around his chest, then his waist, then lower... Graf quickly backed away.

"I'm sure I could be quite happy here. I know I wouldn't have to worry about being bothered by outside forces - but I've only just arrived in the wood. Not that I have any real goals, but I don't want to..." He broke off, unsure how to speak his mind without causing offense.

"You want to look around." There was that strange laugh again. "I had forgotten that you've only just arrived in the wood... a stranger in a strange land."

Had he ever told her that? He didn't remember it. He shrugged. "It's no offense to you, er... Syncletica... I just need to get my head on straight."

She nodded, seeming more amused than offended. "I would come as well, but I am unable to travel far beyond my pond. I'll die if I go too long without water." A rippling shrug. "I don't know what awaits you, but I will warn you... I am not the only entity or obstacle you'll cross. And not all will be as receptive as I."

Receptive indeed, Graf thought... and hoped she didn't hear it.

"Can you at least point us in the right direction? Are there any settlements around? I'm not exactly a 'live-off-the-land' type, and I would appreciate a place where I can at least get established."

Syncie stepped back into the deeper water, transforming and becoming invisible as she submerged.

18

"Take the trail bearing north. Find the man with a thousand names. He will guide you." Her voice echoed in the clearing.

"Well, that narrows it down." Graf threw his hands in the air in frustration. "How will I even know where he is, or if I'll recognize him when I see him? Is he even safe?"

A rippling, gurgling giggle. "That depends on your definition of safe."

Chapter 3

Burl

Graf had several reasons for not staying at the pond. First and foremost was Syncie's unpredictable nature. One moment she had tried to eat him, the next she was molesting him and almost his lover. In his life, Graf had encountered several unbalanced women with poor outcomes, and those women didn't grow tentacles or quadruple in size. With Syncie, the slightest misunderstanding might cause Graf to lose his life.

Then again, maybe I'm just finicky about selecting partners.

Ivory barked. Graf looked down at the dog heeled beside him. They'd been walking for what seemed like hours along the narrow ill-kept path. And every time he became lost in thought she'd bark or yelp or nudge him, as if she could hear his thoughts and disapproved.

"Already jealous of my side women?" Graf joked. Ivory fixed him with an annoyed glare and looked off further down the trail. *She certainly has personality.*

The prospect of making love to Syncie was yet another reason he chose not to stay. In the height of passion, she could easily kill him. It might be unintentional, but death didn't discriminate.

What quality of life could be had living beside the pond? While life had never provided many luxuries for Graf, he was still a man of domestic lifestyle preferences. He was used to sleeping on beds with stuffed mattresses, with a well-built roof over his head, however crooked that roof might be. The romance of sleeping on the ground under the stars could only take a man so far - and a few long trips on guard duty for trading caravans had removed much of the romanticism for Graf, even before his exile.

Getting a meal and listening to the gossip over a pint at a local tavern in town didn't sound so bad either. Graf had taken the companionship of others for granted most of his life and forced solitude had helped him realize just how much.

The path seemed to go on without end, twisting and turning through the foliage. As far as Graf was concerned, every other tree appeared the same. He made camp at nightfall and left camp at daybreak. A week passed uneventfully, with the only notable change being that Graf's hatred of eating rabbit, grouse, and woodland berries had been firmly cemented.

On the other hand, at least he had Ivory. She kept him company, kept him fed, and warm. After another day of pointless, exhausting trekking, she curled up next to him and snuggled close.

Graf patted her head. "You've been awful loving lately."

The dog lay beside him near the fire, her head draped across his thigh. The fire was fairly small. It had nearly died out with the cool breeze wafting through the clearing they'd found.

Ivory roused when he spoke to her, lifting her body and reaching her head up to lick Graf's cheek. She placed a paw on his chest and stared into his eyes.

Graf chuckled. "Okay, Miss Frisk. Time to sleep." Graf patted her rump and reached back to move the pack he'd been leaning against.

The first part of the night passed in silence, save for the hoot of a great horned owl and Ivory's snoring. It kept Graf awake, as usual, but he knew he'd pass out eventually. He didn't bother to put out the remains of the fire. He'd encountered no foe since leaving the pond and was beginning to believe that whatever beasts once inhabited the forest were dead or gone.

He was about to be proven wrong.

A bellowing wail rang in Graf's ears, snatching him from the threshold of dreams. His reflexes slowed by grogginess,

Graf was barely able to roll out of the way as a huge oak limb came crashing into the ground where he'd been lying. It wasn't mere coincidence; the limb had been thrown like a spear. It was roughly the length of Graf's body and stuck up almost vertically from the ground, where it had planted itself.

Graf's body trembled with shock and adrenaline, and he was almost of a mind to check himself for soiled trousers. Ivory barked ferociously, looking up into the trees behind their crude campfire.

Graf followed her gaze. Then he saw it.

Tumbling out of the tree like a spider, a giant form hit the ground on its hind legs with tremendous force. Graf had kept his dagger at his side since the incident at the pond, but the being was on him before he could grab it from his waist. The incredibly agile giant charged into Graf at breakneck speed, stooping low and scooping Graf's legs out from under him. The creature heaved Graf upwards of eight feet in the air before flipping him sideways and slamming him into the soil.

"Damn!" Graf choked out a curse.

The throw was similar to takedowns he'd practiced as a youth and in the Guard, wrestling his associates, but far more violent. He landed hard on his left shoulder, jamming it badly as his breath was knocked from him. He gasped for air, panicking at the thought he wouldn't be able to catch his breath before the beast stomped him to death.

"Aaargh!" A foot the size of a human torso planted itself in Graf's stomach. Then he was released as the giant screamed and backed away.

Graf could see Ivory dangling from the giant's forearm. Obviously, no one messed with her human and got away with it. Graf used the distraction to get to his feet and get his dagger free. Dagger in hand, Graf lunged at the giant's midsection. Darkness made it difficult for him to judge the distance, and the dagger only nicked the beast's side. Ivory's body was thrown into Graf, sending the pair falling to the ground once more.

"Ivory, Go get 'em, girl!" Graf motioned to the giant.

Despite appearing to be an overweight mama, Ivory's reflexes and bite were beyond the norm. Even when compared to some of Graf's best-trained guard dogs, her speed, agility, and overall drive when fighting seemed endless. *What's her secret?*

Ivory jumped on the beast's chest, biting at its neck. Sweat-soaked forearms glistened in the moonlight as it tried to protect its face from the dog. Screams and canine snarls echoed through the forest as the two continued their combat. Even a dog with Ivory's stamina would fall off eventually, and Graf knew he had to do something.

"Hold on, girl!" He moved in.

It had been a while since he'd practiced kicking, but his years of training in all forms of martial arts had ingrained a certain amount of flexibility in Graf. Shuffling forward, he launched off his back leg and threw a vicious kick at the behemoth's groin. The blow was directed at the height of an average man's head, and Graf's hamstrings burned as he felt his boot strike flesh.

"Blah!" The hulking form toppled over.

Graf grabbed the oak limb the giant had tried to spear him with earlier and swung it over his head. He struck down hard, like a man chopping firewood, and one thud followed another as his strike connected and the being fell motionless onto the damp earth.

"What the hell was that about?" Graf dropped the branch and went to Ivory.

The dog was unhurt, but her body language quickly alerted him that the threat wasn't over. Another howl whistled on the wind, followed by a second, a third, and a fourth. Soon Graf could hear dozens of bestial cries.

Graf looked at the dark outline of the fallen monster's body. "You've got friends, huh?"

The wild azalea shrubs beside them suddenly came to life and another gigantic shape tackled Graf to the ground. He heard Ivory's bark and the beast's groan as she latched on.

"Call off the bitch! I'm trying to help you!" Rank breath accompanied an unnaturally low voice.

"Ivory, stop!" Graf struggled to free himself from the giant's grasp, but to no avail. "Who are you and what's going on?"

"No time, gotta go!"

Graf felt himself lifted off the ground and thrown over broad, sweaty shoulders. A sweet and sour musk wafted off the giant's back. Graf struggled to breathe as the creature began to run through the forest.

"Ivory!"

"Don't worry! She's on our tail."

Graf lay stomach down, draped across the beast's shoulder for what felt like hours. His arms were pinned to his sides by the creature's lengthy limb, and the pounding had him cringing in pain. Despite the pitch black of the night, the creature apparently knew the terrain like the back of his hand. He dodged around tree trunks, under limbs, and jumped over bushes and streams like a trained athlete. Graf was on the verge of once more voicing his discomfort when he was dropped on his side once again by an enormous oak tree. Ivory appeared by his side, licking his face tenderly.

"Inside!" Huge hands picked Graf up by his tunic and thrust him through a door that materialized through the folds of oak bark.

Falling on all fours on the cold dirt, Graf looked around, but he could see nothing. He heard Ivory's panting behind him and could feel the vibrations of the giant's footsteps as it walked across the room. A cloth was pulled off a glass jar filled with abnormally large lightning bugs. After several more of the jars were uncovered around the room Graf was able to make out his rescuer's appearance. He stared.

"Care to paint me? It'll last longer." He said.

Graf shook his head. "Don't see folk like you where I come from."

"Imagine what you look like to us."

The creature towered above the height of average men; eight feet tall if Graf had to guess. His body was built much like a human's but stouter and with longer limbs. Obviously male, his skin was the color of blueberries, and he had a short clump of black hair on his head. His nose was an unnatural pink and was covered in bristly white fuzz. His eyes were abnormally large and a solid yellow. Sweat trickled down his arms, chest, and stomach. He was athletically built, but the strain of carrying Graf had exhausted him, and his breathing was heavy.

"I apologize for my cousins' behavior. They're not too fond of humans," he said.

"Guess that makes you the black sheep of your family, huh?" Graf snarked.

A grin spread across the giant's lips as he gestured to Graf's tattoo. "Better than being the Black Rose of yours."

Graf shrugged. "You guys seem to understand the implications of the Black Rose better than I do..."

"You've met my kind before?" The creature looked perplexed. "You came from the west... my people don't venture into those parts."

"No, not your kind in particular. I meant... I've met... nevermind!" Graf winced as he got to his feet and moved to sit on a crude wooden stool in the corner of the room. "What are your people?"

"We are the Crann Fear."

"Say that three times fast," Graf muttered the words under his breath.

"Crann Fear, Crann Fear, Crann..."

"I didn't mean that literally!"

"I know. Humans aren't the only ones that know sarcasm."

Graf chuckled. "What's your name?"

"Burl," he said.

"I'm Graf." He pointed to the dog. "This is Ivory."

The creature smiled at Ivory and the dog fidgeted slightly. Graf assumed the giant wasn't trying to look intimidating, but the fangs didn't help.

"I try to help strangers when they come to the wood. Men and creatures from all manner of worlds. I'm not always successful."

Graf looked at the rough loincloth Burl wore and noticed the rope belt around the giant's waist, from which hung several humanoid skulls of different sizes. Unease leaked through Graf's steely exterior.

Burl noticed and snorted. "Don't worry, human. These are the remains of friends and most died of old age and sickness. It's a custom of my kind to keep the bones of those we care for after they are dead. It's a way to protect their remains from being defiled by other creatures... and each other."

Graf shifted and winced again. "I wish I could say I could've handled things myself, but I barely took out one of your boys back there. Sounded like there were hundreds more coming for us. I was dead for sure."

Burl walked over to a crude iron stove. A rough coffee pot sat on top and from it Burl poured a thick, tarry substance into two bowls carved from giant acorns. He handed one to Graf.

"Coffee."

Doesn't look or smell like any coffee I've ever had. Graf mocked a sip to be polite and nearly gagged from the smell. He winced as the movement jarred his wrenched shoulder.

Burl eyed the shoulder and prodded it. "You'll mend. Got a poultice that'll make it faster." He stalked to another shelf, worked a moment, then set a rough bundle on the stove. Two minutes later, he pulled it off and thumped it onto Graf's shoulder. "Hold it there."

It made him wince again, but after a moment, the heat began to soothe the ache.

"I suppose you'll be looking for more of your own kind?" Burl asked.

"I'm not sure what I want yet... but a human settlement would be helpful so I could get established. I'm not exactly at one with the wilderness."

"You're welcome to stay with me." Burl motioned to the skulls at his waist. "I've housed several travelers throughout my life. We Crann Fear are immortal, at least when it comes to age. I don't get along well with the others, and I prefer the company of other, less volatile races."

"I appreciate the offer, but I'd like to find more of my own kind."

"I understand," Burl said. "You know, some eight hundred years or so ago, another human passed through these parts. Carried the same mark as you carry now."

"Bernholt?" Graf asked.

"Your ancestor?"

"No... but I'm familiar with the name."

Burl sat down on a pile of animal pelts. "He was Briar Dash then. He helped my people fight off the Bleain - terrible wolves that terrorized my people for ages. He too was looking for a man village to settle in. I knew of none then, as I know of none now. I did, however, guide him to one who does."

"The man with a thousand names?"

"I know him only as the Traveler," Burl said. "A strange man, if indeed he is a man, who comes to the wood from time to time. He comes when there are those in need of help... as he helped me learn man-tongue when I decided to separate from my family."

"Does he live near here?"

"Did you not hear what I just said? He doesn't live here... I doubt he lives anywhere. He leaps between worlds the way my people leap from tree to tree. He wields strange magic and keeps bizarre company."

Graf blinked. "I've heard he may not be safe. Is that true?"

Burl shrugged. "He was nice enough to me. Gave me the stove and a never-ending supply of coffee. Didn't care much for the other man-food he offered me, but he did teach me how to read and write variations of your language. He gave me those."

Graf looked to his left, where Burl pointed, and saw dozens of leatherbound books stacked within the exposed root system that made the wall of the room. "You're welcome to some if you'd like to take a few."

"Don't have much use for books... I was never good at reading," Graf responded.

"Suit yourself."

Burl leaned back as if he was about to go to sleep. Graf didn't want to bother the Crann Fear, but he was itching for answers about the Traveler. "Can you take me to the Traveler?"

Burl opened one eye. "I can point you in the right direction... but haven't seen him in almost a century. Not tonight though... sleep now."

"How will I know him when I see him?"

"Man has a gray caterpillar on his upper lip. Now shut up and go to sleep. You humans always talk too much." Burl was clearly tired and getting grouchy.

He must mean a mustache. Soon Burl and Ivory were both asleep and their snoring was fit to wake the dead. Graf made himself comfortable and followed them into sleep.

When Graf awoke, the door to the dwelling stood open and sunlight poured through the threshold. His bag and dagger had been retrieved and sat beside the pile of dirty blankets he'd slept on. Burl and Ivory were both gone when he awoke but soon returned, bringing an assortment of wild berries and nuts with them.

"Eat and drink." Burl tossed him a water bladder made from deerskin.

"Then you'll take me to the Traveler?"

Burl laughed. "You must be eager to be rid of me."

Graf shrugged and ate his crude breakfast.

Burl guffawed again. "I'm just giving you a hard time. You want to be with your people. I get it."

Graf nodded. "It's odd. Back home, it seemed like a blessing to be rid of everyone... but now that I really am alone, I'd give anything to be around my own kind again. Even around those I hate."

"I get that too. Here." Burl tossed a pair of leggings to Graf. "These are a bit more breathable than those wool smocks you're sweating your balls off in. More durable too."

Graf looked at his dirt-stained tunic and breeches. His pants were torn to shreds and the crotch seam had split open. His once-gray tunic had turned a sweat-soaked brown. They were fine for wearing around town, but in the woods, they weren't practical.

The leggings Burl gave him were little more than a loincloth with straps that wrapped around his thighs, where the wearer could strap a knife. Burl also gave Graf a battered short sword. It was dull and dented, but Burl claimed it had belonged to a long-dead friend of his (a human no less) and that it would be more effective than Graf's ornamental dagger. Graf agreed and fixed the sword onto the leather belt Burl gave him to hold up his 'man panties', as Graf thought of them.

"I appreciate your help, but I look ridiculous." Graf held out his hands with frustration as he studied his skimpy leather attire.

"No. Now you look like a warrior instead of a bearded housewife. I would think any who encounter you would take you more seriously now." Burl motioned to his own loincloth, which was even less than what Graf was wearing. "You don't need all those clothes weighing you down and restricting your movements in this forest, at least not until you reach a human settlement. You'll thank me for it."

Graf shrugged and looked at his nearly naked body. He switched his gaze to Ivory, whose tongue lolled out of her mouth as her tail wagged endlessly. From her expression, Graf would have thought Ivory had the hots for his new woodland attire.

"Don't even think about it, girl." Graf kicked playfully at her rear as she jumped at him, smothering his face with licking.

Burl gave them some more dried beans, nuts, and fruits for the road, then took them to the crude path they had been following before, albeit a few miles further along. "Continue on this path and you should meet Traveler eventually. He never comes to the same spot twice, but if you need help badly enough, he'll appear."

Graf raised his eyebrow. "What about your family? You think I'll have any more run-ins with your not-too-friendly kinfolk?"

"We Crann Fear are very territorial. They won't venture this far from their homes in the trees. Beware of other dangers though."

"Like what?"

Burl snorted mockingly. "You want me to powder your ass and burp you too?" He turned and began to walk back towards his home. "Hatch free on your own, little chickadee!"

Then he was gone.

Chapter 4

A Sticky Situation

Graf practiced handling the sword Burl had given him while they traveled. It was heavy despite its relatively small size, and the straight, rigid handle felt odd in his hand. For one thing, he'd been more of an ax-and-dagger user during his soldiering days. For another, sword hilts back home were contoured to the natural grip of the wielder - one reason why blades from Eastern Rising were sought after far and wide.

At least his shoulder was better. He eyed the dog plowing through the undergrowth with him. "What do I need a sword for when I've got you, Ivory?" She bounced playfully at the sound of her name and trotted on ahead.

Through the thick foliage, Graf could make out the shadows of mountains in the distance. The path grew rugged, rising and falling in steep hills. The afternoon and evening chill had set in. The thin strips of leather binding Graf's legs and genitals was hardly going to be enough to keep him warm throughout the night. It looked like a night of cuddling with Ivory was in store if they didn't reach their destination quickly.

He knew something was amiss when Ivory stopped suddenly in the path. She peered into the trees, then sprang into the foliage, leaving Graf to stumble through the wilderness after her.

"Ivory, you mutt, get back here!"

There was the sound of ferocious barking, followed by a yelp. As he rounded a tall ash tree, he saw Ivory fighting to free herself from a rope net suspended in a tree.

"Blast it!" Graf drew his sword to assist and charged forward.

After his previous encounters with the inhabitants of the forest, Graf should have known better than to panic and rush in.

31

Had he taken a moment to take in his surroundings, perhaps he would have seen the hooded man concealed in the limbs of the white oak nearby, not to mention the hastily established snare trap that he stumbled into unaware.

Graf had plenty of time to think about it while swinging from the tree by his ankle.

"Well, well, well! Looks like I caught me a doggyknobber!" The highwayman sauntered into the clearing, yanked off Graf's pack and rummaged through it. "Slim pickings I see… oh, nice blade, this… but I can still have a spot of fun with you."

"Give me back my dagger you… I'm not a damned wild turkey!" Graf tried to lift his body to untie the rope, but it was harder than he'd thought it would be. "You've had your chuckle, now cut me down!"

"Feisty too? I like that." The man stepped behind Graf and grabbed his hips and buttocks. "This is a brilliant outfit, love. I do wonder what you and that mutt were up to."

The man mimicked a dog's panting and whining, a tone Graf was all too familiar with from his days as a breeder. An inkling of the man's real intentions flared in his mind, and Graf lashed out, lurching in his bonds. Disoriented as he was, it accomplished nothing, but he wanted this bandit to know he wouldn't make it easy. He wanted the brute to know he'd go down swinging.

The man stepped back in front of him. He pulled off his vest to reveal a hairy, overweight torso. "You don't have to fight, love. Uncle Sticky can be very gentle." He leered.

Graf felt his breathing speed up, his vision tinged with red from the blood rushing to his face, fury, and the memories trying to break free. "Try it and die." He struck out again as the man approached, lashing out with his free leg and his fists. The fists did nothing, but his leg hit the man solidly on the shoulder.

The man was knocked back a few feet, but quickly recovered. He laughed and began to untie his breeches. Ivory was going nuts in the net, but he doubted her wild bites would free her. To make matters worse, his sword and dagger were both out of reach, having fallen into the bandit's hands when he was snared.

"This'll be fun!" The man snickered as he dropped his pants. "You got any vittles? When I'm done having my fun with you, I'll be mighty hungry, and it's a fair way back to my stash."

"You... you can just eat my fist, you perverted swine!" Graf snarled the words. The red was getting deeper, threatening to sweep him away.

"The only person who's going to be eating any... body... is you!" The man held up Graf's dagger again and advanced, swaggering lewdly. "Do play nice puppet. I don't mind doing you dead... but it's so much more fun if you're alive!"

"How would you like a threesome?" A new voice cut through the encroaching memories, coming from behind the vagrant.

Beside the white oak stood a middle-aged man with a badly scarred face and a long, unkempt mustache that Graf had to admit looked an awful lot like a gray caterpillar. *The Traveler.* Could it be? He looked like the one that Burl and Syncie had spoken of; however, he was scrawny and carried no weapons aside from a walking stick. Graf cursed under his breath. *Hope you got some tricks up your sleeve.*

Got a few up my pants too. Graf was thrown by the thought projected straight into his mind. He knew instantly that it had come from this new arrival.

'Uncle Sticky' snarled. "Wait your turn, fruitcake! Once I'm done stuffing him, I'll be happy to take you over my knee and spank you like a naughty boy."

"Now, now, you should ask nicely about things like that, Eunice," the Traveler said.

The bandit paused, surprised by the man's response. "How the hell do you know my name?"

"It's my job," the Traveler smirked. "And hey, if you're into guys, I don't judge. But it's pretty clear the man isn't interested, and neither is his dog. So how about you cut them down and get lost before I decide to indulge your little fantasy in a way you won't enjoy as much."

"Shut up you wanker! I call the shots in this part of the woods, not you!" The bandit had forgotten Graf and was now squaring off with his new challenger.

"Calling the shots, huh? Well, aren't you a long way from shoveling pig shit for your momma? What was her pet name for you?" The Traveler tapped his staff in a mocking imitation of thought. "Oh, that's right... Jelly Belly! Momma's Little Jelly Belly!" He chuckled. "Notice you haven't lost the belly..."

"Enough!" The brigand roared and charged the smaller man, Graf's dagger in hand. "I was gonna let you both live after some fun, but now you're dead."

As if the portly bandit was moving in slow motion, the scrawny man stepped lazily to one side and stuck out a boot. 'Uncle Sticky' tripped and fell face first into a convenient tree stump.

The Traveler clicked his tongue. "Aww, pumpkin... you'll have to do better than that..."

"Shut up you sissy fighter! I'll squash you easily enough!" The bandit lumbered to his feet and lunged again, swiping wildly with Graf's dagger.

The Traveler seemed to float backward, easily blocking the flurry of clumsy strikes with his staff before disarming the man and bringing him to a stunned stop with a hard kick to his shin. One well-executed twist later, and the rogue was once again laid out in the dirt.

"Well, it seems that now you've got a willing partner to play with, you've got cold feet."

Uncle Sticky rose to all fours, swiping messily at a bloodied nose. He glared at his opponent with watery eyes and let out a cry as he exploded upward with a haymaker aimed right at the Traveler's head.

The man stood still with his hands on his hips, and Graf gaped at him. The bandit was no trained fighter, but that blow was still sure to be a brain scrambler. "Move you idiot!"

Then the unthinkable happened: his fist phased straight through the Traveler's head. Uncle Sticky overbalanced and crashed forward - face first into a tree trunk, knocking him out cold with a jarring thump.

"Wow." Graf eyed the fallen bandit. *He's going to have a hell of a headache when he wakes up.*

The Traveler prodded the fallen bandit with a toe. "Been watching that maggot for some time. Lucky I got here before he had his way with you." He winked.

Blood rushed to Graf's face for a new reason. "Will you just cut us down already!"

The man chuckled and walked over to the oak tree to grab the staff he'd dropped earlier in the scuffle. A moment later the rope holding Graf's ankle disappeared, and he fell in a graceless heap to the dirt, thumping his head painfully on a root. A yelp and a thump told him Ivory's net was gone too.

He grimaced at the Traveler. "You could have warned me, you asshole!"

"And you could learn some manners. You're supposed to thank people who save your life - not to mention other things - when they help you," the Traveler responded.

Ivory yapped at Graf, as if also chastising him. Graf sighed. "Point taken."

"Great. Now grab your things and shake a leg. I'm only in this place until midnight, which leaves us with less than four hours. And it'll take us three to get to my cottage."

"Cottage?"

"Yes. And I know the journey there doesn't leave us much time for socializing, but I don't decide where it lands," the Traveler responded. He turned and began pushing through the woods at an alarmingly fast pace. Graf and Ivory had to run to catch up with him.

As they wound their way through the trees, over hills and streams, Graf noticed the forest was changing. Oak, maple, and ash trees were slowly replaced by evergreens, firs, and other conifer trees. They produced a sharp fragrance that Graf enjoyed, despite the exertion of maintaining such a quick pace.

The Traveler was barely visible to Graf throughout the hike. His stamina seemed endless. Graf lost track of time, trekking along a steep upward climb. Just when he thought his legs were about to give out on him, the path turned down a steep incline. After what seemed like forever, the trio halted at the door of a small log cabin in a thickly wooded valley.

"We have about 45 minutes... come on in and make yourselves comfortable." The Traveler wasn't even breathing hard.

Up close, the cabin was made of roughly cut logs and painted a pale, chalky blue. It had an algae and lichen encrusted thatch roof, and the warmly lit windows were bordered with ornate carvings of mythological beasts - many of which Graf couldn't name. The door seemed to be made of one giant sheet of bark, and a dozen miniature-scale houses were carved into the facing.

The Traveler grinned and stepped aside. "Go ahead. They won't bite."

"What do you mean, they won't... shit!" Graf yanked back his hand, astounded by what he was seeing.

A troll-like creature, maybe an inch tall, emerged from one of the carved huts near the doorknob. He waved a needle sized spear at Graf and squealed in a thin, shrill voice.

"Well, they didn't bite..." The Traveler smirked.

"What the hell are they, and why are they infesting your door?"

"Hey now… I'm just renting them some real estate until I can find them a new home. Cute buggers, aren't they?"

He scratched the troll on the head, and it shivered all over with a high-pitched giggle.

Taking his cue from the man's earlier words, Graf opened the door. "I'm thirsty, and honestly, I'm a bit sick of water. You got any wine or ale in here?"

"I'll do you better than that. Ever had a Coke?"

"A what?" Graf hadn't ever heard of anything by that name.

The Traveler slapped himself on the forehead as he entered. "Of course… I forgot where you're from… trust me, you're gonna love this stuff!"

A garland of holly slapped Graf in the face as he cautiously followed his host. It was hard to tell the difference between the interior of the cottage and the forest; countless bundles of dried herbs and wildflowers hung from the ceiling, and garlands of holly, cedar and ivory bracketed the doors, fireplace, and the bookshelves. Strange miniature trees like nothing Graf had ever seen sat on various stools and tables. Graf couldn't help but poke one with his finger. It looked hundreds of years old, with a single thread of living growth intertwined with bone-colored deadwood. Twisting and drooping over the sides of its sizable shell pot, the limbs nearly touched the ground.

"I've never seen anything like this… not even traveling with the traders, or in lore books as a schoolboy."

"Comes from a continent called Asia, on a planet called Earth. It's one of the more diverse worlds I've been to, albeit slightly mundane. An old work buddy gave those to me. And speaking of Earth, try this." The Traveler walked over to a shiny metal box on one wall.

As he opened the door on the front, frosty air poured out like soup. When he closed the door and turned around, he was holding a small red cylinder which he handed to Graf. It was made of some sort of thin metal, and the Traveler motioned to a tab on the top, which Graf assumed opened it. He tugged, and a loud snap was followed by a fizz. Graf lifted it apprehensively to his lips. The liquid was freezing cold, and had a sharp, sweet flavor. It tickled his throat as he swallowed and fizzled so much as it hit his stomach that he belched hard enough to bring some of the drink back up his throat. He choked, hacking and coughing.

"Woah! Don't drink it so fast." The Traveler helpfully slapped Graf on the back.

"This is that Coke stuff you talked about? I've never had the like." Graf wiped his mouth with his forearm.

The Traveler shrugged. "Well, come sit by the fireplace. We don't have long."

"Wait... I don't even know your name. What am I supposed to call you?"

"What did the locals call me? Surely they shared something with you."

Graf shrugged. "The Traveler. One called you the man with a thousand names."

The man chuckled. "A thousand names? That's a gross exaggeration. The real number is probably somewhere between 75 and 105, but I've lost count. Well, just call me Traveler. It has a nice ring to it."

They stepped into a recessed living room, where they both sat down in plush chairs cushioned in a velvety red material. The chair seemed to wrap itself around Graf's body and the unexpected comfort made him feel drowsy. The chairs were arranged facing the fireplace. Graf noticed the mantel was formed from what looked like hundreds of rough pink diamonds. Graf doubted the Keeplord's entire treasury - or even the entire Keep - was worth as much. Traveler snapped his fingers, and flames sprang to life.

Graf blinked. "What are you exactly? I doubt there are many in the Wanwood who would cross you. Conjuring fire, making ropes disappear... and the way your face dissolved for an instant when that bandit tried to slug you..."

"Liked that, did you? I call that little trick 'ghosting'. Took a while to use it on command. As for your question..." Traveler paused to sip his Coke. "I'm an inter-dimensional guidance counselor."

"A What?" Graf blinked back at him.

"A fairy godfather, if you will. I bounce around to different worlds and dimensions... there are an infinite number of them, but most creatures only ever know the one they are born into, you're lucky enough to know two."

"Two?"

"Well, there was your old town, and there is Wanwood."

"Wanwood is the enchanted forest bordering Eastern Rising. It's not a different world," Graf insisted.

"Isn't it?" Traveler chuckled. "How can you say that after encountering all these creatures' magic with your own eyes?"

"Well... I..." Graf was not entirely sure what to say. He knew that the Black Rose on his arm and the border he crossed going into the woods possessed enough combined magic to stop him from ever returning to his home, but it had not occurred to him that he had stepped into a completely different world.

"Wanwood is indeed very special," Traveler smiled. "It's one of those special places that many other worlds open up and have access to. The creatures you come across here might not necessarily be from here. They could have traveled or stumbled across it from completely different worlds, for one reason or the other, just like you have."

"And you?" Graf asked for clarification.

"I have the power to travel between the different worlds, and I go to different times in the past and present and future. My job is to help those in need where and when they need it, regardless of where and when they are; places and time are not an issue for someone like myself. Sometimes I choose my destination, but mostly my employer points the way. That's what this is for." He rested his hand on a strange globe sitting on a stool by his chair.

The sphere was made of gold and glass, and within the globe Graf could see a countless number of smaller spheres, one within the other, like the strange nesting doll Graf had once seen. Symbols, glyphs, and lines zigzagged across its surface, and a strange device protruded from the glass surface. It looked oddly like a sextant - Graf remembered seeing pictures of the instrument in his school-books, and one actual device on the trading trip - but with an eyepiece.

"What is it? It doesn't look like any tool I know."

"I call it the Navigator. It tells me where I'm going next and gives me a rough idea of who I'll help. Which reminds me..." He put the eyepiece up to his eye and fingered a small switch. "Give me a second while I double-check the next stop in my itinerary."

He pulled a lever and the spheres within spheres began to spin in different directions. There were several flashes of light, and Traveler snorted before leaning back in his chair.

"What did it tell you?" Graf couldn't help asking. He heard Ivory whined and looked down to see her sitting on the floor, staring curiously at the Traveler.

"That I have to go to a third-rate world to help an old colleague of mine. Lazy bum can't find time to officiate a hot-dog eating contest."

"Eating dogs?" Graf gasped. Ivory yipped and covered her face with her paw. "I don't think I'd like that place much."

"No. No, my bad." Traveler held up his hands and laughed. "What I mean is that it's an eating contest for literal hot dogs. A bunch of dogs sit together in this sauna, see, and they have to eat as much ice cream as they can..."

"Wait... why would you scream?"

"No... ice cream, it's this frozen dessert... and they have to eat as much of this stuff as they can in an hour. And I'm gonna be stuck in there with them, sweating my buns off." A distracted expression crossed his face. "Maybe I should take some straws with me..."

Graf shook his head. "Nothing you just said made a lick of sense."

"Trust me, that's a good thing."

"Look, I appreciate the comfy chair and the warm hearth, but I was told you could help me find civilization. If you're just gonna sit there and spout nonsense..." Graf stood and called Ivory to him.

"Woah Nellie! I'm getting there. Sit."

Graf dropped back down and Ivory rested her head on his thigh. Traveler raised an eyebrow with a smirk on his face. "Ivory, wasn't it?" He held out his hand and motioned for the dog to come to him. She wasn't having it.

"How'd you know her name? I never told you..."

"Same way I know your name, Graf." Traveler smirked at his wary expression. "No, I'm not psychic. It was in my briefing." He looked back at the dog. "And I think you should know, your pup's been keeping a bit of a secret from you."

Ivory whimpered and ducked her head.

"What do you mean, a secret? She's a dog. A bit tougher than the rest, and with a better disposition than most, but just a dog nonetheless."

Traveler snickered and rubbed his eyes. "That's what you think." He chuckled again. "Come on, Ivory. You know you won't be able to hide it forever with your love-struck heart. So come on girl."

"What the hell's your deal. You're..." Graf stopped.

Ivory's entire body convulsed. Hair began sluffing off her body as her pelt bubbled and rolled. Her face began to twist and quiver and a cracking sound filled the room as her bones broke and set into new alignments. She stood up on her elongating hind legs, and her forepaws began to transform into humanoid arms. Her fingers and fingernails lengthened. Her sagging nipples reformed into two voluptuous breasts.

Milky white fur was replaced by thick black hair that started from her head and down across her back and across her shoulder blades. It continued down her spine until it thinned out and faded just above her buttocks. Her ears remained small and pointed, the hair around them sticking up in wild tufts like a dark-hued starburst. Two lines of thick, heavy fur-like hair striped down her chest, zinging down her chest before converging at her nether region.

Her face, now a darker ebony color, shifted into something that was a cross between a human and a dog. Despite the smaller jaw, her canines were alarmingly long as she opened her mouth. Her eyes retained a pinkish hue.

When the last cracking sounds faded, a woman stood before Graf. Or rather, a muscular, sinewy beast, a wolf-woman with a sensual musk that seemed to tickle Graf's nostrils.

The wolf-woman smiled. "Hello, my love. I am Amber."

Chapter 5

Information and Destination

"Jeez Louise! I did not think that would be so messy!" The Traveler shot up from his seat, found a broom and a small, flat tool with a wide opening at one hand, steep sides, and a handle at the other, and began frantically sweeping up the slimy white hair littering the ground.

Graf gasped and stared at his 'dog'. "You're a werewolf?"

Amber reached a hand toward his face and gently caressed his rough cheek with her black fingernails. Graf shivered and pushed himself back farther in his seat. She noticed his anxiety and withdrew. "Please don't be frightened, my love. I know my true appearance can be alarming. I hid it from you to prevent this very reaction."

"For what it's worth, Graf, she really has taken a shine to you." Traveler gave him a sly wink and looked to Amber. "What do you call that reaction again?"

"It is an impression of sorts. It happens to the females of my species when they've met their mate."

Graf was stupefied. Did she mean...?

Traveler asked the question out loud: "A soul mate?"

"Yes." She nodded. "We can't help it. Once we've met our mate, we're bound to them for life."

"Listen to that, eh." Traveler paused his sweeping and punched Graf playfully on the arm. "You've got yourself a keeper here! And look at the muscles on this gal... you know, if I were you, I'd be..."

"Just stop." Graf cut him off.

"Please don't be scared," Amber pleaded with him.

He saw her eyes begin to well with tears. "Look Ivory, or Amber, or whoever you are... that whole molting thing was just a bit out of the blue. You need to give me a moment."

She nodded and slumped down to the floor, sitting cross-legged. Her skin glistened with sweat from the exertion of her transformation. As she placed her hands behind her and leaned back, Graf couldn't help but notice her chest - and its attributes - rising with each breath. He quickly shifted a hand to cover a certain rapidly enlarging part of his anatomy.

As terrified as he was of his former dog, Graf wouldn't claim she wasn't a gorgeous creature in this form. He sighed. *What is it with me and freaky women?*

He considered what he'd been told. "Look, I'm not sure about the whole soul mate thing, but I do know you've helped me and defended me several times. I'm not going to try and alienate or abandon you... I just need some space for now."

"Thanks, love." Ivory - Amber - nodded.

Traveler finished sweeping up and used the odd implement to toss everything into the fire. He sat back in his chair and finished off his Coke. He broke off the tab-like thing and began flipping it between his fingers, almost like a nervous twitch. "So... I was never very good at breaking the ice and getting down to business, but now that we're all acquainted, what do you want out of me? What do you want to know? We have just half an hour, so get cracking with the questions!"

"I feel sort of like my head's been trampled on by a goat. You said this place is like some sort of portal to... other worlds or... or something?" Graf had heard the words and the explanation, but he was still confused. Traveler winced.

"How do I say this?" The man couldn't think of a simpler way to explain than he already had. "This forest is like a way station of sorts; a nexus where dozens of worlds collide. It's easy to get here, but almost impossible to leave."

"So, it really is endless?"

"No, but for the likes of you two it might as well be. It's probably disheartening to hear that, but it's the truth. And it only gets worse as you go, with a few exceptions."

"Could you take us to another world?" Amber asked. "One where we could live in peace?"

"Not exactly. I can only return someone to the realm from which they came. My boss's rules, not mine!"

"I wouldn't go back if my life depended on it," Graf scoffed.

"Me either." Amber laughed bitterly. Graf did his best not to stare at her bouncing, fur-covered breasts. "I'm a shapeshifter, and my kind are nearly extinct in my world. To survive I found work in a traveling side-show. A drunk in some backward village tried to have his way with me, and when I didn't reciprocate he became violent. Didn't work out well for him... or me. I was chased by the villagers and I became lost. I had a feeling something strange was going on, because I was suddenly surrounded by plants and trees I'd never encountered in my own world. I put two and two together and began wandering until I found you."

"Your will to escape must have opened up a temporary rift between worlds, and you wound up here. Graf's door to the wood was a bit more obvious. Funny how that works... doors in some worlds are wide open, others are untraceable until the right time." Traveler rose and walked over to one of his little trees, which he began pruning with a pair of shears.

Amber looked at Graf. "So why did you come here?"

Graf remained silent. Then the Traveler shot him a harsh glare, and he realized the strange man already knew the truth.

He sighed. "I was exiled to the forest for assaulting a man. A noble's son. He had... done some terrible things, and was probably going to do more, so I..."

"Graf!" Traveler snapped out the word.

Graf winced at the rebuke. "Fine. The Heir of the Lord's family... he took the lives of my mother and sister, but not before he did other things. 'Had his way with them', in your words." He jerked his head at Amber. "So, I hunted him down, goaded him into a fight while he was drunk, knowing he had no way of matching me when I had years of Guard experience, plus my time as kennel-master, to call on."

The memories Graf had been pushing down for so long began resurfacing.

***

He'd been gone for so long. He was looking forward to seeing Ma and Karie and the dogs again. The months away had been interminable.

The hut his family lived in was quiet. Too quiet. It raised his hackles. Then, the smell hit him. Old rot and blood and worse. Ma would never let the house smell so filthy. It had to be a neighbor... old Jask probably hadn't cleaned up from a butchering session yet...

The door fell open under his touch, revealing a scene from nightmares. Karie, curled on her pallet, with the rags of her clothing and a blanket pulled pitifully around her. Ma wasn't far away, and even from the door, he could see livid bruises and wounds. Wounds that no longer bled.

His breath choked in his throat. "No... no... no..." he staggered forward, his mind screaming denials as the stench washed over him. "No... it can't be..."

***

Graf swallowed. "I beat him good, then castrated him so he'd have to live with knowing he couldn't do that to anyone else. I got exiled, and on my way out of the Keep for the last time, I killed the bastard's father because he admitted that he knew what his son had done. He thought it was better to let my family rot than to discipline his perverted sadist of a son."

There was a heavy silence for a moment, then Traveler sighed. "We all make mistakes, but our mistakes don't have to make us. You weren't warranted to castrate a man, or to kill his father, but neither were they warranted to do what they did to you and your family." Traveler's voice was solemn. "As bad as it was all around, Eastern Rising is behind you Graf. It's time to let it go and write a new chapter."

"Well, I gladly would, but where would I find the quill to write with or the parchment to write on?" Graf rubbed at his eyes.

"So that's what you two are looking for? A place to settle down and start anew?" The Traveler gave them his full attention.

Graf and Amber nodded in sync.

The Traveler muttered to himself for a few moments before raising his voice. "Well, I do know of one place... a small settlement called Sanctuary. It was founded by a young fella I helped out a few years ago. Funny enough, he was from Eastern Rising too."

"Bernholt?" Amber piped up, using the name Graf remembered both Syncie and Burl mentioning.

"That's him!" Traveler snapped his fingers.

"That was hundreds of years ago!" Graf snapped. "You might be immortal, but Bernholt wasn't. How do we know this place hasn't been overrun by monsters, or undead, or demons, or something like that?"

Traveler pointed to the Navigator. "Like I said before, I have my ways of knowing. The village was well established the last time I saw him... but yes, Bernholt is probably dead by now. I don't know the village's exact state, but I do know it's still inhabited."

"Eight hundred years is a long time. How do we know it hasn't degraded into a den of thieves and hedonists, like that Uncle Sticky. We might be walking into a wolf's den." Graf shot a quick look at Amber. "No offense."

"I'm not a wolf, dear." Amber winked at him. "And I can handle people like Sticky. I was holding back so you wouldn't be frightened or feel emasculated." Graf winced.

Traveler shrugged. "From what little was revealed to me, Sanctuary seems to be in good standing. Granted, my boss didn't disclose much - I tried telling him the more info he gave me, the better I could help you, but he's got this whole '*help those who help themselves*' shtick."

"And we're just supposed to take the word of your unknown employer that Sanctuary will welcome us with open arms? We don't know you or your master from a loaf of bread."

"It's an understandable sentiment." The Traveler nodded. "The big guy doesn't make things easy, but he will give you guidance when he feels it's necessary. And I'd be a liar if I guaranteed Sanctuary was free of danger, but it is your best option. That's all I can give you for now."

Amber grunted. Graf shared her distrust. Traveler went back to the Navigator, looked into the eyepiece, and activated the switch again. Graf and Amber were once again temporarily blinded by blasts of light, then the man gave a relieved sigh.

"Boss man says the problems are nothing you two can't handle on your own, so long as you remain together. He was pretty specific about that. And trust me, he wouldn't have told me to send you there if he felt you guys would be in imminent and serious danger."

Amber piped up, "And what happens if we decide not to go to Sanctuary?" Graf was beginning to like the way she seemed to share his distrust of strangers.

Traveler shrugged. "That wouldn't be wise. Like I said, what you've experienced so far was just the beginning. An appetizer, if you will."

Amber and Graf shared a glance before Graf responded, "Very well, I guess we'll have to take our chances with Sanctuary. How far is it from here?"

"A few days journey. I'll make a path for you using my magic. Only you and Amber will be able to follow it."

"What about some clothing?" Graf motioned to his awkward garb and Amber's naked state. "We're not exactly easy on the eyes, or the sensibilities, in our current state."

"We still have a little time, so I think I can find some clothes for you two... and some provisions to last you the journey as well."

"Thanks." Graf paused. "I am curious though."

"About what?"

"You're pretty popular with the locals, as was Bernholt. And I know your powers are extraordinary, but how did you manage to build an entire self-sustained village in this forest? This place is a nightmare."

Traveler leaned back in his chair. "At the time I had several coworkers helping me... several of them were carpenters of sorts, and they helped build some of the initial dwellings and structures. My boss also allotted me a number of gifts for Bernholt and Sanctuary, which you'll see when you get there. There was a pretty serious infestation of monsters in the wood at the time and my powers weren't quite as matured then."

"Infestation?" Amber piped up. "Do you mean the wolf creatures the tree giant talked about?"

"Tree giant?" Traveler blinked a moment. "Oh, you mean Burl! Yeah, same ones. They'd staged a pretty big conquest for world domination on their home plane, and we had to funnel them into the wood to try and stop them. Tried to negotiate peacefully, but the stubborn bastards didn't know when to quit. They're gone now. No need to worry about them."

"Anything else you can tell me about Bernholt? I want to know as much as I can. It might help me relate to the natives." Any advantage Graf could get would help, and all knowledge was an advantage, as his old commander might say.

"He had a way with animals. One of the gifts I gave him was a necklace that could help him talk to animals... He recruited a pretty large bear that ended up being helpful. Don't know the bear's name, but I know it was an important part of the settlement in those days. Maybe knowing about it will help build trust... Who knows?"

Traveler disappeared into another room and soon returned with some more substantial clothing for Graf and Amber. They were similar to hunting outfits Graf had seen worn in Eastern Rising: leather breeches and a sturdy, breathable linen shirt with red thread embroidering on the collar.

The threadwork even matched the patterns his sister had been so skilled at weaving. A single tear spilled from the corner of his right eye, landing on the clean fabric of his shirt. He finished off the ensemble with a sturdy leather belt and tucked his mother's dagger into the leather sheath on the side of one of his new boots.

"I don't normally wear clothing, but this isn't so bad. It's not as restrictive as I thought it would be." Amber shifted and moved, even jumping a bit, then stretched out her arms and legs to make the clothing settle comfortably.

"Hopefully no one panics when they see you," Graf replied. He knew what the response would have been in Eastern Rising.

Amber shrugged his concerns off. "If need be, I can always shift back to my Ivory disguise."

"You said you were a shape-shifter," Graf noted. "Can't you assume a more human-like form?"

"You don't like my natural state?" Amber looked irritated. "I do have more than one transformation... I can do it, but it takes a while and it's rather uncomfortable. I don't assume human form very often."

"We can wait until we get closer. And it's not that I don't like it. It'd just make me a little more comfortable until..." Graf trailed off, flushing.

"Noted." Amber turned away to finish adjusting her clothing. She was obviously annoyed, which wasn't what Graf had intended.

"Here. This could help you out." Traveler returned from the other room carrying a thin strip of black leather. "Wear it around your neck, like a choker, and it should make your transformations more tolerable."

Amber smiled as she put it on. Graf noticed the front of the choker had a small rose affixed to it, made of obsidian. He was less than amused as he looked down at his own Black Rose. "Really?" He waved his forearm for Traveler to see.

"What a coincidence! Oh, you guys match now. It's so cute!" Traveler batted his eyelashes and clasped his hands in imitation of a doting grandmother.

Amber blushed, or made a face that reminded Graf of his own blushes. His body began to itch. He was never fond of public displays of affection. He made a face at Traveler. "That cheese is old and moldy."

"Oh, pish-posh! It's all in good fun." Traveler pouted and crossed his arms. Then he glanced at something else. "But you really need to go now."

Traveler hustled them to the door and the trio spilled out of the threshold. Graf nearly lost his footing as he stepped off the crude porch.

"Watch it!" Graf grabbed at his dagger. "I nearly busted my ass."

Traveler ducked back inside, then threw Graf his pack and sheathed broadsword. "Sorry, sorry. It's just that I'm on the clock, so I can't dawdle. Just follow the trail and you'll find Sanctuary in a few days."

"What path!" Amber called after him as Traveler rushed back into the house.

The door was flung open once again, and Graf could hear shrieking from the minute trolls. "My bad, guys!"

Traveler pointed a finger into the trees and fired off a beam of light. It began bouncing off the trunks of trees as it ping-ponged through the darkness. The trees the light touched were left with a blotch of red stain. Then he paused.

"One other thing. There's an associate of mine in Sanctuary, called the Gardener. Thinks he's a big shot, since he's working undercover, and got promoted... Trust him, above all others."

Graf nodded. "What does he look like?"

Traveler fidgeted, shoving his hands into the folds of his robes. He pulled out a small golden device on a chain. He looked at it feverishly, then looked back at Graf. "He's stuck in the 50s. Don't ask what that means, 'cause it'll take too long to explain, and I really don't have the time. You'll figure it out!"

The Traveler darted back into the domicile and slammed the door.

"Wait! What if..." Graf stopped as the cabin erupted into a cloud of smoke.

The duo shielded their eyes and covered their mouths as smoke engulfed the entire valley. After a moment, the dust cleared. The cabin was gone and in its place was a patch of smashed grass and shrubs.

Amber scoffed. "It's hard to imagine someone with such power being such a bozo."

"That's a kinder word than I would use." Graf replied.

They checked what gear they had. The Traveler had apparently thrown a second pack of provisions at Amber's feet. Graf decided it was time to set up camp for the night. It was past midnight, and Graf had enough experience in the wood to not go tramping around in the dark.

Graf leaned back against the trunk of a tree and closed his eyes. The clothes were enough to keep him warm, and he didn't feel like bothering with a fire. He felt Amber sit down between his outstretched legs as she leaned back against his chest. Her musky odor overwhelmed his sense of smell.

"Hey, what are you..." Her tongue cut him off as she kissed him, the unnaturally long appendage winding its way through his mouth.

Graf gasped for breath as she finally withdrew. He almost spoke, but Amber silenced him. "Oh, shut up, Graf. You know you enjoyed it." They could both feel the evidence of her words, so he didn't bother to refute it.

Soon, Amber was snoring in his arms. Despite his strange arousal at Amber's natural form, Graf was uncomfortable having this hardened, muscular beast so close. Still, he knew better than to protest. This was one woman he definitely didn't want to spurn.

Chapter 6

Encounters of the Stranger Kind

"I knew something was up from the get go," Graf said.

"How so?" Amber inquired. They were passing through a cove, and for a while, the duo's hike was quite pleasant. This gave the travelers time to converse with each other without the stress of tackling a steep mountain trail or fighting off a random monster.

"For one, you knew how to track and retrieve food on your own. All canines have natural instincts, but yours were beyond the norm. When I first met you, I had you figured for a puppy mill... that you'd strayed from a farm and gotten lost. But then I saw you in combat. I didn't see much during our fight with Syncie, but I saw your abilities with the giant. The speed and accuracy in your bite wasn't the defense of a scared, wild animal. It was something I had seen only in some of my best trained working dogs."

Amber laughed. "It took a while to modify my dog form to resemble the momma. The element of surprise always pays off in one way or the other. Was it really that strange though? Surely you've seen far better tricks from your guard dogs back home."

"True," Graf stated, "but there was also our communication. You could read my body language and respond to commands without the slightest hesitancy. Each dog trainer uses different commands, sometimes in different languages, as well as different techniques. You were far too intuitive."

Amber nodded in agreement.

"I guess I should've played dumb," she said, winking at Graf.

"Why, so you could sneak in more tongue action?" Graf remembered all the nights when 'Ivory' lay curled up in his arms, licking his nose and ears. "I hope you know I feel somewhat violated."

"You know I can sense what you're thinking, right?" They stopped at a patch of trees and took a break.

"You can read my mind?"

"It's not full-blown telepathy, but I do get the general impression of what people are thinking when they talk. You act disgusted by my appearance, but I know you're attracted to me."

So much for the privacy of interior monologue.

"I'll admit, as threatening as your initial unveiling was, you are an amazing creature. It's not just the fact that you're not human. Besides my family and fellow guards, I've always struggled with any type of sentient interaction. Too much fighting, I guess."

"Well, in that case, it's just a matter of helping you break out of your shell." Amber inched her bottom along the ground until her body was nearly on top of Graf's. She hadn't made any further transformations yet, and her musk was stronger than ever from their day's journey. "Easier said than done."

It was afternoon, and the warmth of the sun was beginning to dissipate. They hadn't encountered a soul, animal or human, and the entire valley clearing was open. Still, as Amber began to nibble on his ear, he could almost hear the jeers of townsfolk. The smell wasn't helping, either. She backed off, and playfully punched Graf's shoulder.

"It's just not my cup of tea," Graf said. "I'm sorry, Amber. It's just too much like being with a…a…"

"A dog?" Amber finished his sentence with a sigh. "I was hoping I could swing you. What if I transformed into a form more your taste? I can't stand it, but if it helps…"

"You really don't have to." Graf held up his hands in protest.

"I don't assume human form often, so it takes a bit longer than the last one you saw. I'd rather get it over with. It's almost sundown anyway." Amber pointed to the setting west.

"Well, as long as you're not doing it on my account."

She stood up and began to strip her clothing off. *Oh, not this again*, Graf thought. Despite the erotic power this creature held over him, he wasn't in the mood for hanky panky.

"Look, Amber, we hardly know each other, and besides that..."

"Don't worry," she replied. "I'm taking off my clothes for the transformation. It'll take several hours and it gets pretty messy. The more I use a form, the easier my transformations become. Work on getting a fire going and setting things up for the night. I'll be back later."

Amber set her clothing on top of her pack and grabbed the obsidian rose Traveler had given her. She looked at it and then at Graf: *worth a shot*, her eyes seemed to say. She walked behind a cluster of cedars and was out of sight. Time for privacy.

It was dusk before Amber returned. Graf had collected enough wood to start a small fire and ate some cheese and stale bread Traveler had left for them in Amber's pack. He'd set Amber's portion on her blanket and had lain down for bed when he heard the clip-clop of wet footsteps. Graf looked up as Amber's shadowy form approached the fire.

He had to pick his jaw off the ground.

"I'll bet this will make you more comfortable," she said.

While her charcoal colored skin retained its color, the fur that covered her body and face was gone. The fingernails had receded and her hair had grown past her shoulders. Eyes once red had darkened to an intense amber color and only the faintest trace of canines were visible behind her lips. The mounds of her chest were wet, glistening in the light of the fire, and her nipples were no longer hidden by their hairy curtains.

"That's all there is, so don't ask for more. I found a creek nearby and washed off after transformation." She sat down next to Graf, her wet hair molded to her head and neck.

"You didn't have to do that," Graf said. "But I'm glad you did."

The taboo discomfort of intimacy with Amber disappeared with her previous form. Graf tore off his tunic and Amber's warm fingers danced across his chest, finding their way around his neck as she brought her face close to his. Her tongue found his, but not in the canine form it had held the previous night; it was the taste of human flesh and saliva. Graf soon found the rest of his clothes removed, and realized it was the first time in several years he'd been with a woman. This creature enticed him in a way he couldn't begin to explain. Amber paused for a moment atop Graf. On her wet, glistening neck he could see the choker necklace she'd carried with her to her transformation. The dark glass of the affixed rose glinted in the moonlight.

"That charm works in more than one way, I see," Graf said, pulling Amber back to him. "Pleasant surprise," she replied before locking lips with Graf.

There wasn't much sleeping that night.

***

The weather was pleasant the next morning, and after a modest breakfast the duo set off on their path. As beautiful as she had appeared beside the fire the night before, in the daylight Amber was mesmerizing. The additional loss of lupine musk wasn't bad either. Graf wasn't sure how the two of them to have developed such a close bond since Traveler's cabin; their relations the night before had been more than spontaneous. They had agreed to slow it down, however, and Graf was pleased to find someone whose company he didn't despise. Thus, their trek ensued, and soon Amber began prying into Graf's past and homeland.

"So, everything is owned by the Keeplord?" Amber asked.

"No, not exactly," Graf stated. "Under the Keeplord and his Historians are the soldiers and merchants. The Historians and soldiers are given an annual allowance directly from the Keeplord's vault. Being in a higher class than merchants and citizens, they are allowed to keep most of this allowance... one year's pay for them is more than a townsman makes his entire lifetime. The soldier's life was nice for me, but short lived. Bad tempers seem to have that effect on one's career."

Amber grunted in agreement.

"Then below the soldiers are the merchants... they're allowed to take annual trips to other lands to sell and trade. They give their spoils directly to the Keeplord upon their return. This is how he's able to keep his treasury from expiring."

"Wait, I thought you said Eastern Rising was so isolated from other civilizations travelers hardly ever ventured there..."

"Yeah, but that doesn't mean we didn't send our own out and about."

"But what kept your merchants from pocketing the loot and making off? If your home was as bad as you say it was, why wouldn't they split when they had the chance?" Amber asked.

Graf laughed. "That's the double standard of Eastern Rising. For one, the Historians are magicians, and place curses on the merchants pending their return. Secondly, as long as you knew how to work the system, you could live comfortably back home. Merchants are allowed to keep a sizable portion of their profits. Not as much as the Historians or Soldiers make, but enough to keep them comfortable. Their traveling also gives them the necessary goods and wares to keep the city operating. The farmers, serfs and other bottom rung citizens rely on the merchants and their trade."

"How were the rest of you paid?"

"For those like the butchers, bakers, blacksmiths and such, any income they earn is based on how well they conduct business. I was at the bottom of this group after I got booted from the guard. Most of the dogs I trained were bought by the soldiers I'd once fought beside, or bought by other wealthier citizens. It wasn't a bad living for me, as I'd saved a bit of my income from my years as a soldier. Others weren't so lucky. There are unrelenting taxes placed on lower class waifs, like myself. We were lucky to have anything left over. My mother and sister managed to keep a small sack of coins stowed away for food and necessities."

"Sounds rough," Amber stated.

"It was what it was. Folks back home were mostly complacent... Do what the Keeplord says and he leaves you alone. Could have been a bit easier, though."

They were beginning to re-enter the forest, although it would be another day before they were out of the valley and back in the mountains. The sun was high overhead, and soon they stopped in a clearing for a small lunch.

"Tell me a little bit about your work," Amber teased. "Give me a story of Graf the Great, swordsman and dog trainer extraordinaire!"

"It wasn't that glorious," Graf replied. He had cherished his years in the guard, and his family's work, but was reluctant to share too much regarding his personal life.

"At least throw me a bone," Amber cackled. "Get it? Throw me a bone? Ha!"

Graf chuckled at her terrible attempt at a joke and replied, "I'll tell you anything, just stop the lame puns."

***

"I think I was around eight or nine when I watched my father work his dogs at the performance trials. It would be my first and last time, as he died soon after. Every year, my father would take his best working dogs to put on a show for the Keeplord. The hope was that if the dog performed well enough, the Keeplord would give my father a tax-free bonus in exchange for the dog.

"Obedience was first, and was perhaps the most important part of the trial. I'd seen the soldiers command their dogs, but comparing them to my father was like comparing night and day. Nobody could communicate with a dog like my dad. He never had to scream, yell, or beat his dogs. He was an expert in the use of punishments and reinforcers, and he never sold a dog until it was properly trained.

"Orion was the dog chosen for that day. He was one of my favorite play mates as a kid... his merle coat was mottled like an artist's pallet. The obedience portion went by in a flash, and soon they were into the advanced routines. The first of these were retrieving a wooden dumbbell over a hurdle. There stood my father, and in the heel position beside him was my beloved Orion. He called the retrieve command and Orion took off. What happened next still haunts me till this day.

"I don't know why he took the jump so soon. He'd practiced the maneuver countless times before and had been desensitized to distractions. He landed directly on his sternum, a tremendous blow that echoed with thunderous silence. Orion, resilient till the end, landed on his feet, but it was obvious something was wrong. I was shocked to see him continue with the dumbbell, and further still when he jumped back over the toppled hurdle. But his back was arched and his breathing was heavy –"

"Enough!" the Keeplord cried.

"I still remember the anger in the Keeplord's voice, and I remember seeing the short, pudgy man march across the field to confront my father. I remember his gaudy yellow coat billowing forward in the wind, smacking my father's face as he kneeled to tend to Orion. It was my first time ever seeing the ruler of Eastern Rising, and already I disliked the man. Couldn't he see the dog was in distress? Could he not offer help instead of ridiculing my father for a 'shoddy piece of work?'

"My father said nothing as we went home and didn't speak for the rest of the evening. I stayed by his side as he watched over Orion, but the dog's condition worsened, and by morning my beloved dog could barely breathe at all. My father told me his sternum had been crushed, and that there was nothing we could do. It was then that he took out the vial of solution he often used to euthanize sick and dying dogs. I stopped my father before he could finish the job. Orion was my first best friend... it was only fitting that I end his life. To this day, I can't help but wonder if the heartache of Orion's death was what killed my father. That was my coming-of-age moment I could have done without."

***

Amber remained silent after Graf finished his tale. Presence was better than words during moments like these.

"I told you, my stories aren't that exciting," Graf laughed half-heartedly.

"No, I'm glad you shared that with me. It showed your... humanity." Amber's hand rested on Graf's knee. "At least you had a dog like Orion. I'm sure he would've been a great guard dog."

"He would've ruled the roost, that's for sure."

Just then a blood-curdling scream pierced the air, and loud buffeting noises followed. The duo jumped to their feet. Amber shifted in an instant to her natural form; her eyes burned red and her fangs shot out, ready for the kill. Graf drew his broadsword in one hand and his dagger in the other. The screams grew louder, and soon a shocking figure erupted from the trees.

Graf was so flabbergasted, he forgot to hold on to his sword.

A fat, flabby man exploded from the trees, naked as a jay bird and covered in a thick white foam. Whimpering and screeching, he scratched himself furiously under armpits and between his legs, and skittered across the ground on his toes as if trying to pinch his buttocks together. "Red bugs! Red bugs! They're eating me alive!" His voice rose to a high octave.

He had no clue who this man was, but Graf couldn't help but laugh. He lurched over in a fit of hysteria and put his hands on his knees, coughing followed his laughter. Amber, no longer in attack mode, stood dumbfounded by Graf's behavior and the jiggling, jelly-bellied man rolling in the grass.

"Ye gods! They went in my hole!" The man was on his back, humping the air in a bizarre fashion. "By my stars and garters, they went up my hole!"

He jumped back to his feet and ran in circles, flailing his arms like a chicken. Then Graf's attention was diverted to a second figure entering the clearing. It appeared to be a man of average height and weight, though little else could be considered average. This man had scaly orange skin and wore a tattered body suit made of shimmering blue fabric. Several slinky, translucent tubes hung from a strange chest plate affixed to his attire. As he ran after the naked man, Graf saw the creature snatch a bottle off his belt.

"Stand still, twinkle toes! I'm trying to help you!" The creature yelled before noticing them. "Oh, hey y'all. Don't mind us, we'll be out of your hair in a jiffy."

This man had a strange, drawling accent Graf had never heard before.

"Help! Help! They're digging for gold down there!" Graf had never seen a man scratch his crotch as furiously as this fat man was.

"Zip it, bubble butt! I'm coming," the orange creature began shaking the bottle and pointed it at the chubby maniac.

White foam spewed forth, coating the exposed man from head to toe. This had been the strange noise they had heard moments ago. He continued to spray the substance in his portly companion's direction until the screaming man was buried under a white cloud. A muffled cry was heard inside the glob of goo and the scaly skinned man leaned forward.

"I get it?" he screamed. More muffled groans followed.

The man chuckled as he tossed the now empty bottle aside. He dug into the hardening foam and plucked out his friend like a cherry from a pie. The man's itching seemed to have ceased, and he collapsed in a flabby heap at the other man's feet.

The scaly skinned man was knocking chunks of now solidified foam off the blubbery skin of his companion, and at the last moment booted the man in the rear. A litany of curse words flew from the humanoid creature's mouth, some of which Graf had never heard before. The fat man was on his rump yet again, in tears as his companion began to smack him repeatedly in the back of the head. Graf motioned to Amber to follow him as he walked towards the two new faces.

"You bubble headed idiot! I told your fat ass not to wander and you completely ignore me!" The orange man was screaming at the top of his lungs.

"My chest hurts," his companion mumbled. "I c-c-can't breathe."

"I damn well hope you can't breathe. First, you trip into a pile of moss trying to take a piss, then I use up my last round of bug spray chasing you down." The man looked to Graf and Amber, rolling his eyes. "Can one of you put me out of my misery?"

"That bad, huh?" Amber teased.

"Why couldn't I be the one to stick my pecker in a nest of red ants? At least it'd take my mind off this moron." He pulled out a small box from his utility belt and opened the top. "Shit... last one."

The man took a thin white tube from the box, discarded the latter and stuck the stick in his mouth. He yanked a small device from another pocket and pushed a button on its side. There was a spark and flame shot from the device, which he used to light the stick. Soon smoke billowed from his mouth, and Graf recognized the smell as tobacco.

"Blew through that whole pack the last few days dealing with him. Had these cigarettes imported all the way from Earth... was trying to savor them. Damn you!" He kicked a clod of dirt at the sniveling man.

"We've heard of Earth, before. Is that where you come from?" Amber asked.

"Me? No, I'm from a backwater planet on the other side of the Milky Way. I did some training on Earth, though. Most of the galaxy is colonized by humans now... can't turn around without bumping into one. They were always carrying on 'bout how dreamy a place it was."

"What are you exactly?" Graf asked.

"I'm an interplanetary surveyor... I was flying out to the Epagus System to map out a moon for a new mining colony. While in hyperspace I put 'er on autopilot to take a dump and before I knew what happened my ship, or what was left of it, had flown through a damn wormhole and gouged out a strip of land out of the side of some mountain."

"Bad luck seems to follow us too." Amber put her hairy hand on Graf's shoulder. "Join the party. I'm Amber and this is Graf."

"It's a pleasure to meet you two love birds. My handle is Bang-Bang Boomerang, but you can call me Boomer." He pointed to a small patch on his shoulder. "Can you believe I'd just got a promotion?"

"Well, I don't know about Earth or hyperdrives, but you might as well kiss that life goodbye. There's no way back," Graf said.

"Yeah, I figured as much when that scar-faced jackass damn near dropped a house on my head. That fella was kooky as hell... couldn't have talked with him for more than a few minutes. He pointed me in this direction, got back in his little house and disappeared. Said he had some other newcomers he had to welcome. Guess that was ya'll."

"And shortly after that, I reckon, you ran into that bundle of joy," Graf nodded towards the still weeping man, sitting cross-legged in the grass with his face buried in his hands.

"He's a bundle of something," Boomer said.

"Reminds me of someone back home," Graf stated. Graf caught a glimpse of the man's face and thought he vaguely resembled the Keeplord of Eastern Rising.

Boomer shook his head in disbelief. "Dip's been going on about how he's some king or something. He tried to cop an attitude with me when I first bumped into him... all demanding and shit. Didn't work out too well for him."

Graf stepped up to the toppled monarch and glared down at him. "Your reign is at an end, bub. What's your name?"

The man stifled a sob and looked up at Graf. "I don't know you from an apple pie! Be off with you, peasant!"

"Your name, asshole! We're equals now... give it to me," Graf spoke so loudly his voice began to break.

The man looked to Graf, then Amber, and lastly Boomer, who put his hands on his hips and gave the fat man a 'do it or else' stare. For what seemed like an eternity, he was speechless, glancing off as if dazed. Finally, he spoke.

"Buckley," he said, "my name is Buckley."

Chapter 7

Purple People Eater

Boomer retrieved his pack of rations given to him by the Traveler while Buckley found his meager clothing: the rags of a common serf. While the two were scavenging for their supplies, Amber walked into the trees with her obsidian rose, returning after a few minutes having donned her human form. Her transformations did seem to improve the more often she performed them. This aspect of Amber's nature intrigued Boomer, while Buckley was disgusted and horrified.

It turned out Traveler had marked Boomer's path the same way he had for them. This made their journey easy, as they simply followed the red markings on the trees, rocks, and ground. Boomer shared his experiences traveling among the stars. Graf had often stared at the stars at night in wonder, never thinking something like space travel was possible. He was glad there were other realms where this sort of thing existed. The alien spent a lot of time describing the different technologies he had worked with. Graf was especially perplexed by a bracelet that had been surgically affixed to Boomer's wrist, as it had been with everyone in his company, and upon activation would instantaneously teleport Boomer to the bridge of his ship. The scientists had their own name for it, but it had been marketed under the name *Instaport*. It was one of the few devices that hadn't been destroyed in the crash and operated independently from the rest of his ship's systems. However, after popping over to his ship (popping being a slang term used by those in Boomer's profession) there was no guarantee he would ever find Sanctuary or his newfound friends again. It would only be used in a life or death situation. "What are those tubes hanging from your suit?" Amber asked.

"Oh, they're just safety precautions for space flight. Blue tube keeps my body temp regulated, especially since I'm cold-blooded." Boomer pointed to a second. "This green tube makes sure the suit remains pressurized. I hate them flapping around when I walk, but I'd destroy the suit if I ripped them off... I don't feel like walking around naked. I had to discard my helmet, but luckily my utility belt wasn't damaged. They were gifts that came with my promotion."

So, their conversations continued. Buckley avoided the group, only staying within eyesight as he dragged along at the rear. Graf was curious to know what had happened to the man.

"Did princess say how he wound up here?" Graf asked Boomer.

"Something about his kingdom revolting against him. They were upset with how he ran the show. The people revolted and defeated his soldiers and wizards... They tied him to a pole and paraded him around the town stark naked." Boomer paused for a giggle. "They apparently chased him into the woods and he'd been lost for days. He was being choked by a huge snake when I found him. Word of advice: dough boy tries to sneak food at night, so sleep with one eye open."

Graf looked back at Buckley, who was talking to himself, kicking the ground as he walked. The man was twice Graf's age, but acted like a toddler. *Maybe there's hope for Eastern Rising,* Graf thought, *especially after my parting gifts to Gregor and his father.*

"You guys notice anything strange?" Boomer asked.

"About the forest? What's strange about it? I think it's just dandy," Graf retorted.

"No, I mean the last few days have been pretty peaceful... ever since we came into this valley," Boomer said.

Amber raised her eyebrows. "You know, Graf, aside from Buckley the banana slug back there, Boomer's right."

"Sanctuary... maybe we're getting close," Graf said.

"Well, let's not jinx things, eh? When do we stop for..." Boomer paused.

The trio stopped in their tracks at Boomer's sudden silence. Buckley wasn't paying attention, and the blubbery oaf crashed into Graf's back, nearly knocking him on his face.

"What now?" Buckley whined.

"I smell something." Boomer stared into the trees, still as a statue. Boomer hadn't proven to be a serious man thus far, but now the man was stone-cold sober.

A flock of birds exploded from the treetops and a dull roar could be heard through the trees. The noise grew louder and soon Graf heard the rustling of leaves and stomping of large feet. A hulking figure erupted from the forest and leapt into the clearing. This time it wasn't a fat, middle-aged man, but a minotaur. His body was larger than any man he'd ever seen. The pigmentation of its skin and hair was deep violet, and the beast was missing a horn and an eye on its left side. A golden ring dangled from its snout, and around its waist was a skirt of chainmail. The beast rested a not-too-friendly axe on his shoulder and placed its other hand on its hip.

"What are you doing here?" it asked. "Nobody comes here."

Graf was about to say something when Boomer spoke first, "We weren't aware this part of the forest was spoken for. We'll just be on our way..."

Boomer took a step forward but was stopped as the enormous axe planted its blade into the ground at his feet.

"You should've known better... they should've told you," it said. The creature's voice gargled, as if something was stuck in its throat.

"They?" Amber inquired. "Nobody told us anything. Like he said, let us go and we'll be out of your hair."

The Minotaur frowned and shook his head, "You're not going anywhere. It's dinner time and I'm hungry!"

"He's going to eat us!" Buckley's voice quivered with fear.

"Hold it together, numb nuts. I got this," Boomer whispered out of the corner of his mouth.

These loud-mouthed idiots are going to get us killed, Graf thought.

"We should warn you," Amber said. "We're not a group to be messed with."

Graf heard her growl and looked over to see Amber transforming back into her natural form, however her fangs were substantially longer and her muscles bulged, wet with perspiration. The minotaur seemed unfazed by her altered state.

"Enough games! You're all coming with me."

Graf had failed to notice the device Boomer grabbed from his belt.

"Like hell we are!" Boomer screamed.

A small red ball flew from his orange fingers, directed at the beast's face. It exploded, pluming into a ball of smoke as it struck the beast between the eyes. Amber howled like a wolf and flew at her opponent, leaping onto its chest and biting its neck. The minotaur roared like thunder, clubbing its fists into Amber's sides. She held on at first, but was eventually flung to the ground. She regained her bearings and maintained a defensive stance as she squared off with her enraged opponent.

"Run, you idiots... we gotta get the hell out of Dodge!" Boomer had made it a couple dozen yards down the trail when he realized nobody was following him.

"Amber, let's go!" Graf called.

"I got this," Amber growled, "never send a man to do a woman's job."

The minotaur beat his chest and scuffed the ground with his feet. "Who the hell do you think you are, you little brat?!"

Just then Graf saw an explosion of rotting wood and looked behind the beast to see a terrified Buckley holding the stump of a rotten tree limb. The beast snarled and turned on the fat man.

"Well, that explains why it was so light." Buckley dropped the limb and fell to his knees, "Oh, please don't eat me!"

Coward, Graf thought.

A net fell on top of the monster's head and he began to flail. Boomer was back with the group, having deployed another device from his belt.

"Run! I don't have anything else to spare!" He turned on the group and bolted into the trees.

Graf picked up Buckley and slung him over his shoulder. Amber had snapped out of her battle trance and they tore off into the trees.

"No! The trail is that way," Buckley pointed as he was jostled by Graf's running.

"There's no way we'd outrun him," Graf said. "We have to lose him in the forest."

Just then Graf realized something... the trail markings were still visible on the trunks of trees as they ran through the forest, dispersed every few yards. Boomer must have realized this. Their mad dash to the tree line didn't seem so desperate now.

They heard the footfalls of their pursuer behind them, and Graf could hear the saplings and smaller trees being uprooted by his mass. They all knew what awaited them if they stopped. Amber wouldn't be enough to stop the minotaur and Boomer was out of parlor tricks. *Maybe if I left Buckley behind it would give us some time*, Graf thought. *He'd make a decent meal.*

"No, Graf!" Amber called from ahead of him, looking over her shoulder with a chastising glare.

"What the hell have you been eating?" Graf asked Buckley. "You weigh a ton."

"What are you talking about? I'm wasting away here... can't you move any faster? I can see him!" Buckley was a squirming worm.

"Stop moving! I can barely keep up this pace with all your belly dancing."

"I see someone up ahead!" Boomer called.

Graf squinted. As they moved closer to the clearing ahead, he could see the shape of a man dressed in green: a hunter cutting meat from a recently killed deer that hung on a tree.

"Help! There's a monster behind us!" Boomer yelled. The group came to an exhausted halt before the hunter. He looked perplexed, and lifted his cap.

"Monster in these parts?" he asked.

"Yeah," Graf was gasping for breath, dropping Buckley to the ground. "A minotaur."

"Minowhat?" the man scratched his head.

Buckley turned over on his hands and knees, "What does it matter what it's called? Help us!"

Graf drew his sword, remembering his weapon. With this hunter joining their party, they might stand a fighting chance. Amber resumed a defensive stance and Boomer pulled Buckley behind the group. The hunter grabbed his bow and arrow and stood ready beside the duo. The minotaur finally made it to the clearing, its face bleeding and covered in soot from the smoke bomb.

"Oh, it's you," the hunter said, dropping his notched arrow.

Graf didn't like the sound of this, "You know this monster?"

"That's no monster," the hunter grinned, "that's family."

This was bad... really bad.

Amber reoriented in order to face the creature and the now seemingly hostile hunter. Boomer raised his fists, although Graf knew by now the alien was no fighter. Buckley began whimpering, and Graf glanced at the fat man. *Grow a pair*, he thought. His skills in combat were tested mostly against human foes, so the hunter wouldn't be a problem, but it was Amber that gave them a fighting chance against the minotaur.

The hunter began talking to the beast in a language no one in the group understood, but the tone of his voice implied that he was asking a question, and the beast replied with a glare towards the group. The minotaur proceeded to hold its side of the conversation with words that made no sense to Graf and his company.

"What's going on? What are you two plotting?" Boomer demanded what everyone else was thinking. It was obvious the group was being discussed by the pair, and they knew better than to hope it was with good intentions.

"We're just saying that you lot are more than we had bargained for," the hunter chuckled.

"Whatever," the beast huffed, still annoyed at having been attacked. "You skin 'em and I'll cook 'em, I just hope there's enough for a meal."

The hunter looked to the four travelers and winked.

"Sound's good to me."

Chapter 8

Welcomed with Open Arms

The hunter dropped his bow and arrow and pulled a curved dagger from his belt. He looked at the minotaur again before advancing on Graf and Amber. As severe as the situation was, the hair on Graf's neck prickled with excitement at the chance to once again wield his sword against worthy foes.

"It's been a long time since I've done this," Amber whispered. "Get back!"

Before Graf could respond, Amber's flesh and clothing exploded from her body, raining down in a shower of gore. When Graf wiped the blood from his eyes he was horrified at the growing mass of muscle, teeth, and claws. In moments, a towering beast stood before the Minotaur and hunter, sprouting three arms on each side and a wolf-like head with a saber-toothed grin. Her bellowing cry was horrifying, crossed between a wolf's howl and a baby's cry. It rang until Graf's eardrums felt like they would burst. Graf had assumed most of Amber's transformations were variations of her natural lupine form, but this went far beyond anything he'd seen so far.

The minotaur gasped in surprise and jumped back, his hands in the air.

"Hold it!" The hunter dropped the knife.

"I'll hold your severed heads!" Amber's voice was deep and demonic. Even Graf feared for his own safety.

"For cripes sake, we're just trying to help. This is how you repay us?" The minotaur was on the defense, grabbing his terrified companion and moving for the trees.

"Help us?" Amber guffawed. "You attacked us on the trail, threatened to filet us alive and eat us. If that's help, then you're about to get a heap of it!"

Amber leaped towards the two, who dodged out of the way at the last moment. Her six arms flew forward, smashing into the trunk of a red cedar. The wood was pulverized and the tree came crashing down on the hunter's tent. Buckley and Boomer watched on in shock and awe.

The minotaur charged Amber, spearing her in the stomach with his horns. "Attack you? Eating you?! I said it was dinner time... as in you idiots are late for the communal meal..."

"Communal meal?" Graf mouthed.

"Y-yeah," the hunter stammered. "They sent us to find you guys."

"Who sent you?!" Boomed Amber.

"Sanctuary, you heated bitch! They said a group of newcomers wanted to go exploring against Glenna's advice. She sent us to come to find you!" The shock had worn off and the Minotaur was ready for a fight.

"Wait, Amber!" Graf looked to the hunter. "If that's so, what was that talk about skinning and cooking us?"

The hunter looked perplexed and then his eyes went wide, "I was talking about the rabbits I caught for dinner."

"Likely story. You must really take us for suckers!" Boomer laughed.

"Look behind you," the hunter pointed to the tree he'd been skinning the deer on. Graf saw the rabbits' bodies draped over a nearby limb.

He heard a scuffle and turned to see the two beasts wrestling. The minotaur seemed to be winning at first, but Amber's extra limbs gave her an advantage. She hauled her opponent into the air and threw him, spiraling, into a bush.

"That does it!"

The beast roared, jumping back into the fray in another attempt to nail her with his horn.

"Amber, stop!" Graf called, but she didn't hear him. "Stop it! They're telling the truth!"

He jumped between the two mankillers, knowing such a maneuver was suicidal. Amber turned on him in a rage, her teeth bloody and eyes bulging. She grabbed him by the throat and heaved him into the air. She began choking the life from him before realizing who it was.

"Graf!" Amber cried, dropping him.

The last thing he felt before passing out was Amber cradling him in her arms.

***

"... and them things swelled up like a watermelon!" Boomer's voice was followed by laughter as the alien held out his hands in front of his crotch.

Graf's groggy vision began to clear, and he could clearly see the reflections of his companions sitting around the fire with the hunter and minotaur. The alien had no doubt been on a rant about his extraterrestrial misadventures. He looked to his other side and saw Buckley sitting with his back against a tree nibbling what was left of his dinner, making chewing noises Graf didn't think possible.

"It's about time," he said. "I'm so sick of Boomer's voice I'm about to puke."

Graf winced at the fat man's smacking mouth. "You ate my dinner, didn't you?"

Buckley shrugged. "I doubt you would have missed it. Besides, you're probably used to going without food. I need more sustenance."

"Sure, you do," Graf responded.

"Hey, look who's joining the party!" Boomer came over to help Graf to his feet.

Amber was right behind him, once again in her human form. The hunter had given her some undergarments to wear, since her old clothing had been destroyed. Her eyes met his and she smothered him with a ferocious kiss. After an eternity of 'oohing and ah-ing' by the others, they separated.

"I'm so sorry," she apologized.

"She thought you were me," the hunter chuckled.

"No hard feelings. But can somebody please tell me what the hell is going on here?" Graf sat down next to Boomer around the fire. Amber elaborated on what had happened after Graf passed out.

The minotaur's name was Lonnicker, and the hunter was called Berris. They'd been sent by Sanctuary to find another group of new arrivals who'd decided to venture outside the settlement boundaries, despite the advice of the settlement's leader, Glenna of the Woods. These were the newcomers Lonnicker had mistaken Graf's group for, as his prolonged hunting expeditions kept him out of the village proper for weeks at a time. He usually missed new arrivals. Lonnicker and Berris were the village hunter-gatherers. Although the people of Sanctuary apparently had the ability to conjure whatever food they desired, there was a high demand for wild caught game.

"... and our little misunderstanding caused us to miss the communal dinner back in Sanctuary. We'll take you there in the morning."

"What's the communal dinner?" Graf asked.

"Every night the entire village gathers at the Big House for a group meal. Glenna takes it pretty seriously," Berris said.

"What's mom like?" Boomer asked, referring to Glenna. "Is she a battle axe granny?"

"Battle-axe?"

"Yeah... a crotchety old boss lady... a shark-toothed ditch witch," Boomer replied.

"I'm sorry, but your metaphors elude me," Berris laughed.

"She's very kind, but very serious, if that's what you mean. Our words don't do her much justice. You'll get a better feel of her when you get there," Lonnicker added.

After some additional small talk, the party adjourned for bed. After his unintended nap, Graf wasn't very tired. Amber laid next to him.

"Your transformations are becoming very fluid," Graf mentioned.

Amber considered this. "It's been years since I've used that form. It came easily, but I was near exhaustion after only a short time. I wasn't sure I could manage it... pushing it out that quickly should've killed me. The choker must've had something to do with it. After you passed out, I noticed I was still wearing the necklace despite my human skin being decimated by the transformation. It definitely has potent magical properties."

"Keep your eye on it. I know this town is supposed to be peaches and cream, but there might be more to that necklace than we think. I don't want it falling into the wrong hands."

"Noted. I'm getting similar mixed feelings about Sanctuary. I think it's safe for now... the safest place for us in this forest... but something doesn't feel right." Amber went quiet.

Sanctuary indeed, Graf thought.

***

Lonnicker and Berris followed the marked path closely despite appearing oblivious to it. The trip only took a few hours, winding their way through trees and wild azaleas. Graf had never seen these colorful blooms before, and according to Lonnicker the plants grew in abundance near town.

"Sanctuary is in a hollow," Lonnicker stated. "It's surrounded by steep mountains, save for the entrance."

"You should consider getting a job as a tour guide," Boomer called.

"Yeah... I can show newcomers where I buried you," replied Lonnicker, cutting off Boomer's laughter.

Amber patted Lonnicker on the shoulder. "I didn't like you much at first, but for a minotaur, you're not that bad."

"Why does everyone keep calling me that?" Lonnicker puffed. "I'm not a minotaur. Don't you see what color I am? I'm a completely different race."

They continued in silence until they found a crude dirt path. The trail opened up into a grassy clearing set on a gradually inclining hill. Small homes and structures dotted the hill, and Graf doubted there were more than a few hundred people living here, at best. At the summit was a red, wooden frame house, simple in design save for the flaking Black Rose painted above the threshold. Graf rubbed his own tattoo, hidden by the sleeve of his tunic. He'd heard that Bernholt had the same marking but wasn't eager to reveal his own until he'd gotn his bearings. Berris stepped beside Graf and pointed to the house.

"That's the Big House. Bernholt lives there." Berris smiled and continued past the group.

"Lives there? How is that possible for a human after hundreds of years?" Amber asked.

"Glenna will explain. Come on," Lonnicker motioned for the group to keep moving.

Several modest farms could be seen on the edges of the settlement, growing what looked like wheat, corn, and other crops, although Graf thought these were out of season. Further up the hillside were dozens of A-frame houses, painted various shades of green, blue, and purple. Graf assumed the inhabitants of the village had a lot of leisure time, since most of these homesteads were surrounded by immaculate gardens and exquisite decorations. Much of the plant life in these gardens appeared unlike anything Graf had ever seen. *Humans might be a minority here*, he thought.

Graf was still taking in the surroundings when he tripped on something jutting out of the ground. Falling on his face, he felt something hop on his back and attack the back of his head. A stabbing pain followed.

"Intruder! Intruder!" It screamed.

"Cool it!" Boomer said as he picked the thing up by the collar of its shirt. "We come in peace."

Graf looked up at his attacker and then at the ground. The creature that attacked him was a small humanoid, less than half a foot tall, with a red ponytail sprouting from its scalp. The left side of its body was dark blue and its right was white. Lonnicker took the creature from Boomer and patted its head. What Graf thought was a root was actually a pint-sized dugout. His foot had punched a hole in its roof. The thing waved a small, toothpick-sized knife through the air, directed at Graf.

"Calm down, Small Fry," he said.

"Attack! I say, attack! My home is destroyed... kill the intruder!" It shrieked.

Graf was sprawled out on his back, holding hands in the air. "I'm sorry. I didn't realize there'd be such a small..."

"Careful with the 'S' word," Berris called from up the hill.

The creature hopped out of Lonnicker's arms and ran up to Graf's face, pointing the sticker at his nose. "Small?! Who's small? I'll cut you to ribbons! I'll take you with one arm behind my back! I'll..."

"You'll knock off the tough guy act." Lonnicker picked up the creature once again and shrugged at Graf. "He's got a little-man complex. Sensitive to the 'S' word."

"What's your name, friend?" Boomer asked, holding out a finger for the thing to shake.

"He just said it, dummy!" It lunged at Boomer with its poker.

Graf raised a brow. "Small Fry is his name?"

Small Fry went bonkers, flailing his arms and shouting curses at Graf. Lonnicker held on to the teeny warrior, but dropped him on the ground after his hand was bitten.

"Take it easy, Fry. He's a newcomer." Berris had rejoined the group.

"Oh, I see... a newcomer. All hail!" Fry pointed a small white finger at Graf. "You better watch your ass, hot shot!"

After that, the little man stomped his feet, shoved his knife back into his belt and ran back into what remained of his home.

"I think he likes you," Amber laughed as she helped Graf to his feet.

"Terrific! Now I'll have to sleep with one eye open, less that bedbug skewer me in the nuts." Graf rubbed the sore spot on his head and continued with the group.

As they ascended towards the Big House, they entered the town proper. There was a blacksmith, carpenter, and a baker as well as a cooper and an apothecary. On the western edge of the village Graf could see the waterwheel of a gristmill turning.

"The farming, mill works, and bakery are mostly just for show... several of the townsfolk enjoy working for food as a hobby," Lonnicker stated as they neared the Big House.

"So, what *do* you do for food?" Buckley asked.

"We conjure it, of course. Most of the homes have magical pantries and larders that stock themselves with whatever you wish. You just think of your favorite afternoon snack, open the door, and it's there, all prepared and ready to go," Berris added. "Some like to prepare their own meals... so you can summon your food raw if you want."

"That sounds a bit unimaginable," Graf said. He was still apprehensive in regard to Magic.

"You'll see at the meal tonight," Lonnicker said.

They finally arrived at the Big House. It was a two-story home, large compared to the other dwellings. The only thing that stood out aside from the Black Rose painted above the threshold was the front door itself. It was made of stained glass that seemed to glow from within. It depicted a hunter dressed in green, standing beside a bear of tremendous proportions.

"Bernholt built this himself. That's him," Berris smiled as he pointed at the image set in the door.

There was a balcony on the second floor, and a wing extended behind the main front of the house, extending into the forest. The stained-glass door opened and a cool breeze billowed out of the house. An elderly lady stepped out onto the porch. Graf would have described her as grandmotherly, and hadn't expected the leader of the settlement to appear so modest. She wore a white apron over a blue dress, and her snow-white hair was pulled back into a tight bun. Her clothing, like Graf's, was also in the same style as the folk dress of Eastern Rising, and Graf noticed the red stitching on the hem of her white apron. Like the house, she was modest in every aspect, and her smile seemed comforting and friendly. *Like a grandma,* Graf thought.

"We have more newcomers, Glenna," Lonnicker stated, matter-of fact.

Glenna pouted sympathetically and held out her hands to Graf's group. "My darlings, you must be ravished! Have no fear, you are safe. No harm will come to you here."

"Except from Small Fry," Boomer snickered.

Amber seemed to appreciate Boomer's sense of humor. "Oh, he's just smoke and mirrors, honey. Come into the cool, and I'll make us all a nice spot of tea. I might even have some cookies and other delectable treats prepared for you."

Buckley bustled through Amber and Graf. "You heard the lady, come inside! Excuse them, ma'am, they have no manners. Did you say cookies?"

Glenna patted the fat man on the shoulder and winked at the others as Buckley disappeared into the house.

"Would you like to join us?" Glenna held a hand to Lonnicker and Berris.

"Love to, miss, but we need to take some deer meat to the blacksmith. Then we're off for some more hunting," Berris said.

They hugged Glenna and departed.

"Now, please, do come in. I'd love to hear about your journey. I'll even introduce you to Bernholt if you'd like."

"He's alive?" Amber asked as she entered the house.

"All will be explained in good time, dear," the old lady answered.

Something about Glenna's response didn't sit well with Graf. Soon, he'd know why.

Chapter 9

The Undercroft

The house appeared stunningly larger than its exterior. The foyer opened onto a solid marble floor that led to a split staircase made of spalted maple, inlaid with lapis stonework and gold flakes. Stunning tapestries depicted hunting scenes; the bear was a theme repeated throughout the stories in these images. Glenna led them into a smaller room off the main entrance hall. There were several plush couches, lounge chairs, and several tables laden with sweetmeats, pastries, and chocolates. Obviously, Buckley made himself at home.

"Be comfortable and help yourselves to some snacks," Glenna gestured to the candies. "But don't spoil dinner! We're going to the town square later for the meal."

Buckley mumbled something under his breath as he stuffed another macaroon into his cream-smeared mouth.

"Well, there's one of us you won't have to worry about spoiling their meal," said Boomer.

Glenna held up a finger, "Ah, Boomer, I'd almost forgotten. I have a special treat I think you might like."

The old lady snapped her fingers. On the table next to Boomer's chair appeared what looked and smelled like a cow patty. Boomer's face lit up and he dove at the plate, his tongue extending almost a foot out of his mouth. In a few seconds, the plate was clean and Boomer had a brown mustache on his scaly face.

"I don't want to know what that was," Amber said.

"Don't diss it until you try it, sister!" Boomer wiped the gunk from his mouth with a tattered sleeve.

Graf's life didn't often grant him the luxury of the more appetizing of the confectionaries, and so, out of habit, he decided to wait for a more substantial meal. He doubted he'd be able to snack much anyway, with the rate Buckley was plowing through the candies. Glenna looked at him and smiled, as if admiring a grandchild.

The old woman eventually snapped out of her trance. "You must have dozens of questions. I know this is all a bit much for newcomers. I hope I can help you with this transition."

"Lonnicker and Berris said some newcomers had gone missing..." Amber began.

"Yes, they were a group of adolescents. Newcomers often like to explore, or attempt to find a way home. They were here less than a week when they left. I warned them, but you know how young adults can be."

"Anybody see which way they went?" Graf asked.

Glenna fingered a golden teardrop pendant hanging from a necklace she wore. There was a strange look in her eye that Graf couldn't place.

"No, sweetheart. They left during the night," she said, stoically.

Boomer shrugged, stood up, and waltzed around, touching the various ornaments displayed around the room.

"Well, this Bernie fella must've done well for himself. What was his racket, anyway?" Boomer accidentally knocked over a vase, but caught it before it hit the ground.

"Racket? Oh, you youngsters and your euphemisms. He was a hunter and a soldier before he came to the Wanwood, as he called it. He'd been exiled for murder... much as you were, Graf. You came from the same world, didn't you?"

Graf quickly looked to the mark on his forearm and noticed it was still concealed by his sleeve. He looked up to see Glenna smiling.

"My necklace gives me certain abilities, dear. Don't worry, I wouldn't tell anyone without your approval. Some of the locals are rather superstitious... they would take it as an omen."

"So Bernholt was a Black Rose?" Amber asked.

"Yes, dearie. He'd been in the wood for years before he founded Sanctuary. I came later, after the extermination," Glenna added.

"Extermination?" Buckley mouthed.

Graf was momentarily distracted shuddering at the sight of caramel stringing between the fat man's teeth.

Glenna nodded "They were wolf men called the Blaine. They were vicious warriors, and quickly they took over the wood. Many of the forest's denizens were killed, and the Blaine appeared to have taken over until Bernholt came."

"Took names and kicked ass, huh? Sounds like my kinda guy," Boomer chimed in. He wiped the smile from his face when Amber gave him a wicked glare.

"Oh, he hated killing. But in this case, there was no reasoning with the enemy," Glenna said.

Amber shook her head. "How could one man defeat an entire army of monsters? As great a fighter as he might've been, I just don't see it."

Glenna nodded in agreement. "You're right. Bernholt knew this too, and sought out what aid he could. Most of the natives met him with hostility, save one."

Glenna snapped her fingers, and the whole house disappeared. Graf and his companions found themselves in the woods without being in the woods. They were not scared or confused, as it was like watching something with your mind's eye, imagining a story vividly as it was being told.

***

There was a giant bear, and they all knew his name to be Aldo without being told.

It was not a mere bear, though. It was the god of bears and the master of the wood – they all knew it just by looking at him.

He was to a normal bear what a unicorn would be to a pack mule.

Suddenly, Bernholt was there beside Aldo. Graf stared at the tattoo on Bernholt's arm as he reached for the charm around his neck. This was his means of communing with this glorious creature.

There was a flash of light, and the scene shifted: Bernholt and Aldo were chasing the Blaine away, slaying them. The few survivors were driven deep into the forgotten parts of the forest and were never seen again.

The way Bernholt and Aldo worked together... the way they understood each other, was not the relationship of master and beast. They were brothers in body and soul.

***

Suddenly, they were back at the house, and Glenna was wiping away tears.

"What was that?" Buckley shivered, suddenly terrified.

"I cannot speak of them, it's too hard." Glenna shook her tearful face. "So, I thought I'd let you see for yourselves who our heroes were. They were linked in spirit even before the Traveler helped them see it."

Was that what Lonnicker and Berris had meant by being able to see Bernholt? Was that all that was left of him – a magically projected vision?

"You know of the Traveler..." Graf commented. "But why has everyone been so vague about Bernholt's status? Is he alive or not?" Graf was becoming anxious, and wished the woman would stop crying and get to the point.

"The Traveler came with a group of powerful beings who helped build Sanctuary... Helpers he called them. They built this house and most of the dwellings you saw in the settlement. They gave powerful gifts to the first settlers, including ways of summoning food, and constructed the veil of protection that surrounds Sanctuary, guarding it from monsters and the elements. One gift was a necklace given to Bernholt so he could commune directly with Aldo. I wear that necklace now." Glenna lifted the golden pendant she had been caressing while she talked.

"Why do you have it?" Amber asked.

Glenna's face contorted with sadness. "It wasn't until after the Traveler and his minions left that Bernholt became gravely ill. Unbeknownst to us, he had been poisoned by a minor injury sustained during his fight with a Blaine witch-doctor. What started as a flesh wound had brought death. It was then that I arrived at Sanctuary. Having practiced the healing magics of an apothecary in my home world, I tried to place Bernholt in stasis during his final moments before death... but to no avail. Not long after, Bernholt died. We never heard from the Traveler after that. Aldo left the village in anguish. It's been nearly 800 years..."

"... and nobody has heard or seen Aldo since," Graf finished.

"If Aldo cared so much for the people of Sanctuary, how could he just disappear? Why would he abandon the people Bernholt wanted to help?" Buckley was stuffing his face as he talked.

Glenna frowned. "I know not. I wish I could answer. I borrowed Bernholt's pendant with the hopes that one day I would hear from Aldo. I've had no such luck. Bernholt remains in the tomb where I placed him. Not knowing Aldo's fate is a cruel torture for us all."

"Wait," Boomer interjected. "If that was several centuries ago, that would make you nearly 800 years old as well. How could you have lived so long?"

"I'm not human, dearie, although my kind resemble humans. My lifespan is several times that of man, and time works differently in Sanctuary, regardless of species."

"Can we see Bernholt?" Amber asked.

Graf placed a hand on his tattoo. He couldn't explain why, but he felt drawn to this man. He rarely related to anyone in Eastern Rising, aside from his family and a few of the guards. He'd shared secrets with Amber, but it was difficult not having one who fully understood the hell he'd came from. Had Bernholt been exiled for reasons similar to what Graf did?

"All in good time, my dear. Have no fear," Glenna said, standing.

She walked past Graf to a silk curtain which she drew back with a golden cord. Behind this curtain was the portrait of a man that Graf knew to be Bernholt.

The man in the painting appeared in the likeness a hero of old, appearing dwarfed by the bear of unnatural proportions, which stood beside him. The bear was black and stood on its hind legs, displaying a V of white fur that shot across its chest. A necklace of animal bones and bird skulls was draped around the bear's neck, while Bernholt was dressed in green. Behind them, the Big House sat atop the hill. Graf smiled. The painting offered an aura of comfort and hope.

"If only you had met him before sickness took him. The first traces of it had been noticed shortly before I arrived here," Glenna said, stepping beside Graf. "I know you were probably expecting to meet him in the flesh. I'm sorry."

"I rarely feel sympathy for one I've never met, though I feel he and I share a kindred spirit. I never saw him fight or heard him speak. But seeing this painting makes me feel as if I were sitting around the fire with him, sharing ale, and a swapping tales of battle."

Glenna placed a hand on Graf's shoulder, "I'll take you to the undercroft, where Bernholt was laid to rest."

She turned, motioning for Graf and Amber to follow while Boomer and Buckley continued to argue over pie and pastries. They followed the woman outside, where she led them down a spiraling path down the other side of the hill into the woods. Graf was amazed at how swiftly Glenna walked, and as they stepped into the forest Graf saw the opening of a small cave in the earth.

"Bernholt rests here," she said, entering the cave and disappearing in the darkness.

Before Graf or Amber could speak, they saw a spark of flame as Glenna lit a torch. Entering the cave, they were given several more torches taken from the walls. The passage was narrow and irregular, marked with boulders and pits leading into the darkness. After what seemed like an eternity, they came to a large cavern, where they saw a large marble vault set into the wall. Glenna set her torch into a holder beside the marble, and gently rested a hand on the stone. The slab was smooth and polished, and its edges were trimmed in silver and gold. Aside from this, the stone was bare save for a rose carved into the center, painted black. The symbol was an older version of the tattoo Graf now possessed, but it was similar enough for Graf to recognize the dreaded brand of Eastern Rising.

Tears of sorrow had replaced Glenna's smile. "His body is here, behind this stone marker."

"Why were we told Bernholt was still alive... that he lived at the Big House?" Amber asked.

Glenna sighed. "What they probably meant was that his spirit lives here, watching over Sanctuary from the worlds beyond. His deeds were so great in life that his presence never left when his body expired. My magic, as great as I thought it to be, failed to heal him of the sickness brought on from the enemy's blade. But he will always be a part of Sanctuary."

Graf didn't speak; he didn't have to. This man who the Traveler had spoken so highly of, this person who had affected the lives of so many of the wood's denizens, was rotting in a cave, all but forgotten.

Glenna smiled at Amber and walked to her. "Let's give Graf a moment. This means more to him than either of us."

"Will you find your way out of the cave?" Amber asked Graf, resting her hand on the small of his back.

Graf nodded, turning back to cold, dead marble.

He doubted he stood there for more than a few minutes, but it felt like hours. Just as he was turning to leave, he heard a familiar voice. It wasn't loud. In fact, he would've missed it completely were it not for the hollow silence of the cavern. *Touch the rose*, it said.

"Traveler?" Graf looked around, half expecting to see the crotchety hermit whose voice he'd heard.

Graf looked at the emblem on the marble, and slowly reached out his forefinger. Just as it brushed against the black dye of the inlay, there was a loud *thunk*, and Graf looked down to see a small door open up in the rough stone beneath the tomb. Inside, he found a crumbling leather journal. As he turned the pages, he saw crude handwriting of a bizarre language he'd never seen.

Keep it hidden from Glenna, the Traveler's voice returned to Graf.

Graf turned the journal over in his hand. It was slightly larger than his palm and could easily fit his pocket. Graf quickly slipped the book into his pants as he returned to the sunlit lands. Before he reached the entrance, he heard the Traveler's voice a final time.

Beware the Silver Fox.

Chapter 10

Invitations and Warnings

Glenna allowed Graf's group to settle into temporary accommodations within the Big House. Boomer and Buckley were shown their own suites while Amber and Graf were given a bedroom festooned with cedar garlands and carved wooden furniture. The room was also decorated with shoulder-height cedar trees that appeared to grow right out of the floorboards. The room held a cozy alcove bed behind red, heart-shaped wooden doors. Graf informed Amber of what he'd experienced in the cave.

"It's odd that the Traveler would want me to keep the journal from Glenna," Graf said. "Maybe she's not all 'tea and cookies' like she appears to be."

"Should we tell the others?" Amber asked, laying down next to Graf on the bed.

Graf frowned. "Boomer wouldn't care and I don't trust Buckley to save my life. We should keep this to ourselves for now."

"Well, don't act suspicious around Glenna. We don't want to alienate her when we don't even know the facts yet."

"Why would I act suspicious?"

"I can read you like a book, Graf. You were wary about her from the beginning, and now you don't trust her at all," Amber chided.

"You didn't hear what the Traveler said to me."

Amber propped herself up on an elbow and looked into Graf's eyes. "Did the Traveler say Glenna couldn't be trusted?"

"No, but..."

"Then why are you assuming the worst? Why do you instantly suspect some grand conspiracy? Did the Traveler say anything about Glenna being evil? Did he say anything about the wicked secrets of Sanctuary?"

"I already told you," Graf retorted. "He barely said anything. Just the 'beware the Silver Fox' nonsense. I don't even know what he meant."

"Then relax. What does the journal say? Maybe that'll answer your questions."

Graf opened the journal to reveal illegible scribblings. "It's just more nonsense. I looked through the entire thing and I can't make out one word."

"Then calm yourself, Graf!" she playfully slapped his cheek.

Just then the door opened and a dwarf dressed in blue stepped forward, ringing a small bell.

"Dinner will be held soon. Glenna of the Woods requests your presence," the dwarf turned to leave the room. "Follow me, please."

Graf and Amber met Boomer and Buckley in the hallway and proceeded downstairs. They were led out a back door and followed a trail into the woods behind the mansion. Soon, they were in a dimly lit clearing – lit by what, Graf couldn't tell – and a group of several hundred people were sitting at long stone tables.

"You finished fixing my roof yet?" A shrill voice called from the table.

"It's that pixie! You crushed his burrow, remember?" Boomer laughed.

Graf approached the table and saw the small creature sitting on a small stool on top of the table. Set before the bi-colored imp was another miniature table no bigger than Graf's palm. A closer look at Small Fry's face revealed androgynous features that appeared neither male nor female. His body, although humanoid, shared the same unnatural neutrality.

"Look, we got off on the wrong footing. I'm sorry for damaging your home, and hopefully we can…" Graf was cut off.

"Knock off the mushy stuff. I should have seen it coming, as big and oafish as you big'uns are. I should've picked a better spot." Small Fry grabbed a thimble sized goblet and took a sip.

"I see they give you special accommodations," Buckley said. Graf cringed, as a verbal barrage was bound to ensue.

"I'm in a good mood, now, because it's dinner. Don't push your buttons, wide load," Small Fry replied as he pointed a microscopic bread roll at the fat man.

"Attention, everyone!" Glenna's voice was heard at the head of the table.

The citizens of Sanctuary turned to look at their matriarch. She had donned a white dress with red frills at the shoulders and a red sash. She looked the appearance of a kindly godmother, holding in her outstretched hand a plate of buttered rolls for a small boy sitting by her side.

"We've lost one group of newcomers only to be blessed by new additions to our family. I still hold out hope that those youngsters will find their way back safely. Until that time comes to pass, I want you to welcome Graf, Amber, Boomer, and Buckley with open arms." Glenna tilted her head toward them and smiled.

"Amen and oh me! Let's eat already!" Small Fry's squeaky voice chimed in.

Chuckles filled the clearing and Glenna proceeded with helping the children fix their plates. Graf certainly hoped Amber had been right about Glenna. The woman seemed genuine. Her weathered wrinkles, snowy hair, and pudgy figure would make any child run into her arms with unconditional love. With her in charge, Sanctuary really did seem like a happy family.

While Graf and the others snacked on various meats and strange foods, they were introduced to the locals. There were a number of human families that took care of the mill and smaller farms. A pair of pudgy twin girls were fascinated with Amber, who promised to show them her dog transformation later. Between sips of wine, Boomer had begun flirting with a purple fairy, barely knee high, who showed little interest in the alien but seemed strangely attracted to the uncouth Buckley. The portly man was obviously not accustomed to the affections of the fairer sex, and at one point spilled a cup of soup into his lap. This didn't turn off the fairy, who continued to swoon over the flubbed fellow. Boomer turned his attentions to a tree spirit who ended up being male, much to his chagrin, and Amber continued to share stories with the farm twins. There were dozens of other strange creatures Graf had never seen before, and although the entire event was rather intimidating, he did his best to greet everyone he came across.

"So that's your girl?" Small Fry asked Graf. Graf had been so lucky as to sit down next to the obnoxious imp.

"We met under strange circumstances, but we're making it work so far. Do you have a wife?" Graf asked.

Small Fry giggled. "My kind don't have wives. We have over a dozen different biological genders... male and female among them... and my gender isn't compatible to reproduce with males or females."

"A dozen genders?" Graf was surprised by this information. "But everyone refers to you as if you're male."

"Well, my gender more closely resembles that of a male, so I adopted male pronouns. It's rather restricting though, as most of the species I've met here only have male and female." The imp popped a sunflower seed kernel into his mouth.

"How long have you been here?" Graf asked.

"About twenty years or so. Time doesn't seem to affect us here. Took me nearly ten years to learn the common tongue most of you speak... had to take on that idiotic 'Small Fry' nickname too... My real name is 72 words long, in your language at least.

Nobody knew how to pronounce it. Gotta love compromises, huh?" Small Fry continued to devour his small assortment of nuts, cherries and bite-sized morsels of meat.

"Well, what would you want me to call you?" Graf didn't feel like getting attacked by the imp over a misunderstanding.

"Fry... just Fry," he said.

Graf left it at that and continued to circulate amongst the locals. The baker, a portly man named Leon, introduced him to several dwarfs, a gnome, and what at first looked to be a bucket of tar. It turned out to be a gelatinous being that communicated telepathically. Deemed Pitch by the locals, it seemed friendly enough. Its one tragic flaw was its fondness for stale, cliché jokes. They were worse than Boomer's anecdotes, which said a lot. Graf chuckled politely before parting ways with Pitch, which involved sticking his hand into its jelly-like substance. Graf much preferred normal handshakes.

Graf spent what was left of the meal speaking with a young man named Asa, who was a gardener of sorts, and who acted as a caretaker for a nearby shrine made to honor Bernholt. Asa was a human around Graf's age, rather dirty and unkempt, and spoke with a strange dialect Graf had never heard before. His personality was likable enough, however, and the two immediately struck up a bond. They chatted about a variety of topics, but mostly about daily life in their native worlds. Asa claimed he'd worked as a wizard's assistant and had learned a variety of extraordinary uses for common herbs and weeds. Asa had been rather rambunctious with his experiments, and what was supposed to be an expectorant for a mild cough nearly killed his wizard. Once recovered, the wizard promptly fired Asa and banished him from the community.

"Plant life is the ginchiest, daddy-o! I'm always cross-breeding different plants and experimenting back at my pad. You guys should stop by sometime," Asa suggested.

"I'll keep that in mind –" Graf was interrupted when Amber appeared at his shoulder.

She had overheard their conversation. "Just don't tell him if you catch a cold, babe. I wouldn't want him to force feed you some concoction that'd turn you into a donkey!"

Asa laughed and slapped Graf's shoulder in farewell, inviting the couple to 'brunch' the next day... whatever 'brunch' was. As the strange man turned to leave, he muttered something about "beating feet" before Glenna press-ganged him into "lame" chores. Graf's attention was drawn to Boomer and Buckley, who were arguing as usual. Boomer's ego had been bruised when he had failed to woo a new girlfriend. Meanwhile Buckley's lavender lover had to be peeled off the fat man's face.

"Lover's quarrel?" Amber asked the obnoxious pair.

Boomer flung his hands in the air. "I just don't get it! I'm usually a Don Juan with the ladies... human, Martian, or anything! For God's sake, they don't call me Bang-Bang Boomerang for nothing! How does butterball over here get some and I don't?"

"I think it's the other way around," Amber teased. "You're just upset because that girl's driving a wedge between your brotherly love!"

Boomer and Buckley continued to heckle each other as they walked back to the Big House. Graf and Amber were walking hand in hand when Glenna appeared out of nowhere, spooking the pair.

"Oh, my dear, I'm so sorry! I didn't mean to frighten you... I was just hoping I could talk with Graf a bit." Glenna looked to Amber with a smile, squinting her eyes and cocking her head to the side in that petite, grandmotherly way.

"Um... yeah. Sure. I'll go back to the suite. See you soon," Amber pecked Graf on the cheek and continued along the trail.

Graf walked back towards the clearing with Glenna. She remained silent until they were both back at the table, which had somehow been cleared of the leftovers and dirty plates. Glenna sat down at a random seat and looked to Graf. Her kind demeanor had disappeared.

"You met Asa, didn't you?" Glenna raised an eyebrow at Graf.

Since the incident in the cave, Graf felt uneasy around the woman. "Yes. He seems a likable sort."

"Just be careful around him, dearie. He has a kind heart, but he often fills the ears of newcomers with tales of wonder and shoddy wisdom." Glenna's gaze met Graf. "But they're nothing but fables and fairy tales."

Graf tried to remain open minded, but why was Glenna growing so concerned with his conversing with Asa? Granted, Graf knew very little about anyone in Sanctuary. For the meantime, he attempted to remain neutral in his responses until he knew more about Glenna's motives.

She giggled and placed an aged hand on Graf's. "I'm not telling you that he's dangerous, Graf. He's just lost in the clouds. He came to Sanctuary shortly after Bernholt died, and never made much of a connection with anyone. Not that the villagers don't enjoy his company. He's the caretaker of a shrine built for Bernholt just after his death... we pay our respects there."

"I'll remember that, and I'll make sure to take what he says with a grain of salt," Graf answered.

"As you should with any of us," she sighed. "Until you get to know us a bit better, that is... until you begin to build relationships with those you'll be sharing your life with."

"I heard something about time not affecting us here. What does that mean, exactly?" Graf asked.

She stared up at him. "Oh, time still takes its toll, dearie. It's just that here, in Sanctuary, aging is slowed down considerably. A human who might live 70 or 80 years in their world, may live to be several thousand years old. So no, we are not immortal, but we might as well be."

"It's too bad Bernholt isn't still here," Graf stated.

"I've troubled you enough, dearie. Go back to Amber and get a good night's rest. But still, I fear there may be a time when you are needed Graf. I can't explain it, but I sense great power in you, and in Amber." Glenna hugged Graf and walked past him towards the Big House.

"Goodnight, Glenna," Graf said as she departed, but she didn't acknowledge him.

Chapter 11

A Green Thumbs Up

Graf spent several hours that night studying the small journal from Bernholt's tomb. *Nothing more than a mess of dots and squiggly lines,* he thought, slapping the book shut. Graf had studied several different languages and writing styles in his lifetime, but this was literal chicken scratch.

"Never keep a lady waiting," Amber's voice called from the bed.

Graf grunted in disapproval. "I've got to figure out what the hell's going on here. Something's not right..."

"Are you still obsessing over what Glenna said to you?" Amber asked.

Graf stared silently at the crumbling leather cover of the journal. He didn't know what to believe at this point. The Traveler had said nothing about conflict in Sanctuary. Granted, the man admitted to not knowing the current affairs of the village. Glenna appeared as a benevolent matriarch, but life had taught Graf that appearances weren't everything. There was a slyness about her. She reminded Graf of a fox, sliding through the night and stealing away with a mother hen's chicks.

A Silver Fox.

The thought came to him like a voice carried across the wind. Graf wasn't experienced in the art of telepathy, but Graf was certain the thought had come to him from somewhere else. At first Graf thought of the Traveler, but this felt different. No, this thought wasn't from him. But if it wasn't the Traveler, then who was it?

"Graf!" Amber's voice shook his ears.

He'd been in a haze and hadn't heard her yelling at him from their bed.

"Come to bed. We don't seem to be in imminent danger... we'll have plenty of time to figure out what the journal says. Staying up all night and worrying yourself sick won't do a thing." Amber had come to Graf's side, laying a hand on his shoulder.

"You're right. Traveler wouldn't have sent us into a viper's nest without warning." Graf stood up and walked back to bed.

They slept soundly, wrapped in the warm cradle of downy quilts, Amber's head resting on Graf's shoulder. He wasn't sure where fate would take them, but for the moment having this woman at his side helped him forget the loss of his family and home. There was never a night he'd slept so soundly.

***

It was noon when they finally roused to the sound of a meaty dwarf-fist pounding on their door offering housekeeping services. They quickly dressed – Graf stuffing the journal into the safety of his trousers – and allowed the dwarf to make their bed and tend to the trees that grew from the woodwork.

Glenna was reading a book in the lounge downstairs, rising with a smile as the duo entered the room.

"We're sorry we overslept," Amber said, "we were so tired from our journey, and it's been an eternity since I've slept in such a comfortable bed."

Sylvia laughed. "No need to apologize to me, dear. I would've been surprised if you hadn't slept so late. You'll find things fairly easy-going in Sanctuary. No need to stress over the daily routines and rituals that plagued our former lives."

Glenna soon left to tend to Bernholt's vacant quarters. This was to "keep it as it was at his passing," as she stated.

Graf reminded Amber about Asa's offer of brunch, as they were both beginning to hunger. Thus, they proceeded down the hill until they found a cozy purple chalet nestled into a steeply inclining hill. The A-frame hovel was surrounded by a variety of bizarre flora neither had seen before. On either side of the doorstep were snow-white ferns that were icy-hot to the touch, being surrounded by a cloud of frosty, chilled air. There were white flowers that sprouted egg shaped balls in a variety of pastel colors, and a blood-red lily that had a blue duck's head jutting from it. The duck used its beak to attack these eggs, which caused brown goo to spray onto the nearby walls. More striking than this, though, were the rose-bushes that appeared to be made of emerald and obsidian.

"What a marvelous ornament!" Amber exclaimed.

At this statement the front door burst open, and there stood Asa. He appeared grubby, as he had the previous night, with his hair a black web tangled atop of his head. His tattered orange coat was smeared with dirt and grass stains. Graf couldn't help but wonder how such a grungy looking man could keep such a beautiful abode.

Asa's voice issued from the front door, "Ain't no ornament, sweet cheeks. Word from the bird, that's a live plant."

"But it's made of glass, and the other flowers have eggs and bird heads popping out of them," Graf exclaimed. "They're not real plants!"

"They're as alive as you and me, daddy-o! Believe me when I say them things are hard to grow... especially the chocolate eggs! Back home I could sell 'em for a fortune. Hell, I'd be made in the shade!" Asa stepped down and offered his hand to Graf.

As soon as Graf grasped the man's extended hand he felt a sharp jolt shoot through his fingers and up his arm. Startled, he backed away and drew his dagger.

"Hey, daddy-o, I'm just razzing your berries!" Asa doubled over with laughter, holding up his hand to reveal a small metal device held in his palm. "It's just a gag!"

"Forgive me," Graf put away his sword. "My life hasn't been filled with humor."

"You'll have to break us in... slowly," Amber teased, cautiously accepting a kiss on the cheek from their new friend.

Normally, Graf would have been hard-pressed to keep his calm from such a prank. Graf had broken several men's jaws over light-hearted, but ill-placed jokes. However, Asa's lackadaisical nature had a soothing effect. What agitation the hand buzzer had brought was quickly shoved to the wayside as Asa invited them indoors.

They stepped onto lush green carpet, their feet sinking into it as if walking on a cloud. *Wait!* Graf thought, *this isn't carpet at all... it's grass!* It was as thick as any grass Graf had ever seen, and at a closer inspection, Graf couldn't find a single ant, worm, or millipede. He and Amber must've looked completely astounded, because Asa began to laugh and clapped his hands together before reaching up to scratch his greasy hair.

"Grass! Ain't that a gas?" Asa escorted the two further into the room. "My old lady back home was always givin' me the business for tracking mud and grass on the carpet, so I figured I'd save myself the trouble."

Like the Big House, the home was considerably larger than it appeared from the outside. They entered another room with grass of a blue-green hue.

"They call this Kentucky Blue," Asa pointed to several wooden chairs in the center of the room. "Have a seat and I'll go get some tea."

The chairs quite comfortable, as they were cushioned by a thick velvet padding. Looking around, Graf noticed the same type of miniature trees he'd seen back at the Traveler's cabin. He recognized it as a willow tree, but the foliage was a brilliant sky blue. These dozens of small trees were stacked on a variety of redwood stools set in front of an ornamental bamboo wall. Graf had seen bamboo before. Graf's mother had given his sister a bamboo walking stick she'd attained during one of the many adventures of her youth. However, he'd never seen it in such a quantity. Hanging from the ceiling, which seemed to be covered in ferns, were dozens of strange lamps made from thin orange paper.

"I see you're admiring my bonsai." Asa came in, handing them two slender glasses.

Graf eyeballed Asa. In the few breaths it took Asa to grab the tea, he appeared to have bathed and donned new attire. Asa's black hair had been combed and slicked back on his head with the exception of a single curl that fell across his face. Graf had never seen such a hairdo before. Instead of the smelly orange rags he'd worn, Asa sported a bizarre outfit consisting of black pants and a red and white striped jacket over a white undershirt with an unusually high collar.

"Bonsai?" Graf had never heard of the word.

"Yeah." Asa took a long sip of his tea. "They're a horticulturist's hobby back on Earth. Earth is the bee's knees! You ever get the chance to go there, Graf, you gotta do it!"

"Earth..." Graf had heard of that world several times. "Boomer's been there... I think he comes from that universe... and we were also told of Earth by..."

A cough and a kick in the shin from Amber silenced Graf. She was right, no sense blabbing his life story to this man until he knew a bit more about him. Asa saw Graf eyeballing his outfit and chuckled, "Never seen threads like this before, have ya? I used to be in one of them barber shop quartets. Never liked the bow tie, so I ditched it and popped the collar. Now I'm cool breeze, daddy-o!"

Graf stared blankly at Asa.

Amber laughed and reached a hand over to pat Graf on the shoulder. "Asa, I can honestly say neither of us understood a word you just said, and what's the deal with these clothes?"

"Sorry toots! I keep forgetting you cats come from a different place and time. I'll try to tone it down a bit." Asa laughed as he pulled out a small comb, which he ran through his hair. "I take this undercover gig pretty seriously, and when a fella's out and about he's gotta fit the part. I don't like to dress too flashy in public... attracts too much attention. Can you imagine what Glenna would say if she'd seen me dressed like this?!"

Undercover? Graf had heard that reference before.

Asa suddenly looked hard at Amber, squinting his eyes as if trying to make something out. She raised an eyebrow and glanced over at Graf.

"I'll be a monkey's uncle!" Asa slapped his knee. "That's my old lady's choker you're wearing!"

Amber reached up to feel the enchanted necklace the Traveler had given her, and that's when Graf put two and two together.

"You're the Gardener!" Graf exclaimed.

"Jesus H. Christ, you guys just now figuring that out? My green thumb wasn't obvious enough?" Asa snorted, sticking both thumbs up in the air.

"We didn't exactly have much to go on."

"That Traveler in one of his mad-dash rushes again, huh? Ah, hell with 'em! He's just sore cuz I don't gotta tramp across the multiverse like he does!" Asa suddenly glanced up into the air, as if he'd heard something, then said to nobody in particular, "Oh, cut the gas, Benny! You know boss man's taken a shine to me!"

Graf grew more perplexed by the minute. "Who are you talking to?"

"Oh, just Traveler. He's always trying to stick his nose where it don't belong. The rat's probably trying to catch me saying something bad so he can run and tell the Big Cheese! Real brown nose, that guy!" Asa finished off his tea after his rant.

Graf suddenly remembered what Glenna had said about Asa being full of nonsense, but Graf also remembered Traveler's advice of trusting the Gardener above all others.

"For once, the square's right!" Asa laughed and slapped his knee.

Amber raised an eyebrow as she glanced at Graf. "Reading minds? I guess you're in league with Traveler after all."

"Don't throw me in with that bunch, kitten. Those germs call themselves 'Helpers,' but they're just a bunch of cooks. They can sit on it! I fly solo." Asa pointed at Graf. "Anyhow, let's talk business. I see you brought that little book you found in the secret compartment I built."

Graf's hair stood on end when Asa mentioned Bernholt's journal. If there'd been any doubt about Asa before, there was none now. Amber nodded when Graf looked in her direction for support, and with reluctance he pulled out the journal.

"I thought Traveler showed me the journal at the tomb, but it was you after all," Graf said.

Asa snorted as he snatched the journal from Graf and began to flip through it. "Tomb indeed! I take it you had trouble reading this, huh?"

"I can't read it at all. It's not written in any language I've ever seen, and what do you mean by 'tomb indeed'?"

"This journal is written in a language called *Liar's Eye*," Asa said. "Bernie used it all the time."

Liar's Eye? Graf thought. He'd heard of the dead language from his mother's tales of her adventures across the Compass Rose – her name for the continent that Eastern Rising was a part of – but he had never seen written examples. The language had been outlawed in Eastern Rising before Graf was born. It had been used by various groups ranging from thieves and slave traders to black magic cultists and cold-blooded murderers. This upset Graf. He'd hoped Bernholt had been banished for some noble cause like defending his family's honor as he had, or standing up to the corrupt Keeplord. However, his mother had made it clear no decent man in all the lands had ever used the *Liar's Eye*.

Asa closed the journal momentarily. "Why the long face, daddy-o?"

"I know the script, though I've never seen it in writing. It's a language used by bandits and criminals to conceal their foul deeds. I'd thought Bernholt was a man of honor... Then again, he *was* branded with the Black Rose." Graf looked at his own brand.

"Bernie cleaned up his act once got here, but on the outs he was one hell of a hairy dude... I'm talkin' a real, low down hood rat!"

Amber placed a hand on Graf's shoulder. "Don't be too upset. We were all different on the outside. You heard Asa say he changed, didn't you?"

"He sure did. Became a real cool cat once he met Aldo."

Graf had heard others speak of the Great Bear before. "I want to learn more about this Aldo. I heard he disappeared after Bernholt died."

"There you go again with all this death talk! He ain't dead! Didn't you read the journal?" Asa chuckled as he flipped back through the pages. "Oh, I forgot. It's written in the Liar's Eye!"

"What do you mean he's not dead? Glenna said..." Amber was cut off by another snort from Asa.

"What a snow job! Who you supposed to trust, here?"

"Then what's Glenna's story? Who... or what... is she and why did she tell us Bernholt was dead?" Graf stood up and began pacing the turf.

"She probably believes it," Asa said, "See, she's the chick who..."

Graf's attention was drawn to Amber, who'd covered her ears.

"What is it?" Graf asked.

She winced, "I think Traveler's talking to Asa. I can't make out what he's saying, but there's a buzzing noise... like a bee just flew into my ear."

"Zip it, honey. I'm talkin' here!" Asa barked, looking back up at the ceiling. "Well, why can't I just tell 'em now?"

"Tell us what?" Graf asked.

Asa shushed him with a wave of his hand. "But I gotta tell 'em about Bernie and the flower, anyhow! Can't I just spill the beans?"

Asa sighed and rolled his eyes. Without addressing Amber or Graf, he excused himself to another part of the house. Here the argument with Traveler continued. After several minutes of incoherent shouts, the man returned.

"Benny flipped his lid when I started talking about Glenna," Asa said. "He always jumps my bones about 'breaking rules' and all that crapola."

"What do you mean breaking rules?" Graf asked.

Asa began to comb his hair again. "See, boss man don't like us bashing ears."

Amber was growing agitated. "For crying out loud!"

"OK, woman! What I mean is we can only share certain things at certain times. Now, I try to bend the rules to help out nice folks like you, but Traveler is a battle axe when it comes to following rules. That frosted fink thinks he's a damn enforcer!"

"But why can't you tell us about Glenna? It's obviously important," Graf said.

"Well, I don't agree with it, but Traveler does have a point. Big things are happening in Sanctuary, and if you know too much too soon..."

"We might act too soon, and put all of our lives in peril," Amber completed.

"Took the words right outta my mouth, Dolly!"

"So, what can you share with us? Are you going to tell us what happened to Aldo or where Bernholt really is?" Graf asked.

Asa pocketed his comb and stood up. "Follow me, gang!"

Chapter 12

The Grotto

Asa led them through another grass-carpeted room and out a back door made of marble, where they found themselves on a terrace. He crossed the patio to a winding path leading into the forest. Twin statues, made from onyx, stood on either side of the path's entrance. They lowered their spears as Graf and Amber attempted to follow Asa.

"Asa," Graf called. "A hand, please."

Asa looked back and rolled his eyes. "Oy vey! Knock it off, guys, they're with me!"

Asa walked up to the statues and smacked the backs of their heads. They withdrew their spears and Graf hesitantly crossed the threshold into the forest. According to Asa, their destination could only be found on this path and only he had the power to cross these enchanted guardsmen. Anyone – or anything – who attempted to enter the path without Asa's consent would be killed. They were some of the several other-worldly tools his employer allowed him to bring to the Wanwood.

"Nobody can hold a candle to these cats in a fight," Asa remarked as they kept pace on the trail. "Not even Glenna." He seemed particularly proud of that.

Asa continued to make light-hearted remarks about his work on other worlds and about Sanctuary. He made several references to powers and abilities Glenna apparently possessed, and those she lacked. Every time Graf attempted to question Asa further, the man would change the subject or give short, vague responses. Eventually, Graf decided it was best to let Asa share the truth about the woman in his own time.

Despite his illogical ramblings and aggravating dialect, Asa did tell them they were going to a shrine of sorts.

"Bernholt's shrine?" Graf asked. "Glenna mentioned it to me."

Asa gave a strange laugh, as if he knew something Graf didn't.

"She fed you a line of bull, kid," he responded.

"She doesn't know about this shrine! The other is a decoy," Amber stated, matter-of-factly.

Asa clapped his hands and laughed. "Amen and a bottle of pop! Girl, you're just too smart. I gotta spill the beans, Graf, I thought you'd be more intuitive than her."

Graf was aggravated with Asa's remark, but Amber reassured him by quickly grasping his hand.

Graf winked at her, and despite the anger scorching his ears, took a deep breath. His anger had often benefited him in his homeland, but he'd already learned that the Wanwood operated differently. Graf also knew that taking a swing at someone with Asa's abilities may not be a wise decision.

"Honey, I'm home!" Asa smiled at the couple and extended his hand as they arrived at a clearing. "Feast your eyes on this slice of heaven."

They stopped beside Asa to observe the sunken garden they'd arrived at. Two paths crossed in the center, marked with a beautiful fountain carved from iridescent blue stone. The garden was teaming with life: Graf recognized the azaleas, hydrangeas, pink flowering cabbage, and kale. Appearing to mark the four directions were four small trees bearing strange purple fruit. A plaque of marble was set before each tree marking the directions: north, south, east and west. This garden was clearly an homage, not just to Bernholt, but also to his and Graf's world: The Compass Rose. Asa plucked a piece of purple fruit from a tree and took a bite. As Graf walked closer to the fountain, he recognized the figures mounted in the center: Bernholt and the king-bear, Aldo.

"Looks just like the painting in the Big House," Graf said. "Whoever carved this was a master craftsman."

"A colleague of mine did this. Carved it out of blue jasper. Sucky part is it'll all be rubble when we bust Bernie out."

Graf and Amber exchanged glances before the latter spoke, "What do you mean, bust out?"

"See, now that we're here I can give you the rundown! I didn't want to risk someone eavesdropping back at the house. Glenna has no power here." Asa motioned for them to sit on the edge of the fountain. "Hold your questions until I'm finished. We got a lot riding on this, so don't distract me."

"This should prove interesting," Amber whispered in Graf's ear.

Graf looked up at the figure of Bernholt, standing in a pose of victory beside his ursine companion. Instead of a plume of water sprouting from the top of the massive sculpture, the water seemed to be secreted out of the stone itself, cascading in rivulets down the length of Bernholt and the bear before collecting in the basin.

"Blue was always Bernie's favorite color," Asa said. "Don't know why they always paint him in green. And look at those curly locks! Blondie sure could rock that hair."

"So much for staying focused," Graf groaned.

"What? Oh, yeah, we can reminisce later. Now seriously, don't go getting me all twisted. I'm a gardener, not a story-teller."

"Get on with it!" The couple shouted in unison.

"So, Glenna probably told you how she came to Sanctuary shortly before Bernie's death and how he had been poisoned by the Blaine wolves. Then she probably explained how Aldo, the bear, was so grief stricken that he ran away to find some way of reviving Bernie, but never returned. Bernie eventually died. This is probably where she throws me into the mix and claims I'm some delusional outlier that stumbled into Sanctuary shortly after. Are we on the same page?"

"Close enough," Graf said.

Asa nodded, "Well, she lied out of her keister! Bernie wasn't poisoned by the Blaine, and Aldo didn't abandon Sanctuary."

"How do you know? Did Traveler share this with you?" Amber asked.

"No, toots. I was there. Glenna didn't see me because I wasn't in human form yet."

"What?" They both blinked back at him.

"Have some water," Asa nodded with his head to the fountain, "and you'll see it all like you were there."

"Like Glenna's vision?" Graf asked.

"Even better," Asa winked.

Graf and Amber exchanged a look, not fully knowing what to do. The Traveler had told them to trust the Gardener above all others, and if Asa was going to poison them, he would have done so with the drink back at his place.

Both Graf and Amber ended up shrugging at the same time and dipping their hands into the fountain to collect the water, they kept eye contact as they brought the water into their mouths, and the whole world changed.

Graf and Amber found themselves transformed. This wasn't like the vision with Glenna where they were simply seeing things happen around them in a haze similar to that of a dream. They were with Asa, as he was then.

They felt like they were spirits with no bodies, just floating in the air. They could see Traveler and other helpers building Sanctuary under them, they could feel the heart and soul everyone was putting into building the safe haven for all those who needed it. Bernholt and Aldo were named caretakers of Sanctuary, and the others left once there was nothing more that they could add in assistance. But Graf and Amber remained there, because Asa had stayed back then, and that was when Glenna came into the picture.

She walked into the Sanctuary looking very much as she did now: a sweet, loving grandma. She claimed to be an apothecary who had gotten lost in the woods by her home and everyone was charmed by her presence.

Bernholt took a special liking to her. Perhaps she reminded him of the family he had lost in his banishment.

But something was not right.

Graf and Amber knew only as much as Asa had in this moment, sensing that something was not right, and they knew exactly what it was. Glenna lacked the sense of loss all newcomers possessed, because she was not one! The Wanwood had always been her home!

Glenna had more in common with Aldo than with Bernholt. She was the last of her kind. Graf and Amber did not know where they were getting all this information from, but they just knew everything that Asa did, and it felt like facts they had earned.

The spirit-like state they were in flew through the air like they *were* the air, they flew through space and time, and the Wanwood began to make much more sense to them.

The Wanwood was not always what they had initially found themselves in upon entering. It was not meant to be a place of fear or isolation or a survival test. Instead, it was always meant to be a safe haven for refugees from other dimensions who found themselves in it.

But Graf and Amber found themselves being flashed even further through time and space, and the wind they seemed to be riding came to a stop at a time before the Wanwood was open to other worlds, when it was just its own.

***

112

There were two races that ruled the forest as their own: The Ion and the Shoon. They saw Glenna was a member of the Shoon, the moon spirits who would use their magic to ease the mind and provide comfort, rest, and sleep to the lost and weary of other worlds. Aldo was there too, appearing to be as old as Glenna, both seeming to be as old as time, as old as the forest itself. The bear-like race were the lords of the woods and rulers of the natural order. These two races were meant to work together to ensure that the woods would be a peaceful sanctuary; a place where creatures could escape hardship and get a second chance at life. For such a long time, it seemed that that was the case.

Graf and Amber could feel the time slip around them, like they were living for years in this forest the way it initially was, and they didn't want this feeling to stop. The woods were filled with wonderous beings and magic, and there was nothing but peace for age after age. Graf and Amber would not have minded staying in that state of peace forever.

It didn't last.

The Shoon were no longer happy about their role in the woods, unsatisfied with having no authority, despite their immense power. Graf and Amber could feel the envy that separated them from the Ion. They began to abuse their magic, and used their talents to create evil, harmful spells to manipulate and control the Ion to do their will. Their efforts were subtle at first, almost unnoticed, but they grew too greedy, and the Ion caught on to their tricks. Someone akin to the Traveler and Asa were sent down to warn them. He tried to assure the Ion that the Shoon would be dealt with, and warned them not to break their oath and sacred duty of protecting the creatures of the woods. To seek revenge for themselves would warrant them equal punishment, but the hearts of the Ion had been blackened with anger – Graf and Amber could *feel* the uncontainable rage and humiliation. They disobeyed the command and attacked the Shoon.

Graf and Amber watched a great war ensue from above, and they could feel the pain of every creature that was killed in its name.

For the disobedience of both races, and as a result of both of them betraying their natural calling, the Blaine were sent into the woods as punishment. Graf and Amber would have been horrified at the sight of the Blaine, or wolf-men, had they been in their natural states, but in this spirit time they felt removed from the terror.

They saw the creatures in their own world at first, a ferocious race of warriors that were in the process of conquering their own when they were transported into the forest. They were a bit confuddled and disoriented at first, but quickly adapted and sought to continue the conquest they began on their world.

The woods had become a complete mess. Some of the creatures that had found it as a sanctuary were transported to other worlds by the likes of the Traveler and Asa, and others remained. Without the soothing magic of the Shoon, they reverted to their old ways and became just as ferocious as the Blaine. These beings became embittered and vengeful towards the Ion and Shoon and rejected offers of re-location. They joined the rumble and the whole wood was up in smoke.

Graf and Amber watched in shock as several generations passed under these circumstances, and the Blaine had all but conquered the woods. The Shoon were mostly extinct, and only a handful of Ion were left alive: one of whom was Aldo.

Feeling alone in the world, having fallen from the grace of his former position by losing most of his kind, he became a ferocious monster – the only creature the Blaine feared and left alone. A quarantine was declared on the woods. Nobody was allowed in or out for many years. The messenger who had warned the races of this happening in the first place returned and shared a prophecy with the surviving minions of the forest.

"An outsider," his voice echoed inside Graf and Amber, "shall come to the woods. He will form an alliance with Aldo and the woods will be restored to the sanctuary it once was."

Briar Dash was banished into the Wanwood, branded a criminal, slave trader, and murderer; but something happened to him, something that changed him from the inside out. He was gifted a new name by Aldo: Bernholt. This was a symbol of his transformation from evil to good, just as the woods was meant to always transform those who entered it.

Graf and Amber observed the woods and Sanctuary become all that they had been prophesized to be, but there was one thing that they now knew that Aldo had not: the survival of a single Shoon. The envy and anger and ambition of Glenna's race survived with her, and Graf and Amber watched her kill a defenseless old lady in the woods and take over her form. Glenna wore the perfect disguise for getting into Sanctuary.

Bernholt had taken a special liking to her, despite Aldo's suspicions, and allowed her to get close… close enough to stab him in the heart with a poisoned blade! It had been Glenna all along! But the creatures at Sanctuary didn't know that. They were woken by Aldo's roar, and by the time they arrived, Aldo was nowhere to be seen and Bernholt was sprawled out in the yard suffering from a hideous wound to the chest. Glenna claimed a surviving Blaine assassin had somehow slipped into Sanctuary, caught Bernholt unaware and that Aldo had taken off after the assassin to claim revenge and hopefully find an antidote.

Asa's powers weren't as strong now as they were back then, and through the vision Graf and Amber felt him use all his might and magic to place Bernholt in a coma just before he died. He appeared dead to all, even Glenna, but he was merely in stasis.

Graf and Amber watched in horror as Glenna continued with her act, shedding tears in front of everyone who looked and demanding a tomb to be constructed for the man whom she had murdered. It was during that time that Asa was finally allowed to assume a physical form, and he pretended to stumble into the woods like any other creature seeking sanctuary. It was then that other creatures with seemingly similar powers to those of the Traveler and Asa appeared. They built the shrine behind Asa's house, into which Asa secretly moved Bernholt's body during the night and replaced it with a wax effigy in Glenna's tomb.

***

Graf and Amber fell off the edge of the fountain where they had been sitting onto the grass, but it felt like they had just been dropped from the sky. They both struggled to sit upright, gasping for breath.

"Better than Glenna's vision, wasn't it?" Asa smirked at them. "You actually got to be there."

"I..." Graf panted. "I don't understand."

"I just showed you all that and you still don't understand?" Asa sounded genuinely shocked.

"No, I..." Graf shook his head as if to clear it. "Why didn't you stop Glenna from doing this in the first place? We were there! I mean, *you* were there!"

"Hold your fire, Cracker Jack! Like I said, I can only do what I'm allowed. The boss always has a bigger plan in mind. I thought much like you did at the time, but I knew my employer had his reasons for limiting my powers and allowing Glenna to injure Bernie and cause Aldo's disappearance. In time, I'm sure all will be revealed, but for now we just have to make do with what we got. As for Aldo, I'm not sure. I'm not omniscient and I certainly ain't omnipresent. In fact, I was catching a few Z's in an oak tree when I heard Aldo's cry. But I do know Aldo is still alive and that Glenna knows where he is. She's responsible for his disappearance, and I wouldn't be surprised if she was responsible for the other disappearances that occur from time to time."

Graf stared up at the triumphant image of Bernholt and the bear. His suspicions of Glenna and Sanctuary had been well founded after all, and the warrior's mind burned with a passion to free Bernholt and stop Glenna. With his old life behind him, Graf was ready to turn the page and start the next chapter with Amber at his side. Peace was something he'd tasted at fleeting moments since arriving in Wanwood and Sanctuary, and he wasn't about to let Glenna of the Woods stand in his way and all those others seeking it.

"The journal." Amber had gained her breathing under control faster. "The journal is what we have to use to free Bernholt," she stated.

Asa nodded and fished out the journal from his pocket. He opened the book and flipped through the pages before finding his mark. "Yes and no."

"What do you mean yes and no? Just tell us what we have to do, dammit!" Amber snapped.

"Well, look who's froggy all of a sudden! It's not like we're pressed for time. The man's been trapped in there for centuries. A few more days ain't gonna hurt 'em." Asa turned and looked up at the fountain.

"This whole situation has me anxious to take action. Any time a problem presented itself in the past, I could always find a quick solution with a mace or sword. I'm not used to all these secrets and conspiracies." Graf looked to Amber, who took his hand in comfort.

"Don't forget why you're here, Graf," Amber reassured him, "your 'take no prisoner' mentality is what got you banished from Eastern Rising and stuck your ass here with me. Let's listen to Asa, and plan this out right."

Graf nodded and the two embraced.

"Now that she's reeled you back in, let me explain!" Asa teased. "I already know a counter-spell that will release Bernie from the statue he's in and from the stasis I placed him under. It's the ol' fashioned one-two combo. But here's the catch, daddy-o; it won't heal the wound Glenna cursed him with. She used dark, ancient magic to create the poison that nearly killed him, and it'll take that same magic to heal him."

Graf nodded. "So, if we just free him now without an antidote, he'll likely die in a matter of minutes."

"More like a matter of seconds, Billy-bob. So, before we free Bernie we'll need to have the antidote ready. It's not hard to make, and even easier to administer, but we'll need all the same ingredients Glenna used to make the poison. I've managed to round up all the ingredients, save one."

"Which we'll be retrieving," Amber surmised.

Asa smiled. "That's where this little fella comes into play." He lifted the journal. "Bernie explored a great deal of these woods when he first came here, and during that time he came across a rare flower with rather unique properties. He didn't realize the role this plant would play later on, but he was careful to note its location in these pages. He even drew a map."

Asa opened the booklet on the edge of the fountain for them to watch. The page Asa had turned to appeared to be the same scribbling that had perplexed Graf the night before. However, as Asa began to flip the page, Graf saw that several pages had been stuck together. Asa carefully peeled them apart to reveal a small, but very detailed, map. Asa ripped the map out of the booklet and stretched it like sheepskin. Soon, the scrap of paper had expanded almost ten times its original size.

"This should prove rather helpful. Don't worry about the Liar's Eye script." Asa snapped his fingers. "It's all translated for you."

Amber was fascinated with the map. "How will we know the flower when we see it?"

"It's called the Bellows flower. Its properties can be used to form some of the most powerful spells and potions ever known to the Woods. Wizards and sorcerers from countless worlds have died attempting to acquire one. But these bad boys don't just sprout up in every nook and crevice. The flower Glenna used had already been ground into powder several centuries prior. So, for the antidote to work, the flower must be freshly cut. This Bellows flower is one of the last in existence, and in order to reach it, you will have to overcome many obstacles and tribulations. I don't envy you, that's for sure."

"Let me guess, there's a rule that you can't go with us." Graf rolled his eyes at Asa.

"You gotta learn to walk on your own, pumpkin. Besides, someone's gotta stick around and keep an eye on Bernie and Glenna. I wouldn't send you if I didn't think you could hack it. You'll be fine."

"It's just as well." Graf looked at Amber and winked. "Asa would talk us to death long before any monster ate us."

Chapter 13

Call Me Aed

The trail began at the grotto and slithered into the forest. The path was marked by a series of arrows and symbols carved into tree trunks. The trees grew larger the further they went, and soon the trees were so tall Graff could see neither canopy nor sky. The trunks simply shrank until converging at the vanishing point. Despite the absence of sunlight, however, the forest around them remained highly illuminated. Graf had never seen conifers of this size, and the majesty of his surroundings left him breathless. He stopped at one tree and tried to wrap his arms around it.

"It'd take a dozen men to reach around it," he said.

"Asa spoke of trials and tribulations, but this is like paradise. Even Sanctuary doesn't compare to this."

The journey was uneventful, and aside from the occasional squirrel, fox, or deer, the couple saw nothing out of the ordinary. The weather was cool and dry, there were no thorny bushes, vines or other undergrowth hindering the foot trodden path, and even insect life seemed nonexistent. It wasn't until midmorning the next day that the first obstacle presented itself in the form of a strange river that blocked their path. It was only eight feet or so to cross, and the current didn't seem strong enough to prevent one from crossing on foot, but its sickish green color, nauseous odor and random spurts of bubbles alerted Graf instantly.

"Acid," Amber stated.

Graf picked up a large, sturdy stick and plunged its length into the river. He lifted the steaming stub of the twig and held it out. The river had instantly dissolved it.

"There's your answer," he said, throwing the remnant aside. "The map doesn't say the river is acid. Thanks for the heads up, Asa."

"Look," Amber held the map before them. "The map shows that if we follow the river west, we'll come to a bridge. It's not far... half a day's journey."

They decided to take a lunch break before making for the bridge, eating several of the biscuits Asa had given them before departing. Graf had liked them at first. They were sweet, with hints of cinnamon and nutmeg. However, after a day they were getting boring. *What I wouldn't do for a leg of lamb right now*, Graf thought.

They followed the river's edge for several hours before finally arriving at a bridge that appeared to be made of crystal. It was narrow, barely large enough for one of Graf's stature to cross.

"Is it just me or does this seem a bit too easy?" Amber inquired. "Sure, we've had a decent hike, but I'd hardly consider that life-threatening."

Graf was about to respond when he heard a thump. The thumping continued, echoing through the trees until a figure jumped between the travelers and the bridge.

"So much for our peaceful stroll." Graf unsheathed his sword as the figure approached him.

The creature was humanoid in form, with the head and face of a rabbit. His fur was of a grayish brown color and he carried no weapon. Around his waist he wore a skirt of fir needles.

"I am Aed, guardian of the river," it said. "What business do you have here?"

Graf lowered his sword. "We need the Bellows flower to heal a friend. We know the flower is beyond this river and we need to cross."

"The flower you seek is the last of its kind. In order to cross you must prove yourself worthy in combat, for the road before you is long and treacherous. I must warn you, though, I am rarely defeated in combat."

Graf looked at Amber, and from her demeanor he could tell she was preparing for a transformation. He glanced down at his weapon: the shortsword. Graf was well versed in many fighting styles, both armed and unarmed, but favored this weapon in particular. Most of his comrades in Eastern Rising preferred to use a shield with this weapon, often binding or shield striking, bringing them in close range with their opponent to stab or cut. Graf didn't like the added weight of a shield. The whole point of wielding a shortsword was to free oneself from the weight of a broadsword or longsword. Graf grinned and snatched his mother's blue-fire opal dagger with his free hand.

"I wish you no harm, but I must also warn you that you are unarmed and there are two of us," Graf said. He assumed his attack position, light on the balls of his feet and ready to spring into action.

"I'm not at a disadvantage, I assure you," the creature said. "I take it you will not heed my warning?"

"We don't have an option," Graf stated. "We're crossing that bridge."

"Very well, then," said Aed.

Aed's feet smashed into Graf's face and the warrior's weapons fell from his stunned fingers. Graf could hold his own against any human advisory, but Aed's speed was unlike anything he'd encountered before. Jumping to his feet, he shook himself off and grabbed his weapons. Amber had assumed her natural form and was able to keep up with Aed's speed much better than Graf had. Despite this, the battle was still one sided, with the odds in the rabbit's favor.

Amber had latched onto Aed's frame and had attempted to maul him, but the creature pummeled her face with his paws before drop kicking her in the chest. She fell back and Aed landed on his feet, backflipping off the kick. The jackrabbit reoriented on Graf and repeated the onslaught. Graf was ready for it, however, and caught Aed in the sternum with a backhanded pommel strike. The creature gasped, and Graf stabbed and swiped with a speed and accuracy that surprised even himself. Aed had to act quickly but managed to evade the human before the lupine form of Amber jumped onto his back, mauling his neck. The jackrabbit's blood sprayed from the wound as the she-wolf snarled, yanked, and clawed at her target.

"Amber!" Graf screamed.

The wolf's humanoid claw had caught Aed by the mouth with a fishhook, and with a sharp pull swung Aed around to face Graf. He lunged with his sword, but his opponent's speed had returned. His feet left the ground, one foot stepping down on Graf's sword, knocking it from his grasp, and the other planting itself once again in Graf's face. The blow was done out of desperation, and wasn't nearly as powerful as the initial strike. The rabbit had flipped over Amber, tearing away from her grasp and landing behind her. His neck was torn and bloodied, but intact.

"Thought I'd bled him for sure," she told Graf.

The fighters kept their distance from the rabbit as he circled them, throwing a cloud of dirt and leaves into the air as he hopped about on the forest floor.

"It's not wise to let your enemy recuperate," Aed said.

Seconds later, Graf and Amber were knocked on their backsides. Aed mounted Graf and began to unload a fury of strikes to his already bloodied and bruised face. Graf did his best to block out the pain and strike back, but Aed's speed overwhelmed him. Graf's arms flopped about like wet noodles. His vision filled with snow, and his ears began to ring as the enormous paws smashed into his face.

The flurry ended as quickly as it began, and Graf looked up to see that Amber had transformed once again, assuming the form she had used against her fight with the minotaur. Aed managed to evade at first, but Amber soon caught him. Lifting him into the air, she threw him onto the ground before driving an elbow into his gut. He gasped in pain, and pleaded for her to stop, but she was lost in the rage of combat. With a mighty kick, Aed was flung several yards to the edge of the acidic river. Amber shrunk back into her human form and collapsed to her knees.

"Are you ok?" Graf mumbled through a mouthful of blood.

"Two transformations in such a short time... it was too much to sustain." She motioned towards their fallen foe.

Aed had caught his breath and had begun to rise. Graf's sword was nowhere in sight, but his dagger was still in hand. With what little strength he had left, he charged at his foe. Screaming like a banshee, he flung the dagger at Aed. He didn't want to lose this precious family heirloom to the river of acid, but he knew he wouldn't survive another onslaught from the man-rabbit. Aed was caught off guard by the warrior's battle cry and barely had time to catch the approaching dagger before Graf's boot embedded itself into his chest. Aed stumbled back and vanished into the rolling acid of the river.

The splash was surprisingly anticlimactic. There was no cries of anguish or thrashing. The rabbit simply fell into the river with a faint *plop*.

Graf returned to his fallen lover. She was winded, but reassured him she would recover in time, and proceeded to meditate. Graf retrieved the traveling pack when suddenly there was an explosion from the river, raining acid down before them. Aed landed before them once more.

Graf panicked, raising his sword again. *If drowning in acid didn't kill him, what can?* Graf thought to himself.

Aed raised his hands in truce. "Lower your sword, human. You and your companion have proven yourself worthy and may cross the bridge."

"There's no way you could have survived that acid. What the hell are you?"

"I sense time is of the essence. Thus, it would be foolish to waste time sharing tales. Besides, I am needed elsewhere."

"Are you in league with Asa and Traveler?" Graf asked.

"We serve the same master, yes." Aed looked behind him at the woods beyond the river. "Once across you'll find safe lodging for the night, but do not tarry long. Time is not on your side and few who pass this river live to tell about it."

Graf chuckled. "I'm guessing it won't be a walk in the park, then."

Aed responded with a sober look that chilled him to the bone. He tossed Graf's dagger on the ground at the man's feet, and a gust of wind swept past them, encircling Aed in a whirlwind of leaves and earth. When the dust settled, the rabbit was gone.

***

After several hours of walking, it was beginning to grow dark. It was impossible to tell whether the sun had set, but the dimming of the light indicated nightfall. The darkness began to swallow the wood, and just when the duo began looking for a spot to camp, a flickering light caught his eye.

"What is it?" Amber asked. "Is it safe?"

A howl pierced the night air, and Graf's hair stood on end.

He shook his head. "Nothing is safe in this wood, but I'll take my chances. Come on, it's dark as pitch and I don't know how long that light will last."

As they approached the light, they realized it was a sign lit by a strange kind of lamp Graf had never seen before. The sign was wood, and painted on its worn surface were flaking letters.

"Lodging," Graf read out loud.

"The arrow is pointing that way." Amber motioned towards the dimly lit trail. "I see another light in the distance, but it's dim." This time Amber led the way, using her enhanced vision to avoid exposed roots and pits in the ground. The light grew brighter, and soon they arrived at the lodge. There were more of the strange lamps surrounding the building, which was rather small. It had a giant clock built into the wall above the entryway. The setting appeared rather pleasant in juxtaposition with the decaying, tangled wood they had just left. As the two approached the front door a latch above the clock burst open and a giant finch shot out on a perch, chirping. The noise pierced the travelers' ears, and after what felt like an eternity the bird retracted. Finally, the front door opened before them. A man, old as dirt, waddled onto the welcome mat. He wore dingy white clothes and a tall red hat with a flat top and wide brim. He had a long white beard that he kept tucked in between the buttons of his shirt. He was frailly built and crooked of back, with skin so weathered and dry it looked like burlap wrapped around bones. His eyes were yellowed with jaundice and capped with cataracts. A tremendous amount of sleep matter had built up in the corners of those eyes, and the hair around his mouth was caked with dried slobber. He carried a long staff with a small golden clock set on top. He brought the clock up to his face, tapped it several times with his long fingernail, and looked at the duo.

"Oh, thank heavens," he exclaimed. "I was so horrified! There I was, lost in the heavenly peace of dreamland praying for a savior when lo and behold, here you are, jolting me from my sleep well past midnight. How ever can I repay you?"

Graf crossed his arms. "You don't have to be a smart ass, pal. We don't like being stuck out here anymore than you like being woken up."

"Ok, ok! So maybe it's not that serious... but why don't you try taking a blast to the ticker like that when you're my age."

"We're on a quest and need lodging for the night. The sign implied this was an inn of sorts," Amber said.

"Well, it's been ages since I've had any patrons, but I suppose I can spare a bed."

Graf pulled out a sack of coins from his belt – a precautionary gift from Asa – but the old man stopped him.

"Oh, that won't do, son. As you can assume, I don't get guests very often, and at any rate, there's no villages or cities anywhere near here. My larder is enchanted and contains an everlasting supply of food, drink, and other supplies. I have no need for your money."

"Well, if you don't want coin, surely there must be something we can do for a night's rest."

The old man smiled, "Oh, just a little bit of your time is enough payment for me. Like I said, it's been years since I've had a visitor. Having company will take years off me!"

Surprised by the sudden shift in attitude, Graf looked at Amber who nodded in approval. They followed the man into the lodge and through several rooms filled with exquisite clocks, hourglasses, sundials, and other mechanisms built from gold, silver, and bronze, inlaid with gem stones of epic proportions. Graf saw more of the strange lamps lining the walls and hanging from the ceiling. He saw no fire inside them... only brilliant light. The old man walked them to a desk where he opened an enormous tome. He asked for their names and wrote them down as they responded. He then flipped over a giant hourglass that sat next to the book.

"The room is yours for the night," he said. "You must be famished... come to the dining room and I'll fix you a nice bangers and mash with spotted dick for dessert!"

Graf had never heard of either dish, but after the long trek and fight with Aed he wasn't about to be picky. They ate with the old man in a cozy dining room with walls lined in red velvet tapestries. The bangers and mash he served were actually just sausages and mashed potatoes; the dessert was a sort of pastry similar to a dish his mother used to prepare. They ate in relative silence until the man spoke up.

"You're probably wondering about my obsession with timepieces," he said.

Amber shrugged. "Everyone needs a hobby, I guess."

"It's far more than a hobby, my dear," he said. "It's my life's work. Eon upon eon of work."

"In that case, I must say you look great for your age," Amber remarked.

Graf raised an eyebrow.

"You find that to be an outlandish remark?" the man asked.

"Hell, what do I know...I'm just a dog trainer."

"What do you do? What are you?" Amber inquired.

"The question is: what *WAS* I! For seventy-three billion years I served as Father Time for the entire multiverse! I was the best there'd ever been, too, and things were going smooth as silk. The job was fantastic, until management decided otherwise." The man turned his head away, and his voice lowered to barely a whisper, "Crazy they called us... crazy! Can you believe the gall?"

The man glanced up when he noticed the pair giving him an awkward glance and chuckled.

"They say it's ok to talk to yourself as long as you don't talk back," he said, blinking furiously.

The duo sat silently for a moment.

"Forgive me if I find your tale a bit outlandish, Father." Graf pushed his plate away.

"I'm not Father Time anymore. Weren't you listening? I was demoted. Now they call me Grandfather Clock, or Gramps for short. I'm not stupid, though. They only gave me the title to smooth things over... You know how employers are."

"Well, Gramps, with all due respect I'm worn out from our day's journey. Many thanks for the dinner and conversation, but can you show us the room?" Graf pushed away his plate and stood.

"Still don't believe me, huh? I shouldn't be surprised," Gramps said. "Fine, follow me."

He led them upstairs to a small apartment that was cramped, but cozy.

"I just flipped the mattress yesterday, so you should sleep like babies," Gramps said.

The old timer left them with a stiff curtsey and left. The travelers looked at their surroundings: a few leather chairs, a small table with a wash basin and the four-poster bed. Graf's head nearly touched the ceiling. This room obviously wasn't built for two. All discomforts disappeared, however, as Graf and Amber slipped under the plaid quilt. In their exhaustion, they had failed to notice the clock set in the headboard of the bed. As they began to drift into unconsciousness, the hour hand began to move. It was slow at first, but in seconds it had sped up until its movements were invisible to the naked eye.

The whining of the gears fell on deaf ears, however, and the two trekkers slept soundly into the night.

Chapter 14

A Matter of Time

A soft vibration woke Amber from her slumber, and there was a bizarre purring noise coming from Graf's side of the bed. Her eyes adjusted, quickly noticing the blue aura which surrounded their bed, and she cried out in fear when she saw what had become of Graf.

"Wake up!" she screamed.

Levitating several feet off the mattress, Graf's body was rigid and comatose, rotating in midair like a lamb roasting on a spit. The air buzzed and cracked. Blue tendrils of static electricity rippled across his body. With each rotation he aged, and by the looks of Graf's balding, gray hair, crow's feet, and liver spots, he was closing in on his late 70s.

She screamed at the top of her lungs, but to no avail. Graf was in a trance of powerful magic. A string of expletives flew from her mouth, and she reached out to grab and shake him. As her fingers entered the electrostatic field, blue lightning surged through her body and threw her off the bed.

Amber jumped to her feet and shook herself off.

Throw the clock at the force field!

The words sounded off like a thunderclap in her mind, and Amber recognized the voice as that of the Traveler. Scanning the room, she spotted her weapon of choice: a small perpetual clock sitting on the bedside table. It was made from gold and encased in glass but felt heavy enough to disrupt the electric barrier if thrown hard enough. She assumed her natural form. Muscles bulged supernaturally, a wave of hair spread across her body and her fangs dripped with ichor as she hurled the object at Graf with a feral shriek. The projectile would be carrying enough force to kill someone, and Amber prayed it would be enough to break the magic guarding Graf.

A faint pop was followed by a tremendous explosion that knocked Amber against the wall and filled the room with smoke. Graf's coughing could be heard along with groans of discomfort. As the haze cleared, the elderly Graf sat upright on the bed. He waved away the last wisps of smoke and cast a perplexed look on the transformed Amber, sprawled on the floor.

"What the hell happened?" Graf asked. He flung his legs over the edge of the bed and stood quickly. His face contorted in pain as his hand grasped at his back.

She ran to his side. "Careful! Take a moment to gather your strength."

"That bed put one hell of a knot in my back," Graf looked again at Amber. "What was all the noise and smoke about?"

She stood by his side, helping him to the chair in front of the mirror.

"Amber, what's with all the coddling? Knock it off, will ya..." It was then that Graf saw his reflection.

"The bed was enchanted." She rested her hand on his trembling shoulder. "I woke up to find you frozen in midair. You were encased in an energy bubble. I didn't know what to do, so I went berserk and hurtled a clock at you. It disrupted the spell, but not quickly enough."

"I'm old as sin!" Graf screamed. "I must be close to eighty years old now! What did this?"

Amber's mind stumbled at first, but then she figured it out. "Time's not on our side!"

"No shit, darlin'," Graf turned. "What are we supposed to do? We can't go searching for the Bellows like this!"

"It's Time," Amber repeated.

"Time? Time for what?" Graf's jaw hung limp over his chest.

"No, Graf, listen to me," Amber said. "It was Time that did this to you. Time as in Father Time... that old codger downstairs. Time is not on your side. That's what Aed told us, remember?"

Graf's eyes bugged out of his head. "Amber, you're right... and do you remember what that gaffer said when I tried to pay him for a night's lodging?"

Amber's eyes glowed red with fury.

"Having company will take years off me," she growled.

"I'll kill the..." Graf jumped to his feet and grabbed at his sword and dagger, but quickly slowed to a halt.

"How you gonna do that, darlin'?"

Graf stood erect, finally catching his breath. "I might be an octogenarian, but I'm not feeble. I can still take 'em."

"Your attitude is robust, but foolish. If you've aged 50 years in a matter of hours, what's happened to him?"

"I didn't think about that..." Graf scratched his flaking scalp. "But why didn't you age? You were sleeping right next to me."

Amber's neck tingled and her fingers felt the choker Traveler had given her. It took Graf a moment to see her movement in the dim light, but he finally saw her fingers rubbing the charmed necklace and nodded in agreement.

"He must not have realized you were wearing it, or at least didn't know about its properties," he said.

They heard movement downstairs, followed by an ecstatic whistling. Graf attempted to stretch out his sore muscles, but it only made things worse. Amber's hackles were raised, and a strong odor had arrived with the sweat broken across her body.

"He doesn't know about my transformations. His power seems limited to time manipulation, so he may have thought the spell would work on both of us. If you confront him, and I surprise him in this form, he may not have time to react," she said.

Graf nodded. "It might work, especially if you can find a way to sneak up behind him. But what if his power isn't limited to time?"

"We'll have to risk it... We don't have much of a choice."

Graf, despite his old age, picked up the stool by the mirror and smashed the looking glass.

Amber frowned. "I just hope you didn't slap us with seven years of bad luck."

"To hell with bad luck!" Graf grabbed his back again. "Oh, that wasn't nice! I feel like I've been trampled by a horse. I can barely move."

Amber aided Graf downstairs, the sound of whistling and shuffling feet coming from the parlor. Noticing the parlor had two entrances, she motioned for Graf to enter through the first door while she quickly made for the other. He slid the door open. Instead of finding the ancient old man of before, there stood a beardless young man with his back turned to Graf, whistling, and tapping his feet while dusting the mantlepiece. The floorboard underneath Graf's foot creaked under the weight, and the younger, middle-aged man turned on a dime. He chuckled at the site of Graf, winking and dipping into a low bow.

"Top of the mornin' to you, old timer!" Gramps looked at the clock above the fireplace. "Why, it's barely past midnight and you look exhausted. Why don't you lay back down for another forty winks?"

"More like another forty years!" Graf's shaking hand drew his dagger.

"Oh, your sweetheart's not feeling well either?" Gramps laughed again, dancing a jig before his audience.

"She's on the verge of death!" *Thank the gods!* Graf thought, *his powers are limited.* "You're a lying, deceitful pig! I'll kill you for what you've done to us!"

"Lying and deceitful, eh? Why I couldn't have told you more plainly... A little company for the night takes years off me," Gramps said.

"That's dirty, and you know it," Graf said. "How would anyone know that was what you meant? We never would have agreed to it."

The man laughed and slapped his knee before jumping into the air and tapping his heels together. Noticing Graf's feeble advancement, he smirked and stepped closer to the 'old' man. Graf circled Gramps until his back was turned to the Parlor's latter entryway. Amber's head appeared, fangs barred as she advanced into the room.

"It's true, without my staff or other tools handy, I'm at a bit of a disadvantage in hand-to-hand combat... but given your present state, I'll take my chances," he said, raising his fists, oblivious to the werewolf now standing behind him.

"Lucky for you, I'm out of commission, right Gramps?" Amber growled.

Before Gramps could react, she'd grasped his throat in one hand and his testicles in the other. Razor-sharp claws dug into his skin, bringing drops of blood from his neck. A whimper could be heard in his voice as she squeezed his manhood.

"How is this possible?!" Gramps exclaimed through gasping breaths. "Why didn't the bed's charm effect you?"

"I have a trick or two up my sleeves as well," she replied.

"You got one over on me. I salute you for that, but you do realize killing me will ruin any chances at undoing the aging spell, don't you?" Gramps laughed.

Amber throttled the man once more, and the smug look disappeared.

"She can play that game too," Graf said.

"Undo the spell!" Amber screamed. "Now!"

"I can't..." the man gasped.

"What the hell do you mean, you can't?" Amber's grip tightened around the man's neck.

Gramps turned white.

"It's... the mattress..." he stammered. "You have... to flip... the mattress."

"So, the power isn't in you," Graf deduced.

Amber relaxed her grip, and Gramps gasped.

"No! I don't have the power to do anything myself... not since I retired. All the items in my house are enchanted. The mattress affects the age of the user and gives or takes from the owner depending on what side of the mattress is used. Flipping the mattress will reverse the aging."

"How do we know you won't try to find some other way of spelling us?" Graf asked.

"That bed is one of the most powerful objects in this house. If it doesn't work on her, nothing else will either."

Amber refused to release him. "Now that we know how to reverse the spell, why shouldn't we just kill you?"

"No, please!" Gramps cried. "Living in this forest is a curse upon me... to age forever and ever, but not die. I don't mean to be cruel, honest! I'm lucky to get a visitor once in a century, and I'm forbidden to use the bed's mattress myself... I can take the years it steals from other people, and vice versa. Don't worry! I wouldn't risk doing anything to you guys after learning about your resistance to my charms."

"Flip the mattress, Graf goes back to sleep a few hours, and he'll be back to his young self?" Amber asked.

"Yes!"

Amber flipped Gramps around and threw him into a chair, a cloud of dust wafting into the air as he landed on its cushions. The man grabbed his throat and panicked when he drew back his hand to see blood. Realizing it was only a flesh wound, his breathing slowed down as he looked up at Graf and the monstrous woman.

"You don't understand how horrible my predicament is! I didn't retire from my role as Father Time. I was fired and imprisoned here in this hell hole... doomed to age for all eternity, but never die! What few charms you see in this hovel are the only tools they gave me to find some relief. All over a small misunderstanding..." Gramps looked over his shoulder and said in a hushed voice, "Shut up, you!"

"A simple misunderstanding?" Amber inquired.

"I only tried to overthrow the Creator of the omniverse and obliterate the space-time continuum," he said as shirked away from the glaring eyes of the she-beast. "Okay, even I'll admit that was a bit much, but did they really have to send me here?"

"You're lucky they didn't erase you from existence," Graf stated.

"That's what I keep saying," Gramps squawked in his other voice.

If Graf hadn't seen the man's lips move, he'd have sworn it came from somewhere else, but to his astonishment, Gramps looked over his shoulder again and cursed at some non-existent entity.

"I'm sorry," Gramps said. "HE keeps interrupting me!"

No wonder they sent him here, Graf thought.

"There's a crystal knob on one of the corner posts at the foot of the bed. Turn it counter-clockwise and the mattress will flip over." Gramps flopped back in the chair, disappointed.

Amber pulled up a chair and sat down across from their thwarted foe. "Go ahead, dear. I'll babysit our little friend."

Graf was a bit winded after walking up the stairs but was able to make it to the bedroom otherwise untroubled. He glared darkly at the disheveled blue sheets of the mattress. Twinkling in the moonlight, Graf's eye was led to the crystal knob on the bedpost. His liver spotted hand slowly touched the shaped glass. Turning it as instructed, the mattress flew into the air, spinning in a frenzy before slamming back down on the bed frame to reveal a tidy bed with a green comforter and matching pillows. Graf noticed the phrase embroidered in white on the quilt.

"Youth is wasted on the young," he read. "Give me a break!"

He yanked at the covers in disgust and slipped himself under the weight of the comforter. Before he could finish his fiery stream of curses, Graf was drinking oblivion. As the old man began to snore, a dull green light illuminated the room, and the clock in the headboard began to turn back, slowly at first and eventually picking up speed until it once again emitted the shrill drone muted to all but the most astute ear.

Chapter 15

Here Be Ogres

They moved in brisk silence for several hours before Graf stopped to sit on a fallen log. This part of the forest wasn't nearly as beautiful as where they'd fought Aed. It was dense and unkempt, much like the area where Graf first arrived in the Wanwood. Sweat coated Graf's brow and his feet ached, but he was glad to have his youth back.

"Why'd you tell him about the Bellows?" Graf asked. "I was knocking on death's door, thanks to that old fool. We didn't owe him anything."

"We had a long conversation after you went to bed. He's not so bad once you get to know him... and anyways, his magics doesn't affect me. He's a bit loopy, but he's not malevolent. He's confined to that house for all eternity, and another traveler is bound to come across him sooner or later. So, I made a deal with him. I give him a petal from the Bellows flower, and he'll promise never to trick another soul out of their life force again."

"And how do we know he's going to live up to that?"

"The Bellows contains powerful magic. A single petal will keep him young forever. He won't need to use his magic anymore," Amber said.

Graf scoffed, "I suppose he told you that too, eh?"

"No," she said. "Traveler did, through my choker necklace. Turns out Gramps answers to the same superior. He'll make sure Gramps keeps his part of the bargain."

Thanks for keeping me in the loop, Traveler, Graf thought.

Just then he felt a rebuking thought enter his mind: *mercy is shown where mercy is given, dog trainer.*

Amber felt the Traveler's presence then, as well. The duo looked at each other a moment, and Graf gave an accepting nod. Traveler and Asa wouldn't hold their hands every step of the way, but they had both helped them in times of need. Graf knew better than to argue with beings of their caliber. Changing the subject, he addressed other concerns.

"You mentioned that Gramps said something about ogres." Graf looked over his shoulder at the trail ahead.

Amber looked at the map. "It doesn't show any obstacles. Then again, it didn't mention Aed or the lodge, and Gramps seemed certain about it. There's two of us though, and with the choker's protection, my abilities, and your fighting skills, it shouldn't be too difficult."

"We'll need to be on our guard then," Graf stated.

Graf caught his breath after a few minutes and was ready to continue the journey. He stopped occasionally to snack on the jerky and nuts and would handle his sword at times to check his strength and speed. He was pleased with his movements and decided that with his youth regained stamina wouldn't prove a problem in combat. While they walked, Amber shared more about her earlier life: She'd been raised in a desert with little vegetation. Small cities and towns were usually built near oases, which were few and far between. At the time she entered Wanwood she'd been visiting one such oasis with a caravan of merchants. She'd been hiding from her pursuers in a canebrake and when she tried to return to her encampment she became lost and realized she was in an alien world.

"It wasn't that bad. The desert is harsh and unpredictable at best, so I was used to danger. I'd been in the woods several weeks when I saw you arrive from a distance. There was a strange flash of light, and suddenly a very handsome human was there... that's when I felt our souls touch, and I knew you were marked as my mate. I was worried you'd be afraid of me in my natural form, and without the help of Traveler's collar, the only form I could quickly assume was that of a dog."

"Well, there's no love lost between my home and I. The wood may not be ideal, but I'm glad I met you. I feel like we've known each other a lifetime. If only you'd been in Eastern Rising, then I may have kept out of trouble."

Amber stopped Graf, pulling herself close to him. "We have the rest of our lives to make up for our pasts."

They kissed passionately, and Graf could sense himself becoming aroused. *Thank heaven it still works after all that magic,* he thought. Just then, as if moved by their intimacy, a cold wind swept through the trees. Leaves, twigs, and dirt swirled, forming a cyclone that moved past them for several yards before dissipating. When the debris settled Graf noticed something in the ground where the whirlwind stopped. As the pair approached it, they realized it was a sign embedded under roots and years of decaying leaves. It had been buried before the brief storm and would have gone unnoticed otherwise.

"I'll bet nobody's been this deep into the woods for quite some time," Graf said. "Most of the writing is still buried, though."

Amber knelt down and ran her hand across the surface of the wood, clearing off clods of filth and lichen and ripping out weeds, buried moss, and dead roots. Finally, the marker was exposed.

"Here be ogres," she read aloud.

"Ogres... how wonderful. I wonder if they're like the ones we fought back home."

"You fought ogres?"

"They were one of the few nonhuman species I faced as a guard. I killed one once, on a trading expedition out west. They're fat, grotesque blobs... all meat and teeth."

"Humanoid?" she inquired.

"For lack of a better descriptor, sure. They bury themselves into the earth; their bodies are usually covered in moss and grass. One guy walked right over one and before he knew it, the sneaky bastard was picking his bones clean."

"Was it difficult to kill?"

"Not once it's out in the open. They're powerful, but slow and tire quickly. After a few quick stabs it dropped like a cow patty."

"Shouldn't be too difficult for the two of us," Amber laughed. "Unless these are a different breed of ogre."

"More likely than not, you're right."

The footpath became overgrown, insects swarmed, and a foul smell filled the air. Graf knew the smell of rotting flesh, and he likened it to the odor that now berated his senses. It grew to an unbearable strength before the source appeared in the path before them. The rotting carcass of a doe lay half stripped and ripped to pieces; its leg bones had been picked clean and its rib cage had been crushed. Bones laid scattered around the body. Graf's memory was drawn to the way his warrior companions would tear into a chicken or rack of lamb. What little flesh was left on the deer swarmed with flies and maggots. Judging the smell, Graf thought the animal had been dead for three days.

"Something ripped this thing apart like a ragdoll," Graf said. "I think we're dealing with something a lot bigger than the ogres back home."

"This isn't the only one. There are several more carcasses up ahead. Whatever ate this was big... really big," Amber said.

Graf had yet to hear fear in Amber's voice, and although she was remaining calm and collected, he knew she was on edge. They walked a bit further until they stumbled across several more decaying deer, one of them a stag, shredded and mutilated in the same manner as before. Amber stopped suddenly, her nose twitching.

"It defecated in those bushes," she cringed, pointing to an enormous pile of foul matter by a tree. "I think it's humanoid... and probably close to 15 feet tall."

Graf arched an eyebrow. "What makes you think that?"

"You're standing in its footprint," she said.

The footprint he stood in was undeniably human-like but was easily the size of his torso. There were more impressions heading north, as they were, and there was no doubt in Graf's mind that they would intercept this creature soon.

"Any other tricks hidden up your sleeves? Now would be a good time," Graf kicked a shard of bone. Could you take something this big with the form you used against Lonnicker and Aed?"

"My berserker mode? I could hold my own for a while, but I doubt I could overpower him. Perhaps if I had a chance to meditate and gather my energies, with the help of Traveler's choker I could gather enough strength to take it in a fight."

"I don't like the thought of a fight in these parts, but the trees are so dense it'd be unwise to stray from the path, and this thing can run down a herd of deer." Graf was skeptical. "Where would we find a spot for you to meditate? It'll be dark in a few hours and there's no shelter in sight."

"I can't maintain the transformation for long, even with the choker's help," Amber added. "How long do you suppose we have before nightfall?"

Graf looked up. "It's hard to tell, maybe a few hours."

"Let's try to find a secluded spot to sleep, then. We'll need plenty of rest if we're going to cross paths with this guy."

The monster had ripped up several smaller trees in the surrounding area, and a number of other pulverized animal carcasses littered the ground. They came to an enormous tree stump, nearly as tall as Graf and with a considerable diameter. The inside had rotted out over time, but the bark wall was still strong. They made a crude roof out of moss and tree limbs.

Amber decided they'd sleep inside for the night. Graf dozed off rather quickly while she meditated on her transformation for the possible melee. A short time passed before something could be heard moving outside.

"Graf, wake up," Amber whispered.

Her mouth was so close to his ear he could feel her lips brushing against his skin. As his vision refocused, she motioned for him to lean his head out of the tree stump. From a distance Graf could see a grotesque, malformed giant lumbering through the forest dragging the body of a dead elk behind it. He was naked except for a loin cloth, with leathery green skin. Its ears were gnarled and scarred, and a small tuft of moss-like hair sprouted from its head. Its appearance was akin to the ogres Graf fought back home. This provided some relief, as he had experience fighting this kind of beast.

"I can sneak up, jump him, and rip out his throat," Amber suggested. "He's not as big as I thought he'd be and, as you described, he doesn't appear very agile."

Graf shook his head. "Let's follow him at a distance. We need to know where their camp is so we can avoid it. That way we can bypass it and avoid further conflict if the terrain is stable."

They remained about ten paces behind the beast, moving gently and often darting behind trees and bushes. Before long they came upon a crumbling fortress amid the dense foliage of the forest. It was of colossal size, one of the largest castles Graf had ever seen. Judging by the size of the battlements, portcullis, and drawbridge, it wasn't built for humans or the creature they were following. Dwarfed by the structure, the deformed ogre inched his way across the drawbridge and disappeared into the castle.

The duo approached the castle, keeping to the bushes and shrubbery for cover. A crashing uproar arose from within the fortress, and a voice like thunder reached their ears.

"And how am I supposed to fill my gut with that lousy scrap of venison? Damn you, Dingus! I told you I smelled man flesh! You've been gone nearly two days and... STOP SCRATCHIN' IT!"

"It hurts us, Mingus! It itches!"

The feeble, warbling voice that followed the former seemed more akin to the creature they followed to the castle. Graf and Amber exchanged uneasy looks as the voices continued to argue.

"Took a dump in a wad of poison Ivy, likely as not... Stop playin' with it and look at me when I talk to you!"

A thunderclap echoed throughout the clearing and the ground rumbled as the green body flew out of the portcullis and landed on the drawbridge with a *thunk*.

The creature scrambled to its feet, facing the direction of the travelers. Amber yanked Graf behind a collapsed Wagon.

"Sure, Graf, let's follow the ogre right to his lair. That was smart thinking," Amber whispered. "We need to get out of here."

Graf made a quick gesture, running his finger across his throat, and his thoughts rushed into her mind... *SHUT UP!*

The creature sputtered as he stumbled away from the moat. "Why does he smack and wack poor Dingus?"

For the first time, the duo got a clear look at the thing's face. Instead of gasping in fear, Graf fought to suppress a giggle. Its head was shaped like a gourd, with a long, thin forehead and a bunched-up face flanked by fat, pimply cheeks. One eye was crooked and the other was milky and glazed over. His lips reminded Graf of a duck beak, and made the giant look as if it was going to erupt in sobs. Pouting, he sat down, sending a plume of dust into the air as he swung his legs over the moat and mumbled incessantly.

Graf brought his lips to Amber's ear. "They eat humans... Your idea seems the better in this case. We need to get away from here, and I don't want wart-face alerting his *friend*. How quickly can you take him out?"

"He'll never hear me coming, but I'll have to act quickly. I haven't practiced my stealth mode in ages and it's not stable."

Her body became fluid, rippling like a sheet to the wind before returning to normal, only now she was all but invisible. Her smoky figure crawled across the ground like a spider, leaping onto the shoulders of the sniveling giant and slicing his neck in a single quick motion. Springing from his shoulders, she landed off a backflip as the green form flopped back on the ground grasping at its neck, black ichor puddling beneath it. Amber popped out of her lucid state and she fell to her knee, winded. As quickly as he could, Graf ran to her side.

"We need to leave," he hissed. "Can you walk?"

"I couldn't hold it, even with the choker's magic. I can move, but I'll be slow at first."

Then Graf noticed something strange: the creature's body had begun to crumble, and in a few seconds had dissipated into dust.

Amber noticed it as well, and she shot a troubling look at her companion. "Why do I get the strange feeling that's not a good sign?"

"Well, well, well," a familiar, warbling voice said from behind them. "You're quite the smart one, aren't you?"

There was a tremendous blast as bits of rock rained down around them, followed by the louder, deafening voice they'd heard earlier.

"Looks like the trees finally sent us man flesh! A fine delicacy... We'll be eatin' good tonight, Dingus."

"Oh, do let us play wif 'em first, Mingus. It's been so long since we've had company!"

The pair turned on their heels to face their opponents and faltered. This would prove a challenging fight after all.

Chapter 16

Fortress of the Giants

The thing before them was at least twice the size of the ogre they'd followed to the ruins, and far more formidable. Graf judged his height at well over 20 feet, and his body rippled with taught muscle. His skin and hair were brilliant pink, and a putrid smell akin to rotting eggs wafted into Graf's nostrils. He doubted the creature had ever bathed in its life. It was naked aside from a strip of bear skin wrapped around its waist, the head of the bear still attached and resting on its hip. The beast's hair was draped in a thick braid over its shoulder, thick with grease and teaming with bugs and worms. Jutting from its lower lip were tusks stained pink with blood. Aside from these obvious features, however, the creature's face was surprisingly human. *Handsome, even, if you can ignore the smell and creepie-crawlies*, thought Amber. *Though I doubt any woman could survive a night in bed with him.*

Remind me to laugh later, when I'm dead, Graf responded.

"Feast your eyes on a real ogre," the monster told her. A line of snot oozed from the creature's nose as he smiled menacingly. A dark blue tongue raked across its upper lip, collecting the ichor.

As out-sized as he was, Graf wouldn't let the beast's ogling stand.

"She's off limits, Pal," Graf shouted. "We're on a quest for the Bellows flower. So, unless you're hiding one up your rear end, kindly shove off and let us by."

Graf brandished his sword in one hand and his dagger in another.

The beast's glance fell on him. "I must say, few get this far. All for that stupid flower."

"But if you really want by," came the warbling voice, "share your lady friend with Mingus and I for a night and you can march right through!"

"Or a night with you," the giant nodded at Graf. "We don't discriminate."

"And we're oh so gentle..." Both the giant and the other voice erupted in obscene laughter.

"As fun as that sounds, I think we'll pass." Graf grabbed Amber. "Come on, we'll find a way around."

The giant snorted, "Don't you idiots know anything? The woods around this castle are cursed. The way to that bloody flower runs smack through my fortress. You leave that path and you'll be lost forever... good as worm food. You can't go back the way you came, neither. Only way out is through my lovely home."

"Oh, do play wif us," said the other voice. "It'll be fun."

A growl issued from the giant's loins, and something stirred underneath the bear skin wrapped around the creature's privates.

Graf hated to think what "play" the beast and his invisible companion had in store for them.

"This forest is teaming with deviants," Graf muttered to himself, turning up to face the giant once more. "We'll do nothing of the sort. Now let us pass before things get ugly."

"We was gonna play nice," the giant snarled, "but since you won't indulge us, we'll make a nice morsel of you instead."

"Fan out!" Amber mustered her second wind and shoved Graf away from her, exploding into her berserk form.

They were flanking the beast, Amber howling in carnal rage while Graf readied himself in a fighting stance, sword and dagger at the ready.

"Tricks, have you? This should be fun!" The giant reached behind its back. "Let's even the odds, shall we?"

An ogre-faced spider as large as Graf launched from the pink giant's hand, tackling the warrior. Graf rolled from beneath the spider, jabbing wildly to ward off an advance. "Now I know where that voice was coming from," Graf said as he and the spider circled one another. "Nice of you to join the party."

"Look at the scary human with his sticker," it said. "My legs are trembling with fear... all eight of 'em!"

Graf grinned, "Don't worry, I'll be scraping you off my boot, soon enough."

He dove at the spider with his sword, attempting to pierce it to the ground where it had been. It was faster that he'd expected, vaulting over his head and smacking him in the face with webbing. Blinded, Graf tore at the sticky net the spider had cast, peeling the slime from his eyes just as the spider launched itself straight at Graf. Once again, Graf was on his back and his sword was knocked from his hand, but the spider had failed to notice the opal dagger which found its mark in the underside of its cephalothorax. It was a strike of desperation, and Graf knew it wasn't fatal. Startled, the spider backed away.

"Save us, Mingus! He's stings us!" It cried.

But Mingus was in a predicament of his own, fighting Amber.

Graf's companion was dwarfed by the giant even in her berserker form, but proved the more agile, having mounted his shoulder. Black ichor oozed from his ear, which Amber now mauled, and meaty, pink hands struck at her in a frenzy. Diving away from one such blow, the giant struck its own injured ear as Amber dove away, crawling around to his stomach and onto the ground. His equilibrium off, the giant staggered. She capitalized at the widened stance, and her muzzle dove underneath his loin cloth, her canines sinking into grotesque genitalia. Black blood surged from between the monster's legs, and she tore at her prize violently until it released.

Immediately, Mingus dropped to his knees, screaming wildly. This distracted Dingus long enough for Graf to retrieve his sword and stab Dingus through the abdomen. The blow had been so mighty it had driven through the spider entirely and embedded itself into the wooden drawbridge they stood upon. Withdrawing, Graf kicked Dingus, sending the dying spider into the foul waters of the moat. Graf caught his breath and glanced at his companion. Amber stood in front of Mingus, having spat his torn appendage onto the ground before him. Graf quickly recognized it for what it was, and nearly puked at the thought of the pain that Mingus was now enduring.

She reverted to her natural state. "What's wrong? I thought you liked it like that."

"You bitch!" Mingus lunged forward.

The blow was unexpected, catching her square in the face. She fell backward, half conscious. Mingus, unaware of Dingus' demise, had failed to notice Graf's left hand throw the dagger, and soon the hilt was buried in his eye socket.

There's nothing more dangerous than a wounded animal, and Mingus fought on with all his might. His two-fold pain forgotten in the frenzy of rage, he swung at Graf. Graf was hard pressed to avoid the blows, one catching his shoulder, sending him spinning backward. Mingus stomped and smashed the ground with feet and palm, sending dirt and stone flying into the air as Graf tucked and rolled into a forward handspring, landing on his feet. He spun, swiping his sword at the advancing giant, severing several fingers. Mingus cursed, throwing a right cross which Graf side stepped. Graf returned with an arcing strike that partially severed the giant's hand. Graf surged forward, leaping into the air and smashing the hilt of his sword into the beast's remaining eye. Mingus crumbled to the ground, and in rage Graf dropped his sword and pummeled the ogre's face with several hard heel stomps.

Amber had shaken off the giant's blow and stood next to Graf.

"I should've known better than to gloat," she wiped Mingus' blood from her lips. "Going to put him out of his misery?"

He wasn't sure. Looking down at his felled opponent, Graf was almost sorry for the thing, but then thought twice. It had planned on raping and eating them, after all. They had delivered irreversible damage, though, and he doubted Mingus would be so eager to conduct mischief the next time a traveler sought passage through the wood.

Graf put his foot on the giant's forehead, grabbed the bone handle of his dagger and ripped it free from the eye socket. Mingus screamed in pain and fell back, his partially severed hand clinched under an armpit and his other hand, minus two fingers, clutching his bloody nether regions.

"I forfeit! I forfeit!"

Graf glowered down at the beast. "Give me one reason why I shouldn't kill you."

"Took my manhood, you'uns did," he groaned. "Ain't it enough?"

Amber nodded at Graf. "He won't be doing any harm for quite some time. Let's focus on the Bellows."

The path led through a crude tunnel within the castle that led underneath the keep and into the wilderness on the other side. Had the fortress been built to human scale, it would have been considered quite small, but in its super-imposed size, it took them quite a while to work their way through the tunnels to the other side.

They continued for several hours unhindered. The forest grew around them as they trekked further in, and soon all but the faintest glimmer of sun passed through the canopy leaves. The trunks became gnarled and deformed, and little by little all noise faded around them until not even the sound of leaves or the buzz of insects could be heard. The silence wailed in their ears, and it seemed even the rustle of debris underfoot had been muffled. Graf's shoulder had begun to ache shortly after his battle with Mingus, and it slowed his pace considerably.

"We have to be getting close." Amber stopped to sit on a protruding root. "I don't like the idea of any more surprises."

Graf laughed. "Don't tell me you've lost your taste for adventure."

"Don't get me wrong, lovekins." Amber pulled Graf down beside her. "I love the occasional obstacle, but this is a bit much."

"What does the map say?"

She pulled out the folded parchment and laid it flat between them. The image that had guided them thus far had all but faded, and any attempts to find their position failed.

"Another trick of the forest, perhaps?" Amber flung the map aside. "But how do we return to Sanctuary when we find the Bellows? The map has been enchanted by the wood and it's rotten magic."

Graf rubbed his eyes. "And if we go back the way we came we'll become endlessly lost."

"It's a lot to chew on."

The pair sprang from their seat at this voice which rang in their ears. Sitting on its rump and leaning against the very tree they had stopped at sat a bear of enormous girth, larger than any Graf had ever seen. The fur on its torso and head was brilliant orange with a bit of gold around the eyes while his paws were black as coal. Vines had grown up around its legs and stretched onto his midsection. Next to the bear was an equally large pile of fruits, nuts, and plants the bear repeatedly ate from.

"Did I frighten you? So sorry," it said as it stuffed its mouth with an enormous paw-full of beechnuts.

"You were sitting there the whole time?" Amber gasped.

The bear shrugged, "I know, right? Shan't imagine why anyone would notice a tub o' goo like me."

"Who, or should I say what, are you?" Graf asked.

"What does it matter," it said. "You won't care. I suppose you're here for the Bellows?"

Graf looked up the trail. "Are we close?"

"Ah ha, I knew it! You humans are all the same." The bear nearly choked on a mouthful of blueberries as it laughed. "No concern for a poor wretch, like me. It's all about you."

"There's no need to be salty. I asked a simple question and expect a simple answer."

"Now who's being salty?"

Graf's hand rested on the pommel of his sword. "I didn't come all this way for some bubble-brained bear to cry me a river. Our friends lives are at stake, maybe even the safety of the entire wood. Now are you going to stop stuffing your face and help me or do I need to top off your dinner with my metal?"

Graf whipped out his blade and the bear feigned a gasp.

"First off, you naked mole rat, I'm not a bear! Secondly, do you honestly think I'm here by choice? Look at how thick these vines are around my legs... I haven't moved for centuries. Cursed, I am. Should've heard what he called me: a selfish, egotistical, gluttonous slug. I'm to live out my punishment here, sitting and gorging myself on the delicacies of the forest until the end of time, directing travelers to the Bellows; never to move and never allowed to die. A cruel punishment for one foolish error in judgment. I can't be killed, even if I let you; my tissue instantly regenerates. I'm impervious to all weapons, magical or otherwise. My cousin is nothing, if not creative."

"You're an Ion," Amber stated.

Graf looked from the creature to Amber and then back again. The epic size of the bear, coupled with the unnatural colorations of its pelt should have made this fact obvious for Graf to deduce. Graf's agitation had hindered his intuition.

"Who cursed you?" Graf asked.

"None other than mister 'Holier-than-thou' himself," the bear smeared his face with honey from a jar at his side.

Graf groaned. "Forgive us, but we have no clue who that is. Do you mean the Traveler?"

The bear licked the last bits of honey from a claw and rolled his eyes. "The Ald Marc, you nimrod. That puffed up crow's cock with his human lackey trailing him like a snot-nosed cub."

"Aldo and Bernholt," Graf said.

"Yes, yes... that's what all the underlings call them. The Ald Marc is my cousin, you see. Got all pissy when I refused to fight in that icky war with the Skulk... the vulpine spirits."

"He must be talking about the Shoon," Amber said to Graf.

"Gor blimey! You outsiders and your silly names..." He was obviously disgusted by the titles used by Asa and the rest of Sanctuary.

Amber sought a friendlier approach, hoping to comfort the bear enough to point them on their way.

"Listen, friend, we're awfully sorry about your predicament, and would love to stay to listen to your troubles, but your cousin Aldo might be in serious trouble. We really do need the Bellows. Do you know the way?"

The bear's eyes went wide and its jaw dropped, spilling a mash of half-eaten nuts and berries. "In trouble you say?"

"Been missing for centuries," Graf said. "Lost to untold dangers and possibly dead. However, if he does live, the key to finding him might lie with the very flower we're searching for."

The bear brought a claw to its muzzle, staring at the ground in contemplation before Amber spoke.

"If you help us, and we find him alive, we could put in a good word for you... tell Aldo and Bernholt how sorry you are."

"Aldo might even retract the curse," Graf added.

Amber winked at Graf, acknowledging the grim warrior's cooperation. The bear became excited.

"You'd do that for me?"

"Why wouldn't we?" Graf did his best to muster a smile.

The bear sat silently, apart from the occasional crunch of an acorn in its jaws. Finally, it nodded and spoke.

"Ok, I'll take the bait. You'll find the Bellows in that direction," he said as pointed a mighty claw into the darkness.

"But there's nothing..." Amber was cut short when a soft light appeared in the trees.

"If you do find my cousin, tell him I said I was sorry." A single tear fell down his cheek. "Tell him Chuffy said he was sorry."

"Will do." Graf nodded his thanks.

The pair turned towards the light that now guided their path and left the last living Ion to his penance.

Chapter 17

Within the Rose

They reached the Grove of Ages. The branches of white poplar trees met above them, forming a tunnel leading into the dazzling light. The air cooled. Birds, squirrels and chipmunks once again marked their presence and all memories of hardship were obliterated. The silvery grove that now surrounded them seemed to encompass more terrain than all their journeys in the Wanwood combined. Minutes turned into hours and hours seemed like days. There was a strange euphoria about this place. It was needless to speak. As the magic of the grove surrounded them, the spirits of Graf and Amber began to coalesce into one, and the couple walked hand in hand. Finally, they had reached their destination. A rush of air blew past them as they returned to reality, finding themselves standing in the soft grasses of a glade.

"This place is holy."

Graf could display neither protest nor approval at Amber's statement. In fact, he couldn't speak at all. It wasn't appearance that sanctified the glade, although it was truly breathtaking. It was something in the air; in the vibrations felt as each foot was cushioned by grass; in each blade seeming to possess a living, breathing soul. This place was at the heart of the wood, and the holy blossom of Sanctuary's salvation was within their grasp. The grove encapsulated the glade, and before them, at its center, was a lake. In the center of this lake was an island wrought of gold, and even from their distance he could see the enormous, gilded monuments of two mighty bears. The firmament above them was a remarkable night sky yet, despite this darkness, their surroundings were remarkably illuminated.

"I can't explain why, Amber," he looked at her, "but it all seems worth it now."

Amber shook off the awe of their surroundings and motioned for them to continue.

"The sooner we get that flower, the sooner we can save Bernholt and figure out what to do about Glenna," she said.

Graf could have stood in that exact spot until his skin had turned to ash and his bones to dust but remembering the comforts of Sanctuary and the threat Glenna imposed, he moved on. He pulled himself out of the trance and ran with Amber towards the lake. The water was not deep once they arrived – barely waist high – and they quickly made their way for the island.

The island was in fact a platform, built with a skill and precision Graf had never seen equaled. Every square inch had been shaped from gold, and the two monuments he had seen from the forest's edge, golden statues of two mighty Ion, stood on either side of an object in the center of the island. Surrounding these were dozens of man-sized statues. The creatures these depicted were all too human.

"Are these the Shoon?" Amber inquired.

They were all female, with fox face and bushy tail. Their voluptuous bodies and stately features would have been something to behold, and Graf doubted the statues – opulent as they were – did the real creatures justice. These statues were enrobed with delicate, pastel silks, and despite the untold ages the garments had been present, they displayed not the slightest weathering or deterioration. If these were indeed the Shoon, Glenna had gone to great lengths to conceal her true nature.

"Come. I can see the Bellows," Amber called.

Rising from the center of the courtyard was a stately pillar, about waist high, and set at its top was a small basin barely a foot in diameter. It was filled with earth, and a single lush stem rose from the moist soil. At the top was a black pod the size of Graf's fist.

"That's it?" Graf asked.

Amber walked forward. "Do we break off the pod or rip the whole plant out?"

"*YOU"LL DO NEITHER!*"

The platform trembled with the sound of the voice and water rained down upon them as a creature flew from the lake and landed on the outstretched paw of the Ion statue. It was a mighty beast: a man above the waist and something resembling a serpent below. It was heavily armored in a shell-like armor and wielded a spear. The beast slunk down the statue to separate the pair from the flower. When the being spoke, its mouth didn't move. Rather, it communicated through telepathy: thoughts which echoed within Graf's mind like thunder.

"*HOW DARE YOU APPROACH THE HOLY BELLOWS WITH SUCH FLAGRANT DISRESPECT! THIS BLESSED RELIC IS THE LAST OF ITS KIND AND SHALL NOT BE DESTROYED BY A BARBARIC HUMAN AND HIS SHAPESHIFTING CONSORT!*"

Amber had spoken brashly about how to obtain the flower, and Graf knew better than to try and sway this creature with intimidation. *A little flattery might work,* he thought.

"*NO, IT MOST CERTAINLY WILL NOT! THERE'S NO NEED TO SPEAK, MORTAL. I KNOW THE DARKEST DEPTHS OF YOUR MIND AND MEMORY. I KNOW WHY YOU ARE HERE AND I KNOW WHY YOU MUST RETRIEVE THE BELLOWS.*"

"Then certainly you know our intentions are pure," said Graf. "We seek the flower only to aid our sick friend. We have no desire to destroy the flower. Please tell us how to properly harvest the petals without killing the plant."

"*THE BELLOWS WILL YIELD ITSELF TO YOU, YOU NEED NOT TOUCH THE STEM NOR THE POD. HOWEVER, THIS CAN ONLY BE DONE AFTER YOU HAVE BESTED ME IN COMBAT.*"

"I take it there's no other way," Amber stated.

"*IT WAS DECIDED AT THE FOUNDING OF THE WOOD THAT I, THE CUSTODIAN, SHOULD GUARD THIS HOLY*

FLOWER WITH MY LIFE'S BLOOD. YOUR INTENTIONS, BE THEY GOOD OR EVIL, ARE OF LITTLE CONSEQUENCE TO ME. I EXIST TO DEFEND THE BELLOWS AND NO MORE. SHOULD YOU ENDURE TILL THE END, YOU WILL RECEIVE YOUR JUST REWARD."

Their walk through the Grove of Ages had been an enraptured experience, but upon entering the glade the pains of their journey had returned. Without the adrenaline of battle, the blow Mingus had dealt to Graf's shoulder smarted fiercely, and the cuts and bruises from his brawl with Aed hadn't healed despite the maniacal machinations of Grandfather Clock's mattress. Graf's legs were weak from the untold miles of their hike, and Amber, who'd returned to her natural form before entering the Grove, had performed so many transformations that Graf doubted she'd sustain another. This creature would be their most challenging foe yet, with Mingus' size and strength and no doubt Aed's speed and precision. To make matters worse, Amber's transformations had been so rapid in their battle with Mingus that her powers were now spent and she had to revert to her natural state. Unlike the Jackrabbit, this guardian gave no ultimatum. The pair had presented themselves to the Bellows and would fight to death or victory.

"Can I speak to my companion before we battle?" Graf asked.

The Custodian nodded his approval.

He turned to Amber, gripping her shoulder. "Can you take berserker form?"

"Sure," she laughed. "Only by the time I completed the transformation I'd begin reverting. My energy is spent, Graf. We'll have to fight him naturally."

Graf sized up the Custodian, and for the first time in quite a while felt butterflies in his stomach. He was a trained warrior and didn't scare easily. However, despite the gravity of their previous conflicts, this was the first time he felt truly unsettled.

"Be honest." Graf looked into her eyes. "Do you think we can beat him?"

"If your shoulder wasn't jacked up and I was fully rested, it'd be unlikely. Now? I doubt even a miracle would help us."

Graf nodded, embraced, and kissed her, despite her beastly appearance. Releasing himself, he drew sword and dagger while Amber crouched on all fours, hackles raised.

The Custodian sprang towards Graf, thrusting his weapon at Graf with expert aim and precision. Barely diving out of reach, he felt the burn of the spear's tip graze his arm, tearing his tunic and flesh. Amber jumped into action, aiming to latch onto the creature's back, but was instantly knocked to the ground by the snake tail. Graf put away his dagger and rushed the Custodian while brandishing his sword. He grabbed the spear with his free hand, but the creature easily muscled it away from him before jabbing the butt end into the man's sternum. The blow sent him sprawling backward into a Shoon statue.

"HOLD HIM!"

Upon this command, the arms of the statue he'd fallen into encircled him in a bear hug. Another statue became animated, grabbing his legs. Soon, four curvaceous, vulpine women of pure gold held him aloft. Graf struggled hard to free himself, but their embrace was unyielding.

"Amber!"

Graf's cry was one of desperation, and he knew there was no way she could hear him amidst the rush of battle. Despite her agile performance, he could tell she was depleting. Without his help, she would be gone for sure.

"You call this a fair fight, Custodian?!" Graf screamed.

The creature faulted a moment, barely avoiding a swiping claw to the face by an airborne Amber. In fact, Graf now realized the Custodian had the same twitch each time they'd spoken aloud. Before, the Custodian had done a better job of suppressing the distaste of their voices, but now it was obvious.

Watching the battle more intently, he noticed more subtle cringing of face every time Amber snarled and growled. An untrained eye would have missed it all together, but not Graf.

The creature's weakness was sound!

That must've been why it told us there was no need to speak, thought Graf, *it couldn't tolerate the sound of our voices.*

The Custodian sensed the thought and swung towards Graf with a look of frenzy. Knowing time was critical, the man screamed with all the power in his lungs.

"Amber, make noise!"

The Custodian charged at Graf, and for an instant she stood confused, panting.

"Noise!" Graf's voice rattled. "He can't stand noise!"

The confusion in his love's eyes was traded for one of awareness. Dropping again to all fours, she craned her neck and stuck her face into the air, letting a wind piercing howl escape her lungs.

Even for Graf's ears, the howl was mind-numbing and deafening. Their foe dropped his spear and clutched his ears.

"STOP! STOP! STOP!"

The grasp of the golden statues loosened and Graf fell to the floor. Realizing he needed to act quickly, Graf reoriented himself and retrieved his sword. The creature was writhing in pain, clutching his ears and spinning about on the platform. Graf fought past Amber's howling and charged, only to be caught by the brunt of the Custodians tail. It was a wild, desperate blow, but Graf could feel his nose crack and teeth break as the scaly hide connected with his face. He fell back, his mouth filled with blood and for a moment he was unable to breathe. Graf had suffered an injury to his lower jaw in his youth as a member of the guard, having extensive repair done. This injury wasn't as serious – he could live with a busted lip and a few missing teeth – but the time it would take him to recover would be his doom.

Graf was grabbed by the ankles and thrown across the podium, landing near Amber. She stopped for a moment, noticing Graf's bloody mouth. He looked into her eyes and pleaded with his mind.

Keep going!

The howl was renewed, as was Graf's attack. His foe now rolled about on the floor, his energy exhausted. Graf raised his sword above Custodian's head, praying the creature's flesh didn't contain a supernatural dexterity. The head was severed by that blow, sword ricocheting off the gilded floor. The body thrashed about in the throes of death, the snake-like tail knocking Graf from his feet once again, but after a moment the body lay still. Amber's howling ceased, and Graf closed his eyes for an instant. They had won.

She knelt beside Graf, sitting him up on her knee and tore a strip of cloth from the sleeve of his tunic to wipe his lip. They held each other a moment before they were startled by a buzzing noise. They were equally astonished when the Custodian's body disappeared in a flash of light. The voice of the being was then heard, coming from the black pod of the Bellows itself.

"YOU DISCOVERED THE WEAKNESS OF MY AVATAR AND PREVAILED. IT HAS BEEN CENTURIES UNTOLD SINCE I WAS LAST DEFEATED BY A WORTHY RECIPIENT OF THE BELLOWS. THE FLOWER IS YOURS, FREELY. HOWEVER, REMEMBER MY WARNING: TOUCH NOT THE POD, NOR THE STEM. THE POD SHALL OPEN, AND YOU MAY THEN TAKE YOUR REWARD."

So, the creature they had fought and defeated had only been a physical manifestation of the Custodian. Graf held no doubt the Custodian was yet another of Traveler's associates. The pair had grown accustomed to supernatural interference within the Wanwood and didn't question it. Helping each other to their feet, they did as the Custodian commanded and walked towards the Bellows pod.

"I would've expected something a bit grander after all that," said Graf.

Before Amber could respond, a crack appeared in the hairy surface of the pod, and it popped open to reveal dozens of thin petals. There were petals of every color of the rainbow; some were striped and polka dotted, some shone like silver, and still others contained images of people or scenes of nature. Thinking this the Bellows flower, Graf reached to grab the mass of petals, and upon doing so a small hand, no larger than Graf's fingernail, reached out and smacked his fingers with shocking strength.

"What did I tell you?"

Following the small hand came the head and torso of an elf-like creature, with skin like alabaster and blue hair, dark as the night sky above them. There were stars in its hair, which twinkled relentlessly, and when the elf lifted its head it revealed eyes like glowing embers. The petals Graf had reached for were not Bellows, but the creature's skirt.

"Let me guess," Amber laughed. "You're the Custodian."

The elf smiled. "It's not often that travelers prove themselves strong enough to free me from my pod. It's been an eternity since I've had a breath of fresh air."

Graf nodded respectively at the elf. "You stated you knew why we were here, so you must know we can't risk waiting here any longer than necessary. I lost all track of time passing through the poplar grove, and heaven knows how long we've been gone from Sanctuary."

"No need to rush. You've only been in the Grove a few weeks." The elf scratched its chin. "But yes, time is of the essence. I suppose it's time I handed over your well-won prize."

Waving its hand in the air above its head, a rose much like the one on Graf's tattoo materialized in midair. Following the elf's instructions, Amber reached out and took the blossom in her hand.

"Don't worry about crushing the petals, dear," it said. "It's quite sturdy. Oh, and this one's for Grandpa Clock."

The small hand produced plucked a metallic petal from its skirt, held it in the air, and blew on it. It vanished with a spark, and the elf clapped his hands.

"He'll find it on his bedside table when he wakes up tomorrow. I figured since you defeated one of my avatars, the least I could do is save you the trouble of taking it back to Grandpa Clock. Not that you could return the way you came."

Graf nodded. "Much obliged."

"Now, all you have to do is follow the Porter's instructions and you'll be back in Sanctuary in a split jiffy," the Custodian said, beginning to retract himself back into the pod.

"Wait!" Amber exclaimed. "What instructions? We never met anyone called *the Porter*."

"Well, of course you did. Don't you remember? He was that rather stout fellow at the beginning of the Grove... stuffing his cheeks. He showed you where the Grove was."

"He must mean Chuffy," Graf said. "Aldo's cousin."

The Custodian nodded.

Amber rolled her eyes. "But that's the thing. He never said anything about how to get home."

"Of course he did, sweetheart. You just weren't paying attention."

"Do you know how we can return home?" Graf asked.

The elf nodded with a smile, "Uh-huh."

"Can you tell us?" Amber pleaded.

"Nope!"

Graf's ears burned. "Why not?"

"Rules are rules, Graf. Much as I'd like to tell you, I can't."

With that the elf retracted into its pod and spoke no more. They stepped away from the planter, looking down at the rose in her palm. Aside from its velvety shade of black, there was nothing at all remarkable about the flower.

"I've half a mind to rip that damn pod out and throw it in the lake," Graf said.

"I HIGHLY ADVISE YOU DON'T."

Graf looked back at the pod. "Shut it!"

Amber snorted loudly, fighting to suppress a laugh. Graf put his hands on his hips after wiping blood from his chin. Despite his agitation, he couldn't help but admire Amber's body, soaked in the blood and sweat of battle. She'd regained enough strength since defeating the Custodian's avatar that she could reassume human form, and her glistening wet skin gave Graf inappropriate ideas.

"What's so funny?" Graf asked.

"You're arguing with a flower."

Graf nodded solemnly and walked with Amber to the platform's edge where they took off their footwear and stuck their aching feet in the water. They talked for a few moments, attempting to piece together their conversation with Chuffy. It seemed like ages ago, however, and as hard as they tried they could remember nothing significant. So, they took advantage of the calm moment and sat in each other's arms. They finally came to the decision that despite the warnings of Mingus and the Custodian, the pair would attempt to return the way they came as best they could.

"I suppose we can spare a moment, eh?" Amber held his hand.

"I don't see the harm," Graf said. "After all, what could go wrong now that we have the Bellows?"

A cool breeze wafted up from the waters of the lake, and they kissed passionately. So passionately, in fact, that Graf hardly noticed the rotting hand rise out of the water by their feet.

Chapter 18

Chewed Up

The corpse crumbled under the blow dealt by Graf's sword. The next was broken in half by an earth-shattering heel stomp. Amber was tallying up her victims into the double digits, but the myriad of reanimated corpses was endless, and across the lake dozens of zombies emerged every few moments. They wouldn't have been much of a challenge in small numbers, as they were sluggish and fragile. However, after their recent battle, Graf could feel exhaustion creeping in.

"We can't keep this up forever!" Amber cried, kicking the head off an approaching zombie.

Graf screamed violently as he swept his sword out in front of him, laying low several foes. She was right. They couldn't fight forever, and the number of fiends emerging from the water weren't slowing down. Was this some sort of a trick by the Custodian? The Traveler and his ilk were unpredictable at best, and there would be little surprise if this current trial was an unfortunate by product of their failure to return home. Just then, the thoughts of the Custodian flooded their minds as they fought.

"THIS IS NOT MY DOING, GRAF. SOMEONE, OR SOMETHING, HAS BROUGHT A CURSE DOWN UPON MY HOLY FLOWER. IT IS DARK MAGIC, FROM ANCIENT TIMES, CAST FROM AFAR. I DID NOT SENSE IT UNTIL IT WAS TOO LATE, OR ELSE I WOULD HAVE WARNED YOU. YOU MUST ACTIVATE THE MAGIC OF THE BELLOWS TO RETURN TO SANCTUARY IMMEDIATELY FOR I AM TOO WEAK FROM OUR BATTLE TO AID YOU. THIS IS AN ARMY WITHOUT END. THEY WILL STOP ONLY WHEN YOU ARE DEAD OR GONE."

"We can't activate it, you idiot!"

"YOU MUST REMEMBER THE PORTER'S INSTRUCTIONS!"

The mass of undead warriors grew tenfold, and both Graf and Amber were fighting two and three foes at a time. His shoulder ached and his mouth was swollen and bloody. He barely avoided getting his head sliced off by the rusty wet sword of a monstrous foe.

"We told you already," Amber cried out. "He didn't tell us a damn thing."

"HE TOLD YOU ALL YOU NEED TO KNOW, CHILD. YOU MUST REMEMBER!"

Graf spun towards the Bellows pod, ignoring the throng of rotten bodies. "How are we supposed to remember anything when we're fighting off endless enemies? I can barely think!"

The Custodian was silent for a period, and the duo continued to fight off the horde. Most of the army was humanoid, while others resembled wild beasts or rotten amorphous blobs. Amber, exhausted, fell under the crushing blow of a mace. Graf rushed to her side but was instantly intercepted by the corpse of a centaur, its flesh half rotten to reveal its muck-covered ribcage. It carried a mighty club which was brought down on Graf's hand, breaking several of his fingers and knocking his sword from his hand. Just then, reinforcements arrived.

The trunk of a mighty fir tree – sharpened to a point – spiked itself into the water, sending a shock wave across the golden podium and disintegrating hundreds of zombies. From the mass of branches and needles erupted the familiar form of Aed the rabbit.

"The Custodian sent for me. I have slowed the enemies advance, but they will regroup. A curse has been placed on this glade and they will continue to regenerate until you've left."

Graf looked at the rabbit. "Who is capable of such a spell?"

"There is little time." Aed shook his head. "You must follow the Porter's instructions."

"Again with this *Porter*."

Looking over his shoulder, Graf could already see bodies rising from the murky water and inch towards the island. In moments they would be overwhelmed.

"Think, man. He had to have said something to you. Think!" Aed pleaded.

Graf racked his memory for their conversation with Chuffy but could remember nothing aside from the Ion's complaining and incessant munching and chomping. His eyes went wide with epiphany and reading his thoughts Amber looked at him and smiled in shared recognition.

"It's a lot to chew on," they said in unison.

Aed nearly collapsed with relief. "Quickly, then. I'll hold them off as long as I can."

With a speed he had not displayed even in their previous combat, the jackrabbit sprang into action, pummeling corpses at a pace that dazzled human eyes. Graf snapped back into reality when Amber shoved something rubbery and bitter into his mouth. It was a petal from the Bellows.

"Chew," she commanded, likewise stuffing one into her own mouth.

The petal seemed to grow with every bite, and despite Aed's prowess, dozens of zombies broke through his defense and lumbered towards the beaten companions. Graf kicked hard into the stomach of the nearest zombie, which fell backward and was trampled by the enormous feet of a troll-like creature. He gasped for breath, fighting to swallow the petal, but his mouth was jam-packed and bursting with black mush. Finally, after being pulled out of the way of a rotting fist by Amber, he swallowed the gooey mass and embraced his mate as they were blinded by light and encased in a cyclone of wind and water.

***

It was the second night in a row that Buckley had missed dinner. Now that he thought of it, Boomer hadn't seen his corpulent friend at all since the night of their arrival following the communal dinner.

First Graf and Amber, now Buckley, he thought. *Smells like the Milky Way's gone sour.*

Glenna appeared noticeably worried about the whereabouts of his companions and had stated the trio had been seen leaving the boundaries of Sanctuary. Lonnicker and Berris had supposedly been dispatched by Glenna upon learning this news, along with a small search party.

"We can only hope they haven't strayed too far," she'd said at that night's dinner. "Why do newcomers insist on venturing outside Sanctuary!?"

Boomer had a sixth sense when it came to people. As genuine as the old lady's concern appeared, he knew an actress when he saw one, and this dame was a damn good one. Graf and Amber had made it clear they were in no hurry to return to the wood. Likewise, it was also unlikely that Buckley would want leave his newfound comfort. The man was a nuisance and proved himself useless in the many fateful encounters with monsters before they met Graf and Amber. Despite this, Boomer had grown fond of the whimpering man-child. Over time, glimmers of personality began to appear through the incessant squalling and crying. His three companions, however short their relations had been, were the closest thing he had to a family. So, if they had not left of their own accord, where were they? Boomer wasn't about to take a shifty hag's word for it that they'd just gone exploring.

It was time for this scaly orange space man to do some sleuthing.

He'd been given his own quarters in the Big House, separate from the others, and after dark, Boomer grabbed what was left of his gear and slipped out into the hallway. The house would undoubtedly prove full of surprises, but with this as his only lead, he slunk in the direction he'd last seen Buckley walking. After several turns, and several empty bedrooms, Boomer reached a wooden door at the end of the corridor. After verifying he hadn't been followed, he turned the handle and stepped inside expecting to see a bedroom. Instead, he nearly plummeted face-first down a spiraling stone stairway.

"Jumpin' Jehoshaphat!" Boomer shouted, falling back into the hallway.

Boomer suddenly felt a strange sensation – like a sixth sense – as if he was being beckoned by some unknown force to follow the steps. The spaceman cautiously descended the dimly lit stairs. It didn't take him long before he reached the landing and opened another small door. Upon entering, Boomer found himself in a moderate chamber lit by crystals embedded into the walls. Opposite him was a stone archway leading into another dark chamber, and above the entrance, etched in stone, were strange markings in a language foreign to him.

"Liar's Eye."

Boomer swung around at the sound of the strange voice to see Glenna blocking the doorway he'd just entered. However, the voice she now used was not that of a kindly grandmother. It was powerful and foreboding. She stepped towards Boomer and nodded at the inscription.

"It says: as the bear lives, so does Sanctuary," she snickered. "Briar Dash's secret alphabet. What Aldo saw in that despicable parasite, I'll never know. You know him as Bernholt, but I refuse to acknowledge that name."

A noise came from beyond the threshold, a resounding grunt and a burst of hot air that smelled like the rot of death. The grunt was followed by a growl and then a deafening roar. The rattle of chains followed. Boomer had heard recordings of bears in his studies of old Earth and he recognized it here, but the noise that had shook ground beneath him was of no ordinary bear.

Glenna noticed the recognition on Boomer's face and stepped closer. "Naturally I couldn't kill Aldo like I killed Briar Dash. Had I done so, the holy barrier protecting Sanctuary would have died with him."

"So, you found a way to bewitch him," Boomer concluded. "Trap the bear down here where nobody would ever find him."

Glenna's elderly appearance melted away, replaced with a form both erotic and deadly to behold. She stepped towards the dumbstruck Boomer and caressed his scaly face with a single silver fingernail, its edge razor-sharp. Boomer could hear the point of the nail rake off the front of his chin. He wanted to make a run for it, to tackle the witch, make like a tree and leave. Magic was new to the extraterrestrial, but he could tell it was by the spell of this enchantress that he stood motionless and mute.

"It's nothing personal, Boomer. I've grown rather fond of your presence in Sanctuary, and I'd hoped you'd let sleeping dogs lie... But your concern for your friends has proved your undoing."

"You... you..." Boomer struggled to speak through the curse.

"Aldo needs to feed, dear," she kissed the alien's cheek. "As fond as I was of your stout friend, I had to put business before pleasure."

"*YOU BITCH!*" Boomer screamed, spit flying from his mouth.

She chuckled, wiping the spittle from her cheek with the back of her hand and licking it off. She walked around the frozen Boomer and stared into the dark void beyond the archway.

"It took great magic to bind Aldo here... magic that can't be duplicated. It took a part of my soul, which I can never get back. He is forever trapped here, as long as the house stands, held in a severely weakened state and robbed of the independent use of his magic. The chains I only use as a matter of principle... a tool to work on his mind. He was stubborn at first, refusing to kill or eat live prey. So, I had to ration out meals of raw meat a week at a time, then two weeks at a time. I must've brought him to the brink of starvation hundreds of times before I broke him, but after a few centuries he finally caved in."

"You'll get yours," Boomer stammered.

"I don't blame you for being mad. It really is a rotten business, sacrificing innocents to keep this bastard alive, but it's a fitting punishment to the beast for giving such authority to one like Briar Dash. I fought back tears when he tore into Buckley."

Boomer shook with anger, "And Graf and Amber. I'm sure you wept for them too!"

"On the contrary, Boomer. I wasn't lying when I denied knowing their whereabouts. Although I do have my suspicions, which I'll address should they ever reappear. I wouldn't have sacrificed specimens of their caliber, anyway. Sanctuary needs strong, sturdy, and skilled citizens like Lonnicker and Berris, Graf, Amber, *and* you. Buckley was rather helpless, a lost waif. He had nothing to contribute aside from comedic relief, and we have enough of that already."

"And I suppose now that I know your little secret, you can't take the risk of letting me live, either."

"It does pain me, Boomer. Your will is so strong. Even now, you're on the verge of breaking my freezing spell. No, you're too much of a risk. I worked too hard to win Briar's graces... too long to harvest the materials needed to devise a spell to kill him and contain Aldo. Sanctuary is mine, and I mean to keep it so."

Suddenly, Boomer pushed through the spell holding him in stasis and spun on his heels, charging at Glenna. She anticipated this, however, and sidestepped just in time, tripping Boomer and sending him sprawling into the dark chamber.

Boomer jumped to his feet, rushing for the doorway in an effort to escape the clutches of the crazed Aldo. The bear's rabid roaring bellowed in his ears and shook his brain, but a steel wall dropped down before him, halting his escape. Through a single slit in the steel, he could see Glenna staring back at him, transformed back into her guise of the harmless grandmother.

"Goodbye, Boomer," she said.

He watched as she walked back through the door and up the stairway. The sound of chains dragging against stone alerted him to the beast behind him. Hot breath wafted against his neck, followed the overwhelming scent of rotting human flesh, of which Boomer was familiar – though not by choice. Boomer turned slowly to behold the giant muzzle before him. In the dim light that spilled into the chamber, he could see it was ten times the size of any bear he'd ever seen. No man could withstand an assault from this creature. The slightest move would trigger Aldo's wrath, and Boomer had to make a choice quickly if he was to survive. His supplies had mostly been spent on the way to Sanctuary, and what he did have would prove useless against a beast of this caliber. His only hope lied in the small red dial on his Instaportwristband. The survival rate had been rather high in the Beta tests. In fact, only one percent of test subjects had resulted in fatalities.

Knowing my luck, I'll be in that one percent, Boomer thought.

Before he could reach for the dial, Aldo attacked. In a bite that encompassed Boomer's entire torso, the bear came down on the humanoid. Boomer parried to the side, desperately trying to get out of the way, but Aldo's speed was unlike anything the alien had ever seen. Fangs pierced into his shoulder, chest, and stomach as he was thrown across the room by the maw of the monstrosity, his head ricocheting off the nearby wall. Scurrying across the bones of Aldo's victims, he barely escaped another ferocious attack.

"Didn't your momma tell you not to play with your food?" Boomer teased, despite his agonizing wound.

A mighty paw that covered his entire torso came crashing into him, sending him sprawling back. His skeletal system being very similar to humans, he could hear several bones in his sternum break, and felt the claws tear away both space suit, scales, and flesh. His blood spilled onto cold stone, and Aldo roared even louder than before.

If he's this powerful in diminished capacities, I'd sure hate to square off against him when he's up to snuff, Boomer reflected through anguished breaths.

The Ion bit down on Boomer's left shoulder this time, lifting him into the air and jostling him around like a rag doll, but this didn't last long. With the spacesuit mostly gone and his bare flesh and blood exposed, the bear got a good taste of Boomer's species, spitting him onto the ground in disgust. A thought entered Boomer's mind, and he knew even while in immense pain that the thought came from the bear.

TASTE BAD!

Aldo was done toying with his meal and would soon destroy his unsavory dinner. Using what little strength he had left, and capitalizing on the beast's unfamiliarity with alien blood, Boomer fell to his side and activated the dial on his wrist. A wisp of flame shot up from the spot where he lay, singing the whiskers of the enraged Ion. Despite this, when the smoke had cleared and Aldo reoriented for the final attack, he paused in shock.

Boomer had disappeared.

Chapter 19

Homeward Bound

Drifting through a white-hot void in the moments after swallowing the Bellows, the full memories of the death of Graf's mother and sister flooded his mind. Naked and broken, he had cradled his mother in his arms, fighting back tears as he said farewell to the one who raised him, promising to avenge her death.

"Brunhilde," he said.

It was the first time he'd said her name aloud since that excruciating discovery, and for the first time in over a decade, Graf cried. His mother had been a distinguished shieldmaiden in Calm Frost, a civilization far to the north of Eastern Rising. Tattoos of runes in the old northern tongue coated her face, neck, and arms, as well as dozens of scars she wore proudly. These markings were the trophies of many victories in battle. She would sit Graf on her knee telling him stories of the monsters and armies she'd defeated in her youth, and his plump fingers would trace the strange war brands as she would tell him of the humble stable hand from Eastern Rising who'd stolen her heart during her darkest hour: his father. Having been greatly wounded in battle by a dragon, her days of battle were long since spent. Thus, she'd left her place of prestige among the hardened warriors of the Calm Frost and traveled to Eastern Rising, where she met the lowly commoner whom she would soon wed, and bore him a son, Graf, and a daughter, Karie. His father would soon after die.

Graf the Undefeated, his sister had called him. He was his sister's hero, and the only person he loved as much as his ma was Karie.

Graf sought the right words to give her, but an anvil had become lodged in his throat. He looked around him, saw the battle she and his sister had given the man before he overpowered them. It was too much to bear, and his eyes stung from the bitter tears welling in the corners of his eyes. He knew who had done this, had seen this same act before, and hated himself for not stopping Gregor sooner.

"I will end the man who did this to you." Graf pulled her to his chest and embraced her. "I will make you and father proud."

Laying Karie gently upon her bed, he covered her with her quilt and retrieved her blue-fire opal dagger, which he'd kept in his chest for safe keeping. He gave his sister a quick last kiss on the forehead, knowing the sorrow of tarrying any longer would undo him. Looking at his blood-stained hands, he turned and bolted from the room like a whirlwind into the night.

It was time to pay Gregor Firstborn a visit, and Graf knew just where to find him.

***

The breath was ripped from Graf's lungs as he struck the ground, flat on his back. Amber was a step behind, landing on top of him and sending a second wave of pain through his sternum. Seeing stars, he couldn't make out the figure that had hauled him to his feet and set him on the stone ledge. The person's voice rattled inside his head until his brain settled and he caught his second wind. He realized the person flapping their gums was Asa. The petals had transported them back to Bernholt's shrine.

"Took you long enough," Asa said. "Thought you lovebirds gave me the shaft and ran off."

Graf grabbed the collar of Asa's collar in anger, but Amber intervened before the Gardener could retaliate, wrestling her lover to the ground. Graf's anger quickly abated when the pains of their journey made themselves known.

"Your map wasn't exactly foolproof," she stated.

Graf rose to his knees. "We've been to hell and back trying to find that damn flower, and damn near got ourselves killed a half dozen times."

Amber shoved the Bellows flower in Asa's face. "Say 'thank you' like a good boy."

Asa frowned but accepted the flower.

"Yeah, well before you get all hot and bothered, there's something you should know," he said, turning to face the Lapis statue of Bernholt. "Your friends are missing."

"Boomer and Buckley?" Graf asked.

Asa nodded. "They disappeared without a trace not long after you left. Top that with my happy ass covering for you two the last few weeks and..."

"How long have we been gone?" Amber interrupted.

"Like I said, a few weeks. Glenna was pressing me hard about you two," Asa said. "Luckily, her magic can't read my thoughts, so I eventually convinced her I was clueless. Everything's hotsy-totsy now. As for your pals, Gigglemug and Applesauce... Let's just say they're likely wearing pine overcoats right about now."

The Gardener could tell by their expression they didn't understand his nicknames for Boomer and Buckley, nor what he was trying to insinuate, so using his thumb he pantomimed slitting his own throat. Their eyes went wide as they caught the hint that their friends were dead. Asa nodded apologetically.

"It's a raw deal, daddy-o," he said.

"I'll bet Glenna was responsible," Amber stated.

"Do rattlesnakes bite gently?" Asa threw his hands up in frustration. "Common sense could've told you that much."

"What do we do now?" Graf stared earnestly at the statue.

"Not much to do, except for this," Asa held up the flower and walked over to a mortar and pestle he'd set aside.

He ripped off several petals and slowly worked them into the mixture, then taking his fingers, he molded the paste into a small waxy ball. He handed the sticky orb to Graf. It was about the size of a small pebble, just big enough to fit in someone's mouth. Asa nodded at the statue, and his tone became more serious, even dropping the strange accent Graf had grown to hate.

"We'll have to work quickly. Once I free him from the statue the stasis will wear off in a matter of seconds. When he wakes up, shove this in his mouth and down his gullet."

Graf looked crossways at Asa. Asa smirked, and a bit of his jovial attitude returned.

"I mean it," the man said. "It's hard on the body, coming out of stasis. He'll be dancing the Clambake when he wakes up... twisting and shouting. Just make sure he doesn't bite your fingers off."

"Can't you do something to calm him down?"

"No time for that, pooh bear," Asa responded.

Turning to the statue, he snapped his fingers and a ripple of energy cast itself out from the statue, shaking the ground beneath them. The lapis surface of the statue cracked and crumbled, falling into the basin of the fountain to reveal a skeletal figure standing in its place. The greasy, emaciated corpse quivered and spasmed before falling to the ground at Asa's feet. His skin, withered, translucent and filmy, and clinging to the bones; muscles, bones, arteries, and organs were clearly visible. A black mass covered the chest right at his heart, and when Graf stepped closer he saw an open cavity infested with black worms and a wasted heart struggling to beat under the mass of parasites. The thing gasped and writhed on the ground, spit flying from the mouth and cataracts capped eyes bulging. Asa fell to his side and pinned him down.

"Now!"

Graf dove to Bernholt at Asa's command. Bernholt's sickness had caused him to lose most of his hair, only a few wisps remained on his mottled head, fluttering in the air like cobwebs. Graf reached for the sickly scalp, tilting the shivering head back to insert the pill. Graf felt the membranous skin of Bernholt's scalp break under the pressure of his hand. His hand slipped from Bernholt and he stumbled forward onto the writhing body.

Asa snatched the pill from Graf and threw him back.

Graf was surprised by Asa's strength, and before he could blink saw Asa shove the waxy ball deep into Bernholt's mouth. Fingers dove further into the man's mouth than Graf thought possible, and seconds later Asa pulled back and clamped Bernholt's mouth shut.

Bernholt grunted and whimpered, undulating on the ground with arms flailing in every direction. Asa brought his face close to the man's and with lips nearly touching, blew gently on his face. Bernholt quieted and finally went limp. Color quickly replaced the deathly pallor of his skin, which had soon been restored to a healthy appearance.

"Look at the wound in his chest!" Amber screamed.

Graf looked to see the black worms dissolving before his eyes, and quickly the heart could be seen growing back to normal size, with a healthy rhythm returned to its beat. The wound closed, leaving a hideous scar across Bernholt's left breast. Asa withdrew from the man. Bernholt's sudden gasp for air startled them, but Asa held out his hands to stifle their reaction.

"Cool your jets... he's ok," the Gardener said.

Bernholt had undergone a drastic improvement upon taking Asa's pill, and Graf had even noticed a thick helmet of curly blond hair sprouting from his scalp. However, the man was still dreadfully thin and severely malnourished, with little to no muscle mass. Graf had expected Bernholt to be fully revived upon taking the concoction, but he was lost in a deep coma.

"Why is he still unconscious?" Amber stammered.

Exasperated, Graf stood.

"I thought you said this would cure him, Asa," he said.

"The Bellows acted as the quick release, stopping the effects of the curse and saving his life. He ain't out of the woods yet, though. It'll take a while before the other ingredients of the capsule restore his body to full health and heal him of the damage Glenna's magic has done to his body. He was in stasis for centuries. Sure, his life was intact, but the parasites you saw... they've been working on his body ever since I put him in that statue. That's why he looked so bad when I busted him out."

"He didn't look like that when you put him in there?" Graf asked.

"Hello no, daddy-o. He wasn't a pretty site when I put him under, but he sure as hell wasn't the walking dead."

"How long before he wakes?"

"No telling. But we need to get him inside, where it's warm. It could be days or even weeks before Mr. Sleeping Beauty is well enough to get up and about, and until then he needs to stay out of sight and mind."

"Will Glenna detect Bernholt's presence?" Amber asked.

"She couldn't spit in the direction of this grotto, let alone break in to harm him. She'd have better luck finding Hoffa... But Bernie here's been worm food for hundreds of years. Buddy-roo deserves a comfy bed. Unless of course you wanna leave him here on the cold, wet grass."

"Are you sure there's no way for Glenna to get in here?"

"The only ones that can gain access to this house are myself and those I deem trustworthy, which include you. I'll also enchant the house so Bernholt can't leave."

Working together, they carried Bernholt into the house and tucked him into a bed in a backroom. Asa snapped his fingers once again, and a glass and pitcher of water appeared on the bedside table. At Asa's request, Graf touched the pitcher; it was chilled.

"It'll stay cold too," Asa said, dimming the lights with a nob by the door. "He'll drift in and out for a while, and he's gonna be thirsty as hell once he comes to."

Asa led them back out to the terrace leading to the grotto. They sat down on a stone bench Graf hadn't noticed before, and the trio developed a game plan for Graf and Amber's return to Sanctuary. Exhausted and troubled by the freeing of Bernholt, Graf let his better half do most of the talking.

"I'm worried about what she already knows of our journey," Amber said, "and whether or not she'll be able to read our thoughts."

Asa nodded. "Her powers ain't what they were, sweetcheeks. Besides, omniscience and divination were never her strong suit to begin with."

"How do you mean? Isn't her magic powerful enough to look into our minds? You said yourself, she's incredibly powerful."

"She used to be, but in order to create magic strong enough to curse Bernholt and efface the Big Bear she had to relinquish a part of her soul. Her powers were permanently weakened."

"Then she can't read our memories?" Amber asked.

"Nah, toots. She meddles a bit in telepathy, but mostly she can only read impressions of thoughts in the moment. Memories are off limits, and with that choker your mind is locked up tight."

Amber looked to her companion. "Graf... What about his mind?"

"Good point. Even in her present state she could sense something." Asa snapped his fingers. "That reminds me!"

Asa reached into his pocket and pulled out a ring he slipped onto the middle finger of his left hand.

"Put 'er there, pal!"

Graf hesitated, disliking the notion of shaking his hand when he remembered the zapper Asa had used before. Eventually, he reached for Asa's hand only to retract it with a yelp; instead of an irritating shock, Graf was blinded with an instant of searing pain. Looking at his palm, a small symbol of a horseshoe had been branded into his flesh. Looking at Asa, the man held open his palm to reveal that the ring had a red-hot horseshoe charm facing inward.

"You're welcome," he said.

"What the hell was that?!" Graf shouted, clasping his still burning hand.

"It's for luck and protection, Daddy-o! Witches like Glenna hate horses."

Graf's stern look drew further explanation from Asa.

"Hey, cool your jets! That ring didn't come from no Cracker Jack box... It's got some souped up anti-magic. Now your thoughts are safe from the Silver Fox, too."

Graf looked at his palm again as the pain subsided. The brand had quickly healed, and only a feint white outline of the horseshoe emblem remained.

"Now you're both safe, and don't worry," Asa winked. "Glenna's magic can't beat mine."

Needing to relieve herself, and choosing the more human route, Amber inquired as to the location of the facilities.

"The crapper? Down the hall from Bernie's room. Can't miss it."

Alone with the Gardener, Graf was able to finally catch his breath and reflect on what had just happened. Bernholt was only partially recovered, but Graf could tell that even when fully recuperated the man's appearance would be underwhelming at best. The notion of this man's status as an ordinary person – ordinary in every sense of the word – had never crossed his mind. He'd expected someone tall and imposing, like the man in the portrait at the Big House, with a demanding presence and a supernatural aesthetic that made him something more than human.

"A bit let down, big daddy?" Asa draped an arm around Graf.

"I don't know." Graf put his hands behind his head and leaned forward until his head was between his knees. "The way everyone described him, I'd expected a sight to behold: a superhuman demi-god who'd snap into action the moment you launched your counter spell."

"He's a man like any other, Graf. His hair will finish coming in, and he'll gain a bit of weight once he's mended, but what you saw is what you get."

Graf shook his head. "He just looks so..."

"Pitiful?" Asa finished.

Graf nodded. Asa laughed and slapped Graf's back.

"A warrior like you should know not to judge a book by its cover. I know he don't look much now, but just wait until that cat starts swinging a sword! When he's ready to rumble, he will be Glenna's kryptonite."

"What makes him so special?" Graf asked. "Without Aldo, what could he possibly do?"

"He has Aldo's blessing, kid! That man was always a warrior, not always an honorable one. But when Aldo gave him that gift, the wood became a part of him."

"What was Aldo's gift?"

"Giving him his new name! A name carries great power, especially when it comes from an Ion. It's sorta like a tradition among Aldo's kind. Once you're renamed by one of those bears, nothing's the same."

"I've heard him called Briar Dash several times," Graf chuckled, "I suppose that's his original name, and it sounds right for a man from Eastern Rising. I can't help but wonder what got him exiled."

Asa's voice lost its vibrant accent and became serious.

"His old name died with his old self. Bernholt's exploits before coming to the wood make even Glenna's atrocities seem tame, and thinking about those times will help nobody."

"What changed him?"

Asa shook his head. "Ain't my place to say. Only Bernholt can share that."

Asa stood up and walked towards the house, Graf following. Stopping at the door, Asa turned to Graf and whispered a final affirmation in his ear, his accent returned.

"Things are gonna get sticky, kid, so don't lose your head. It'll all work out," Asa winked. "Boss man said so himself."

Chapter 20

Winds of Change

They stood in the grotto near the rubble of Bernholt's statue. Despite the desire to bath and borrow clean clothes from Asa – who was about Graf's size – the Gardener insisted the blood, dirt and grime of their journey would make their story more believable to Glenna. The plan had been set: Asa would teleport them to a location just outside of Sanctuary in the midst of Lonnicker and Berris' hunting grounds, where they would be seen and returned to Sanctuary. There, they would stick to their story of accidentally stepping outside the boundary of the settlement and becoming lost. Amber was unsure of this, but Asa insisted that her obsidian choker and Graf's horseshoe brand would ensure Glenna believed them despite any inconsistencies in their story.

"But be careful not to share anything to Lonnicker and Berris," Asa warned. "They're well intentioned, but Glenna's been brainwashing and bewitching them for centuries. They'll do her bidding to the grave and believe anything she says, as will most of the townsfolk. Anything you tell them will beeline straight to that frigid bitch."

"Noted. Thanks." Graf shook Asa's hand a final time, surprised not to be burned or shocked with another brand.

Finished with their farewells, they stepped onto the podium where Bernholt's statue had stood. Asa snapped his fingers and after a flash of light engulfed the pair, who opened their eyes to find themselves surrounded by the familiar Wanwood.

"Let's hope it doesn't take them long to find us," Graf said.

They rested by a nearby tree until late afternoon, as the sun began to set through the trees. Amber had reassumed her human form, and the pair napped despite the pain of their injuries, which at this point were really making themselves known. The pair were alerted by the rustling of leaves and the crunching of twigs when the minotaur and his hunter appeared through the vegetation of the forest.

"Sweet snake oil," muttered Lonnicker. "Didn't think we'd see you again."

Berris knelt down to observe their wounds and apply some crude ointment. "Sure didn't, especially after your friends went looking for you," he said.

Graf knocked away from the man's hand, which was irritatingly rubbing a cut on his face with a rag. Berris apologized and helped the man to his feet.

"Our friends went looking for us?" Graf asked.

Berris had given up on trying to help Graf with his wounds and instead began to clean and bandage a wound on Amber's forearm. The hunter exchanged a worried look with his companion and responded to Graf's question.

"Then they never found you."

The minotaur stepped forward. "You'd been missing about a day when your portly friend went looking for you. Glenna said she tried to warn him, but he wouldn't take no for an answer. When he didn't return, your scaly orange friend in the funny clothes went after him. Glenna's been having us patrol the territory all around Sanctuary looking for ya'll. We'd given up hope."

Looks like Asa wasn't kidding, Amber's thoughts flooded Graf's mind. *We can't let on that we're aware, especially if they're in Glenna's pocket, like he said.*

Graf had grown used to her projections and remained passive while her thoughts were transmitted to his mind. He acted quickly to her warning, casting a worried glance at her and looking back to their so-called rescuers.

"This can't be true!" Graf cried.

He began to pace before the pair and was relieved to find them convinced of his despair.

Amber interjected, "You haven't found a trace of them?"

"Not one stitch of clothing," Berris said. "Not one drop of blood."

"We should get you to Sanctuary. Glenna will be relieved to see you! You're the first ones who've gone missing and that we've ever managed to recover... First in my lifetime, anyway," Lonnicker said.

Weaving them with uncanny precision through the forest, they guided the pair through the dense trees, Berris in the lead and Lonnicker at the rear. In a short time they were entering the settlement near the same point of entry they'd taken when they were first led to Sanctuary by the hunters. Berris ran ahead, light on his feet. By the time Lonnicker, Graf, and Amber reached the Big House, Asa, Glenna, and many townsfolk had gathered. Asa, covered in dirt and once again donning his grubby orange robes, had appeared in deep conversation with the old woman when attention was alerted to the 'rescued' duo. Asa, like a true thespian, ran forward and embraced Graf.

"Thought ya'll were taken off the payroll for sure," he slapped Graf on the back several times. He smiled at Amber. "And you, dollie! Aren't you a sight for sore eyes?"

He leaned in for a kiss from Amber, who pushed him away with a playful grimace. Glenna came forward, placing a hand on Graf's shoulder and tilting her head in a consoling look.

"Lonnicker told me about your friends, dear," she dabbed her eyes with a neckerchief. "I promise, I'll not let them rest until they're found."

"Thank you, Glenna," Graf said.

Looks like she and I are tied for an Academy Award!

Asa's thought was so loud it nearly knocked Graf off his feet. Glenna stabilized the man with surprising strength, and her warm smile turned cold. For a moment Graf feared she'd broken through Asa's anti-magic, and for the first time since being in Sanctuary her eyes changed. Cool blue irises flashed rich amber and the pupils stretched into slits. Graf recognized the eyes for what they were: a fox's eyes. As soon as they'd appeared, however, they were gone in a blink, and Glenna was again the doting grandmother.

"Oh, sweetheart, you must be famished! Come inside, quickly, so you can be tended too."

A group of dwarves similar to house staff he'd seen on his first night led them into the Big House and to their quarters where they were bathed and given fresh clothes. One of the dwarves, an apothecary, took great care in tending to their wounds. He momentarily noticed the horseshoe burn on Graf's palm, but quickly dismissed it as an anonymous battle scar. Afterwards, Glenna returned with trays of food and drink.

"Here's a little something to soothe your stomachs," she stated, "and after you eat, it's off to bed for you two! Heavens knows how you two haven't come down with death of cold already."

Graf took a large bite of a sandwich and a swig of wine. Like the meal he'd shared with his traveling companions on his first night in Sanctuary, the food was absolutely delectable. In moments both he and Amber had devoured their dinner while Glenna checked their fresh bandages.

"Oh, I suppose they'll do. I should have tended to you myself," she said.

Amber smiled at her. "You've done enough, Glenna. We're just happy to be back."

"Not nearly as happy as I am, although I do fear for your dear friends. How fond I was of the portly one," she whimpered as she once again dabbed her eyes. "The poor dears!"

Must've rubbed onions across her eyelids while making dinner, Amber's thought shot through Graf's mind.

Glenna didn't notice this transmission the way she had Asa's. Instead of reacting, she stood stoic and misty eyed, glancing at the two as if they were her grandchildren.

"Perhaps we can aid in the search for Boomer and Buckley," Amber said.

Graf added, "Once we've recovered of course."

"Of course, poppets," Glenna nodded.

"Perhaps Asa could help," Graf suggested.

Glenna flinched at the Gardener's name, but quickly changed the subject.

"Off to bed with you now! All this talk of rescue won't do a bit of good if you die of exhaustion. Don't worry, for I put a mild sleeping potion in your drink. It is harmless and will help you sleep."

She walked to the doorway as the two crawled into the closet bed. As she reached the doorway, she turned to face them. She thought: *What are they hiding? Why are their minds closed to me?* The only other person who had shielded his thoughts from her was Asa. Glenna had suspected his interference for some time. She didn't know his full nature but was aware of at least some the power he wielded. Her spies had in fact witnessed the pair visiting Asa on the day they'd vanished, and their return was no coincidence. Someone of Asa's abilities could easily harm or even end Glenna altogether, and the fact that he hadn't yet done so concerned her.

What is he waiting for? she contemplated, and *how will he use these two?*

The pair had shown an incredible tolerance for the potions she infused with the nightly communal meal, as was displayed in Graf's untrusting demeanor after that night's meal. Most newcomers would have been eating from the palm of her hand after their first bite. Boomer had shown this same resilience, unlike the weak constitution of Buckley, who had followed her straight to Aldo without question.

Sleep well, my dears. You'll soon join your friends, she smiled, *but first I'll deal with that meddling Asa.*

Whatever reasons Asa had for not confronting her openly, she would take advantage of it soon. There was the possibility his powers rivaled even hers, but his lack of direct interference gave her the assumption he wasn't liable to use them in combat. Then there were the thoughts of the Traveler and his Helpers.

Could he be one of them? Glenna thought.

She would have to act sooner than anticipated. A few simple spells would plant the evidence needed to condemn the pesky gardener, and the people of Sanctuary would be easily convinced of his crimes. Then she could turn her attention to these two. The bear would be excited to have feedings so close together.

Fear not, Aldo, Glenna fondled the pendant on her necklace. *The main course will be there soon.*

Her necklace glowed, and this message was passed to its recipient deep underneath the Big House, into the sad, horrific heart of Sanctuary.

The Great Bear stirred.

***

It was approaching noon when the duo finally woke to the violent fanfare outside. Amber couldn't make anything out through the small window above the bed, so they quickly gathered collected, and went outside. The citizens had gathered before the Big House and Graf could make out Lonnicker's shouting.

"Black magic," he called. "A sick cannibalistic ritual conducted in plot against Sanctuary!"

As they pushed their way through the crowd, they could see the one horned minotaur in the center of the gathering, with

Asa on his knees, bound and gagged before a large wooden block. In the beast's hand was his axe. Berris stepped forward, his face twisted with anger.

"We discovered him steeped in his experiments, the remains of our beloved brothers and sisters littered in an unholy circle around him..."

Lonnicker finished his sentence. "Demonic prayers spilled from his lips, and he tried to bewitch us when he saw us. But with Glenna's protection, we overpowered him."

The whispers and murmurs of the citizens quickly erupted into jeers and curses. Graf was all too familiar with the dynamics of a crowd with 'gang' mentality, but these claims were too sudden and unsubstantial. No evidence had been brought forward and no investigation had been done; the crowd was simply taking these two by their word. Everyone Graf had met in his short stay in Sanctuary appeared to possess sound, rational minds – a quality espoused by their leader, Glenna – and this reaction to hearsay was too dramatic for him to believe. These people were incensed and no doubt bewitched.

"We have to say something," Amber whispered.

Graf reached to his belt, relieved to know in his haste to come outside he hadn't forgotten to equip his sword. He gripped the hilt tightly. Graf gathered himself to speak out over the crowd, but he faltered when he made eye contact with Asa.

There was no fear in the man's eyes, only a vexed annoyance. Why wasn't he fighting back? Surely, the Gardener had an unlimited number of abilities at his disposal that could combat his captors and provide escape. Instead, he sat motionless and content in this inconvenience. As if reading Graf's thoughts, the man winked at him.

"It is as I have feared."

The crowd opposite Graf and Amber parted for Glenna, who circled around the three figures in the center of the throng to stand before Asa. Her eyes met Graf's and once again he noticed the fiery tinge and slit pupils. The traces of a smirk touched the corners of her mouth as she turned back towards her prisoner. She grabbed the handkerchief with her hand and yanked it off Asa's mouth, her silvery nails leaving deep scratches in his face. Graf hadn't noticed these nails before.

"We've opened our homes to you, deceiver. We welcomed you with open arms, invited you to take communion at the sacred meal, and you spit in our faces."

"We didn't want to believe it, Glenna," Lonnicker stated. "But we've seen his wicked practices with our own eyes. We fought off demons summoned by his own hands."

It was then that Graf noticed the strange look on the beast's face as Glenna pretended to lay a comforting hand on his shoulder; this same look was shared by Berris the hunter. Their stare was blank and distant, as if a black curtain had been drawn behind their eyes. Their faces mocked emotion, but their eyes remained glazed over. Graf stared around him at the faces of the townsfolk, and Amber quickly caught on to his observation and nodded in agreement.

"She's controlling them, without a doubt," Graf whispered. "The question is how, and what do we do about it?"

They were unable to finish their conversation as Glenna's voice grew louder over the noise of the crowd. "There shall be no forgiveness for this crime. No mercy. Sanctuary is a place of peace, a peace we all enjoy. But this... *savagery!* It must be answered for in blood. Lonnicker... bring the axe."

Graf tensed but felt Amber's hand grip him. "We can't give ourselves away... not yet," she whispered. Harsh words, but true nonetheless.

Still, Graf felt the frustration tearing at him inside. Asa wouldn't even look their way. Graf watched as Lonnicker vanished into a nearby store house. A huge clank echoed from inside it. Something heavy hit dirt, and with Lonnicker's resumed footsteps, the steady churn of earth being chewed up followed. Lonnicker emerged and brought with him a large axe of execution, covered in ceremonial markings. The townspeople gasped in horror and wonder. Tears ran from Lonnicker's eyes, and his nostrils huffed with rage.

Berris met Lonnicker halfway there. "Let me, brother. I know your anger consumes you. But my skill remains true. Let us give our people the peace they need." Berris took the great handle of the axe from Lonnicker and took up the mission of dragging it toward Glenna and Asa. Again, Asa did not look up or react, even as Glenna stared down at him, awaiting any sign of weakness or despair.

"We can't let them kill him, Amber." But she would not let go of Graf's arm. As if in response, finally, Graf saw Asa glance toward him. The Gardener gave a weary smile, then turned his face back toward the ground. *He's resigned himself,* Graf thought. *Why... why must all in the Wanwood be so resigned to their beloved fate, To their destinies and prophecies that doom them to misery...*

Berris reached Glenna and Asa. "Ma'am." Glenna nodded. Berris took firmer grip of the handle and steadied himself.

Glenna turned back toward the townspeople, slowly moving her gaze across them. "With this blood, let us soak this treasured earth and remind ourselves why we must never let evil doers trespass against us. Berris, feed the blade of the Woodsman's Axe." With her speech finished, Glenna's eyes landed on Graf and Asa. Graf swore he saw the curl of a smile on her lips – but then she turned back to Asa.

At last, Asa looked up at his executioner. He spoke in a voice only she was close enough to hear. "You can't keep the wool over their eyes forever, foxy lady. I'll be back like a thief in the night... and I'll have friends."

Darkness flooded Glenna's features. She looked to Berris and nodded. With a great groan of exertion, Berris lifted the Woodsman's Axe from the earth. A battle cry filled his lungs as his great biceps swung to bring it up, over his head, and down it came upon its target –

And yet! Just as the Axe reached Asa's neck, a great gust of wind blew through the valley of Sanctuary, and Asa's physical form vanished into a colorful collage of autumn leaves. The Axe crashed into the ground, inept, as the wind carried the leaves that were once the Gardener away into the sky. Even more, the wind took Glenna off her feet, and she fell to the ground twenty paces from where she once stood.

The townspeople cried out in alarm. Graf and Amber looked into each other's eyes and they both heard the voice at the same time. *Run. To Asa's cabin. Now!*

The wind howled louder now, a cyclic moan of natural fury that crested across all of Sanctuary. Homes rattled at their foundations. Dwarves clung to giants, and fairies were twirled through the air as a mighty cyclone touched down.

Graf and Amber made a run for it, not far from Asa's cabin. They shut the door behind them, the chaos of Sanctuary still echoing. A moment of peace, as Amber held tightly to Graf and they both sunk down into the grass that carpeted the Gardener's floor. "Graf... what was that?" But before he could answer he house shook.

The knickknacks and doodads that Asa had filled his home with fell from their shelves. Glass shattered. A heavy creak issued from beneath the floor and soon Graf and Amber felt their stomachs lift up and their hearts race. The cyclone was ripping the house from the earth.

"We need to get out!" Amber cried.

Graf shook his head. "Too late now, bolt the door! And hold on!"

Amber slid the bolt lock shut just as the house ascended into the air. Through the windows they watched Sanctuary disappear beneath them. The howling winds grew in velocity and terrible power, and the house seemed ready to tear apart at the seams and explode into a million little pieces of debris...

But then all grew quiet. The wind grew gentler, and their airborne ride steadier. Graf caught his breath. "It's as if we're in the eye of the cyclone..."

Amber stood and looked out the window. "You're right... We're coasting on the breeze. We're... we're flying through the sky, Graf! How is this possible?"

With a great boom, the back bedroom door swung open. From it, a man sheathed in dirty blankets stepped forth. He pushed his curly blond locks back from his face and met the eyes of Graf and Amber. Graf couldn't believe it. He could see it all now, how the stem of the Black Rose spiraled and grew in thorny glory all the way up the man's arm.

"The North Wind rises and Mother Nature cradles us in her bosom. We live to fight another day, comrades. And I owe you both my thanks as well. I have been known by many names. But please... call be Bernholt. And in this respite offered by the elements, allow me to tell you my tale."

Chapter 21

The Chains That Bind

He was not a good man. The Eastern Rising had known many like him, but his evil had a particular flavor to it: a hint of selfishness and a healthy seasoning of pride. All in all, the taste was sour and overwhelming, and any who faced him knew its accompanying stench.

In that time, he was known as Briar Dash. Wherever his troupe of no-good mercenaries went, the rattle of chains followed behind. They were slavers, and cruelty was both payment and reward. The Eastern Rising had its wars, and in their wake Briar Dash and his men would travel to the weakened villages, the ravaged cities, and those forlorn outposts left behind in burning campaigns of fire. There they would do their business, claiming lives not in death, but in servitude. Briar Dash liked to watch his victims squirm, beg, and cry. It made the clank of the heavy chain more satisfying, the dire note to end his symphonies of terror.

As their wandering troupe moved across the land, it grew in size, with hundreds stretched behind the wagons. They were bound together, fed scraps, used, and abused by his men at will. And in the end, as they reached the city centers, the prosperous fortresses and castles where the victors of the unending wars dwelled, the prisoners were sold. Briar Dash liked his coin, sure, but he always felt empty when his slave train emptied. A hunger would gnaw in his soul and command him back into the bloodied fields, seeking the next round of instruments in his unholy music.

Briar Dash was a monster. No man at all. And even in a world of greed and horror, monsters cannot be tolerated forever. In times of peace, Briar Dash would still rage and rampage. Those who kept his business alive tried to tame him. He was put in charge of an underworld of horror, where even in peace times souls were sold into sex slavery and trafficking across the Eastern Rising.

Yet Briar Dash could not be trusted not to bite his masters. In his view, he had no master aside from himself. The Lord of the Chains has no higher power or allegiances. All he cares for is that sound of the chains clanking in the dark... the knowledge that he controls all he sees.

So, one night, as he dreamed of his particular shade of violence, Briar Dash was set upon by the royal guard of some lowly lord. He was brought to the edge of the city, and before many he had wronged and many who just shared his taste for pain, Briar Dash was branded with deep, dark ink. The first mark of the Black Rose was bestowed, and the first Black Rose was exiled beyond the barrier into the endless, knotted chaos of the Wanwood.

For the first time in his life, Briar Dash was stripped of all his power. The fear he utilized and the tools of his trade were locked away, beyond a dark magic veil he could not pierce. Like many Black Roses to follow, Briar Dash could only wander into the Wanwood and accept the fate he had been given.

Wander he did, for many moons. Try as he might, all matter of the hunt avoided him. They played a game of shadows, the small, yet fast creatures and the larger ones that even Briar Dash feared to confront. Such a hopeless chase left him malnourished, thinner than usual, as mangy and ragged as a street dog. He drank from the rivers and ate the leaves of plants that only sometimes left him poisoned and stricken with bouts of madness... Briar Dash had met his match in the Wanwood.

It was in such a state that he was captured, set upon in the night by those who wore dirty greaves and dinged armor, stolen from corpses. It was a gang of ravagers, scavengers... *slavers*. Wolves without mercy: *The Blaine*. Unlike the Eastern Rising breed, these slavers served no higher power, as there was none in the Wanwood. In its place was an endless selection of new things to ensnare and chain. And now Briar Dash was counted amongst them, hands and legs bound, tied to the prisoner in front of him and the one behind. Fed from the same dire trough every night with privacy eliminated and dignity erased. The man behind him, a shrunken creature covered in fur, barely remembered how to speak; the one in front never stopped laughing. Soon, Briar Dash felt himself caught between these two extremes – laughter or voiceless despair. His life's days blurred. His memories of his own wrongdoings became a prison.

It was torture beyond anything he could have ever imagined. It was the same torture he had inflicted on countless others. In the Blaine, he saw the glee with which he too used to work. Their leader, a sniggering, disgusting fool called Mad Jack, sometimes let his men eat the weakest of the slaves. A few months in, they dug into the hairy, hapless creature that walked behind Briar Dash. They cut loose his lower limbs and roasted them over a fire. They let the creature live, and now Briar had to shoulder the burden of keeping the legless body afloat in the great chain as they crossed the treacherous terrain of the Wanwood.

It could've been a year. It could have been many years. The unyielding misery made it impossible to know. What Briar Dash did remember was that it was nearly dawn, when the first arrow flew from the bush and blew through the throat of Mad Jack's lieutenant. The Blaine hit the ground and readied their own weapons... but no assault came. Not yet. Only a low, unsettling growl. It was deep enough to rattle gravel free from the earth and set some of Mad Jack's men to pissing themselves. The slaves all laid still, dead-eyed, their souls broken...

All except Briar Dash. That growl did something else to him. It awoke within him a fire he long thought extinguished. He couldn't name it, or define it, but he knew how it felt. It felt like life. It felt like a fight still worth fighting.

The first tree fell. Then another. Mad Jack cried out for his men to be still, but a few broke out in a run. That's when the Ion came forth, ready for battle. His claws shone in the dawn light. His roar shook birds from the canopies above. A great black bear with a crest of white fur in the shape of a 'V'. Briar Dash knew that mighty growl had come from this one. As this defender of the forest tore into the slavers, Briar Dash rose to his feet. The laughing one tried to pull him back down, but Briar Dash persisted. The heavy weight of the legless creature weighed him down, but still he pushed with every fiber of his being, until he stood upon his two feet.

Mad Jack saw this. A feral, spiteful cry issued from the slaver's mouth. He charged, blade drawn. Surprising even himself, Briar Dash answered with a battle cry all his own. He pulled up his chains and caught Mad Jack's blade, halting the attack. The laughing man finally fell quiet. And the legless slave, the one Briar Dash had carried for so long, his voice awakened: "Kill him. *Kill him. Free us!*"

This was it, the fight, the purpose. Briar Dash understood it all. He understood he was no longer the man he once was. He was a slaver no more, no man of the chain. He never would be again. Now, he would live or die in the pursuit of only one thing – the freedom of those he had once violated.

He felt the eyes of the great black bear fall upon him, and with the help of the two men on either side of him, lending him their own strength through the links of steel that bound them together, the man once known as Briar Dash twisted Mad

Jack's hands into the gnashing steel, and shattered them. Jack's blade fell to the ground, useless, and the slaver king's eyes went wide. His former prisoner leaned in close and spat in his face. "Never again."

The former demon of the Eastern Rising swung the chain around Mad Jack's neck and choked the life from him. It was as if all the weight finally dropped away. The tension the slaves had carried together for all this time... it was gone. And it was only when he looked up did the Black Rose realize this was literally true. The great black bear was snapping the chain away from each prisoner, one-by-one. Soon enough, they were all freed.

The Black Rose fell to his knees before the great bear. He bowed his head. "I am a disgrace of a man. I have done great evil throughout all my days. Only this morning, when I heard your roar of freedom, did I understand... did I finally see... what life could truly mean. So, I offer it to you now: my life, my future. Do with it what you deem worthy. For I trust no judgment beyond your own."

The Black Rose awaited the blow that would kill him. But it did not come. Instead, the great bear kneeled beside him and lifted his face with his paw. The two fighters, the justice bringer and the former slaver, met on equal ground. And the bear's voice emerged with that same rumbling of the growl in his chest. Somehow, the Black Rose understood it.

"The Wanwood is not the world you once knew. And your life need not be what it once was. That choice is yours. It is the choice we give to you, to all of you here this morning. That it was why we fight and you must decide why it is that you fight. It seems to me... you have made this choice."

The Black Rose could not help it as tears ran down his cheeks and he looked up at his savior. He nodded.

The great bear nodded in response. "Then tell me, Man with the Black Rose. What is your name?"

He tried to respond, but his voice caught in his throat. "I... I don't know anymore."

The bear considered this, then nodded. "No need. I hear it now, carried on the wind, whispered by forces far greater than the two of us. Your name, now, is Bernholt. And you may call me Aldo."

Chapter 22

Mother Nature's Son

Nearly a thousand years later, that same great wind whispered outside of the Gardener's house, still held aloft high above the Wanwood. Graf and Amber clung to one another as Bernholt tended to the fireplace and finished the tale of Briar Dash.

"Aldo redeemed me. The Wanwood was a new world, but I couldn't see it until I saw him... until I saw what good people can do in this world." Bernholt finally turned back to Graf and Amber. He settled in one of Asa's old chairs and let the flames flicker beside him. "This is another such inflection point of fate. A moment where we all must make decisions about who we hope to be..."

Graf couldn't help himself. He'd kept quiet, at Amber's urging, for too long. He agreed with Bernholt. It was time for *action*. "Then you know what Glenna has done."

Amber issued a dark laugh. "I'm sure he knows *all* Glenna has done."

"Amber... that's your name, yes? You're correct. I know Glenna's treachery more intimately than most. When the task of guarding Sanctuary was given to me, I thought Glenna nothing more than another seeker, like all in the Wanwood.: a lost soul looking for a home. I never expected her betrayal of the Ions, the disruption of the Wanwood's natural balance, the corruption she intended to seed through Sanctuary... Her jealousy drove her to that point. While I had once known such terrible impulses, many years had made me forget what it fuels in people. I ignored Aldo's impressions of the *old woman*. It cost us both... It cost us both dearly. Only Asa's foresight saved me, although I must say, being imprisoned in the form of a statue did leave me a little worse for wear."

Graf couldn't help it. He stood and strode over to the window. "This is a waste of time then! We must return to Sanctuary. Asa must be avenged! I think you've spent a little too long in that statue to realize... Glenna is going to cement her rule, tonight!"

"Graf, don't be so rude. Bernholt's still recovering. He's –"

Bernholt laughed now. "No, it's okay. I understand the way he feels. Graf, please. Imagine it yourself: being stuck in one place, unable to move, unable to even truly think. All I had were my memories, the good and the bad. It was an imprisonment unlike any I had ever been subjected to... or subjected anyone to. Can you imagine such an unnatural state?"

Graf's frustration cooled. *I have to admit... he's right. Such a thing would drive me insane.* Graf looked at Bernholt and truly took him in for the first time since he had awoken. It was undeniable that the skinny, aging man did not appear the legend Graf had hoped. Yet there was a power to Bernholt when he spoke about the voice of Aldo and how it had made him feel.

Graf felt the same about Bernholt. In all of his time since he had come to the Wanwood, Graf had felt caught up in something beyond himself. He had fixated on the legend of Bernholt as a traveler might upon a compass. It gave him direction. *Purpose.* And now here the man sat, yet Graf was so quick to judge. Instead, he decided to listen.

"I see... I hadn't considered it as such. Forgive me, Bernholt. It's only... it's been..."

Amber came to Graf's side and caught him as he nearly collapsed. "We lost a friend today, Bernholt. We lost Asa."

Bernholt picked up a rod to tend to the burning logs. "I know that pain as well."

"Of course. Aldo... he's gone then? Dead?"

Bernholt stared deeply into the flames. He bit his lip, lost in thought. "No. I fear... it may be a fate worse than death for my old friend. I believe Glenna has him in her clutches. I believe it may be his very life force that fuels her dark spell cast over Sanctuary... and now Aldo too is lost to it... Things are worse than I could have imagined."

Graf leaned into Amber, letting her carry the burden he felt in his heart. "Asa was a good man. Somehow he lived all of these years, waiting for help... lying to Glenna... carrying this terrible truth... and we let him die. We just let her kill him..."

Amber cradled his head and kissed him gently on the forehead. "He wanted us to live, Graf. Our fight isn't done."

"I could've done more... I... I could've..." Graf stifled a sob. He held back the sadness and the pain with everything he had. He didn't want to appear weak, not in front of Amber and Bernholt. But a single tear fell down his cheek and landed in the soft grass that coated the floor of the House of the Gardener. "I failed him. Traveler would never forgive me. Asa... he..."

"He had so much to live for..." Another voice joined the collective mourning. Footsteps in the soft grass sounded, as the voice spoke again: "And he was a real dreamboat too!"

Graf, Amber, and Bernholt all turned their eyes to the doorway that led into the kitchen, and from beneath that archway, Asa stepped forward. He wiped away faux tears from his eyes and sobbed to an exaggerated effect. "Whatever will we do without him?"

Amber was the first to react. She ran to Asa and wrapped him in a big bear hug with enough force to lift him off his feet. "Okay, okay, enough!" Amber laughed and laughed as she dropped him down.

Graf slowly approached in turn. Unlike Amber, he was angry. "Is this some kind of cruel joke?!" He grabbed Asa by the cuff of his shirt and drew him close.

"No, not a joke. Never a joker. Okay, maybe a tiny, tiny joke, yes." He mock sniffled again and blew his nose on Graf's shirt sleeve.

Graf pulled away in disgust. "Aw, come on!" But then, despite himself, he was overcome with a belly laugh. Amber collapsed into him, and the two's laughter became contagious. As they tried to recover, Bernholt stood.

Asa held out his hand. "Long time, no see Daddy-O... at least apart from while you were a statue or mostly unconscious." Bernholt took hold of Asa in another hug.

"Loyal friend. True Guardian of Sanctuary. I give you my thanks." Then even Bernholt joined the laughter. "You clever son of a bitch."

Asa shook his finger in reproach. "I'd watch your mouth. Weren't you just singing Mother Nature's praises?"

Graf finally caught his breath. "What's that supposed to mean? I saw you die! You... you..."

"What? Became a lot of leaves? Is that how you think people normally croak?" Asa pointed out the window. The house began to pick up speed on the wind, in a slow, controlled descent. "My brother, the North Wind, he thought it'd be easier to carry me in that form."

Now Amber spoke with bewilderment. "Your brother, *the North Wind?*"

"Yes, yes, surprise, surprise. Not everything about old Asa was as it seemed. I'll admit it now: I'm Mother Nature's son. Literally. The elements stroll with me and watch my back. Glenna never had the power to harm a hair on my pretty little head. Though it sure razzes my berries that she thinks she could. It gives us the one-up."

"Look!" Amber pointed outside. "We're landing back in the Wanwood!"

Bernholt moved for his room. "I need a blade –"

"Not so fast!" Asa drew them all together into a huddle in the center of his room. "We're far from Sanctuary. I asked my brother to bring us here."

"Why?" Graf asked. "If we have the elements on our side, surely we can overpower Glenna!"

"Come, come, Graf. Surely you must not think Mother Nature fights in worldly wars on behalf of mortals? No, while she's happy to protect me, this fight is still yours. That's why I thought you might like a gun-slingin', wild cowboy alien on your side."

Graf ran to the window as the house settled to the ground. "Boomer's alive?!" Outside of the window lay an unimaginable sight: a huge twisted hunk of purple and orange steel, with a rattling jet engine hanging from one wing and a gunmetal black turret from the other.

"Word from the bird, he's alive and well, if half-chewed counts as well. He had an encounter beneath the Big House at Sanctuary."

Bernholt once again drew away into the shadows near the fireplace. "So, it's true... Aldo lives... *kept* as a pet of that fell witch..."

"Yes, I'm afraid so. Boomer had a run-in, and barely escaped with his life, thanks to his teleporter. Traveler'd be jealous of such a handy tool. Although Boomer's all out now. He's been tinkering away in that ship of his for hours now, though. And he's hankering for a fight."

As if on cue, a great whoop arose from the hunk of metal that was once Boomer's ship before its crash landing in the Wanwood. The alien himself leapt from a hole in the roof and slid down the wing. Asa opened the door of the home and waved. "I've brought company!"

"Well good goddamn, it's about time!" Graf and Amber ran out to greet their friend. "Lookie who we have here!"

"We thought you were dead, Boomer! You and Buckley both."

Boomer grasped his friend's hands but looked down at the ground. "I may be alive... but I'm afraid Buckley's bear food...

He was a fearful little guy, but I have to admit I'd grown to like him."

Graf took hold of Boomer's shoulder. "We'll avenge him. I swear it."

"You're goddamn right. I've been working on a little something inside the *Neon Cowboy*, for just such an occasion."

Asa emerged from his house, skipping toward them with positively jubilant energy. "This reunion's nice and all, but we are on a tight schedule. Allies need to be gathered. Bernholt can rally the most valiant defenders from the Wanwood. My business will take me further afield... but you three... you'll be the vanguard."

Graf stepped forward, gripping the handle of his blade. "No place I'd rather be. And no one I'd rather fight alongside." Amber and Boomer both stepped up alongside him.

Finally, Bernholt stepped forth from Asa's house, steady on his feet, shoulders thrown back strong and defiant.

"Then let us fight, as I know one thing for certain: before the sun sets on this day... my friend shall be free from his chains."

Chapter 23

No Sanctuary

Glenna watched the horizon line over the hill rise at the edge of Sanctuary. The wind had finally died down. Now… all was silence. Behind her, Berris and Lonnicker approached.

"The townspeople are frightened, Glenna."

Without turning toward them, she shook her hand dismissively. "That was only prologue…"

Lonnicker stirred, an anxiety building across his huge features. "…What do you mean?"

"The evil raised by Asa… we are not yet clear of it. It comes for us still."

Berris gripped the blade he kept around his belt. "So, what now?"

Glenna smiled. "Now… I call upon my own magic. Sanctuary will not fall without a fight."

In the dense thicket of woods that encircled Sanctuary, Graf crouched close to the earth, lost in thought.

"Graf… it's time."

Graf met the eyes of his lover and partner. She looked beautiful in the fading light of day. Amber nervously toyed with the talisman that Traveler had given her and Graf felt the full weight of his journey press down upon him. "Amber, it's been a long few days… but I'm glad you've been the one at my side for it all. I love you."

Amber kneeled down next to Graf. Without hesitation, he kissed her. She chuckled when she pulled away.

Graf laughed. "What is it?"

"I can feel your thoughts, remember? I've always known… I was just wondering when you were going to admit it."

Graf went red. "I... I, well..."

Amber cradled his cheek in her palm. "It's okay. I know. I love you too. More than anything."

Graf tried not to, but he couldn't help himself. He smiled, and felt his face blooming red. "All right, all right. You got me."

They both stood with renewed energy. Amber nervously toyed with the Traveler's choker. "Graf... is this going to work?"

"It has to, Amber."

They strode forward through the foliage, each step landing with intention. Soon enough, the outer limits of Sanctuary came into view. All was quiet – too quiet. The blooming azaleas seemed dimmed of color, drained of life. It was as if the forest was retreating into itself... as if it knew that blood was about to be shed.

Finally, the hills sloped downward into the hollow that kept Sanctuary safe from the dangers of the Wanwood.

"It's deserted," Graf observed.

"No..." Amber raised her nose to the breeze. "I can sense them all. The dwarves, the fairies, Berris, Lonnicker... they're hiding."

Graf gave a short laugh. "From us?"

"No."

That voice sent shivers down both of their spines. It seemed to come from nowhere and everywhere at once. It was Glenna's, but also not her voice... It was deeper, melodic, voluminous. It was clear as a bell, and as ancient as the darkest woods of Wanwood.

"Not from you."

It broke out into a cackle that reverberated through the valley of Sanctuary.

Graf's fury grew with each echoed laugh. "Enough, Glenna! This ends today." But Glenna didn't answer. "Coward!" he cried out.

Amber tensed up. "Graf, listen..."

She was right. Something was beginning to fill the silence. A tearing and ripping, a rending of earth, like a quake shaking through the land. It didn't come from Sanctuary. It came from all around them... and beneath them.

"Graf, look out!" Amber pulled him out of the way just as a sharpened branch shot past his head like an arrow.

Before he could draw his blade or even react, another five sharpened branches zipped through the air around them.

"The trees!" Amber shouted.

"They're in the trees?!"

"No! They *are* the trees!"

Horrified, Graf realized Amber was correct. From the woods stalked mutant trees, with roots scurrying across the ground like spider legs. They had no faces, no eyes, just maniacally waving branches and blazing red light issuing from the darkest recesses of their cracked and scarred bark.

"That spiteful witch has dropped the Barrier around Sanctuary! She's opened it to the hell beasts of the Wanwood!" Amber cried.

"Get to the houses, Amber! Now!" They made a break for it, using the slope of the hill to their advantage.

"How do we know if we can trust them?"

Graf looked over his shoulder. From the treetops behind the mutant trees rose great, winged beasts, demonic in appearance. Their screeches were ear-splitting. "I trust the people of Sanctuary more than those things. We need time!"

Graf guided them both to the door of a small home and he pounded upon it. "Please! It's Graf and Amber. You need to let us inside. Look at what Glenna has done!"

The door swung open. At first, Graf saw no one.

"Ah, come on! You see me!" Graf looked down. It was Small Fry. "Get outta here! I'll not have you destroy my new home!" Small Fry hopped up, trying to shut them out.

"Wait, Fry, please!"

Amber pulled Graf back. "Be careful. He could be under her spell!"

Small Fry spat out in derision: "Her spell? What are you talking about?"

"Glenna's! But hold on... his eyes... he's not hypnotized, Amber!"

"Of course I'm not hypnotized. I just woke up. What in heaven's name is that racket out there –" Small Fry peeked beyond Graf and Amber. He saw the beasts coming down the hill and screamed. "What in the holy hell?!"

"Get inside, Fry! Now!" Graf and Amber pushed Fry back into his small home and slammed the door shut behind them. The horrid sounds of Glenna's eldritch beasts muffled.

Small Fry glared at Graf. "I'm gonna need an explanation – *now.*"

"That's going to be a hard one to answer. Here's a better question – *how have you've been asleep all day*?!"

"I had a big dinner!"

"A big dinner?!" Graf had to laugh. "What, like half a potato?"

Small Fry leapt up to attack Graf, but Amber caught him mid-air. "Enough! Both of you. This isn't the time, clearly. Fry, you need to understand – Glenna isn't who you think she is. She never has been. This morning, she ordered the death of Asa. She hypnotized the other villagers. And now... she's bringing hell down upon the Sanctuary to finish off the people who know the truth."

Small Fry began to hyperventilate. Suddenly, Graf felt bad for the little guy. He patted him on the head. "Sorry, Fry. We're all just worked up right now."

"You're gonna lead those things right to my doorstep! I just moved in!"

Amber snuck a glance out the window. "Not yet. They're amassing around the Big House... like they're forming a protective circle."

Graf and Amber exchanged a look. "Aldo..." Graf spoke, under his breath.

Small Fry grew more agitated. "How do you people know more about this place than I do?!"

"Trust us, Fry. Knowledge is a burden."

Outside, one of the demonic bats landed atop the Big House, then stretched out a long, spindly finger right toward Fry's home. Amber's eyes widened. She looked at Fry, then Graf, with love in her eyes. "But knowledge is the only thing that will set you free."

With that, she pulled the choker from her neck and threw it to the ground. She kicked open the door, and with a mighty roar, began her transformation.

Fry screamed again and hid under his bed. Graf lurched out to grab her, but it was too late. As Amber's wolf form took over, she bounded toward the demonic bat, that swooped down to meet her halfway. They came together in a great clash of claws and blood.

Graf stepped out of the house. So much for buying time. The Battle for Sanctuary had begun. With that, he drew his blade.

***

High above the battlefield, the North Wind blew, and carried with it the stripped hunk of metal once known as the *Neon Cowboy*. It creaked, it groaned, it rattled – but it was once again airborne. Boomer stood atop his ruined star cruiser, searching the ground below for a sign.

"All right, all right. Slow 'er down, Northie. We're coming up on it now." Boomer hopped back down into the *Cowboy*. He quickly navigated the crushed and crowded hallways by memory. He made it into the cockpit and plopped down in his old chair. The clouds zoomed past them at such a speed that they turned to vapor. While he missed the old sound of the engines roaring, he had to admit this was much more fuel-efficient.

"Angle the nose down a bit, Northie. There we go..."

He saw the circle of dark figures surrounding the Big House.

"How convenient. They've marked a target for us.... perfect. It's go time."

Boomer patted his old command console with fondness. This ship and him had been through a lot.

"And North, I gotta thank ya too. Never thought I'd see this old girl airborne again. It's a beautiful feeling." Boomer hopped up and headed for the stern, where he stored the escape pods. He'd already loaded one up with necessities earlier. Boomer had been sad to realize his ship was out of missiles and ammunition. He'd wanted to help Graf and Amber make their initial push. But then he'd stumbled upon a better idea.

As Boomer climbed into his pod and strapped in, he smiled. He knew someday, somewhere out in this vast multiverse, the *Cowboy*'d fly again.

"Until then, sweetheart. It's been a trip."

***

Graf stood at the ready. Two of the tree beasts broke from the line surrounding the Big House and charged him. As they approached, their twisted branches and bark cleaved into various parts, birthing three smaller tree druids each from the larger ones. Their branched arms sharpened to blades.

Graf raised his own sword. "Guess I get what I asked for. Worthy opponents." As the demonic bat lifted Amber into the air with a pained flapping of its wings, Graf's clashed with the tree druids. He dodged and weaved, instincts from his past on the Guard kicking in. For once, it wasn't anger that fueled Graf's fire.

He knew Amber was in danger. He knew they all were. He had no idea the extent of Glenna's true power, and he knew nothing about the true source of Asa's supernatural confidence in fate. But still his body moved in perfect rhythm, the druid's blades slashing only the air he left in his wake. Still, he survived and fought and, yes, triumphed. With a final twirl of his blade, a jet of dark plant matter shot across the blue-fire opal inlaid in his dagger. Two druids fell. Without needing to look, Graf twisted his arm backward and buried the blade to the hilt in the chest of the third druid.

He withdrew the blade with a satisfied sigh, giddy with adrenaline. He turned his face to the sky, where Amber tore open the throat of the eldritch bat. As it fell from above with a final scream, Amber rode it down onto the ground, landing on its chest to absorb the blow. The bat exploded into viscera.

"Nice work, girl."

"Not too bad yourself," Amber growled, her voice in that strange timber between woman and wolf. She bounded toward Graf, when suddenly another animal cry filled the landscape. Amber turned, but it was too late.

Bursting forth from one of the barns, Lonnicker leapt with the Woodsman's Axe raised high above him. "Traitor!"

"Amber!" Graf picked up speed, but he'd never make it in time. Amber managed to slide to a halt, but Lonnicker landed atop her and brought the Axe down into her shoulder. Graf fell to his knees. The pain was overwhelming. *I feel it, Amber. I can feel it just as you can.*

With the black of Glenna's spell still filling his eyes, Lonnicker withdrew the Axe from Amber's arm. She swiped with her other arm, knocking him off her. "Snap out of it, Lonnicker! She's using you! She's using all of you!"

Graf pushed himself to his feet, only to see the other doors of the village opening. The townspeople were emerging, all of them with the same black-eyed stare. "Amber, it's too late... she has them all..."

"Yes," came Glenna's voice. But this time it emerged not from the ether, but from the Big House. Two of the large tree druids parted, and Glenna stepped out from between them.

Graf smirked. "I see you've wiped that pleasant old lady grin off your face."

"This is no time to smile, Graf." With each step she took, the villagers also moved. Step-by-step, encircling Graf and Amber.

Amber's injury took so much of her life energy that she was now caught between human and wolf form, bloodied and beaten. "Your lies are not eternal, you bitch."

Glenna shook her head. "You mistake me. I am not the villain of this story, wolf woman. Sanctuary is a place deserving of protection. That supposed *hero*, Aldo... he handed it to Bernholt. A man with a past like his... you know of it, now, don't you? He was a monster."

"He changed," Graf muttered. "He changed his heart. And you couldn't accept it. Because you never could. You're rotten to the core."

"Shut up," Glenna spat out the words like venom. "I see the Black Rose upon you. You're just another in his lineage. A fool, a rabid *dog*, if not a monster yourself."

Graf cleaned the blood of the forest from his dagger until it gleamed. "We won't stop, Glenna. Not until Sanctuary is free."

"Sanctuary is already free," Glenna said with a twinkle in her eyes. "Free from the burdens of so-called heroes. Free from the chance of discovery." She raised her arms in the air. The sky darkened. More rumbles issued from the surrounding woods. "Free from all those who would disturb the tranquility I have achieved." The spellbound villagers closed in around Graf and Amber. Some carried knives, others pitchforks and scythes.

Graf made it to Amber's side. "I think she's calling more to her aid. I can hear it from the forest..." He leaned close. "Amber, look at you..." He caressed her shoulder near the gaping wound. It did not matter that she was not fully human. In this moment, nothing mattered more to him than the wolf-woman sprawled before him, in pain, bleeding out.

"I don't want to fight them, Graf. I don't want to kill them."

Graf couldn't answer. He didn't either. But he'd die before another laid their hands upon his love. He gripped the blue-fire opal blade and thought of his sister and mother. He tried to summon that buried and boiling rage, ever-present in his heart. He tried to project the face of Gregor upon the villagers he'd once called friends.

"Halt!"

Even the dumbstruck villagers froze. The twinkle faded from Glenna's eye. Graf and Amber looked, as the mass of villagers and monsters around them parted to give clear view of the sight.

Two huge tree druids tumbled down the hill, hacked and chopped to bits. Atop the crest stood a man.

"The terror of the Wanwood ends now, you foul bitch." Bernholt raised a greatsword in the air. Behind him was an assemblage of heroes: Burl, the Crann Fear with a giant club in hand; Aed the Rabbit-Knight and his hero's blade; Grandfather Clock carrying a staff topped with a ticking clock face; and Chuffy, the Last Ion, with revenge in his eyes and not a crumb of food in sight. Graf had to stifle the cheer that rose in his chest, but Amber didn't.

"Yes! You see that, Glenna?! We're not so alone after all."

Bernholt pointed his sword down the hill. "Your backup will not be arriving Glenna. We have cleared the path. Now, I come for you."

With that, Bernholt charged down the hill, and the heroes of the Wanwood followed.

Chapter 24

Legacy of the Shoon

At first, Glenna stood stock still and silent. Her tree druids and eldritch beasts rushed forward to meet the challenge of the heroes, but Glenna did not. The villagers did not stir either, held in their limbo state with her. Graf thought it could mean that Glenna's resolve had broken, that she had finally seen the light.

With a great smash, Burl knocked off the head of a demonic bat with one fell swoop of his club. He whooped with joy. "The Crann Fear eat creatures like you for breakfast!" With another swing, he cracked open the ribs of another demon. "Lunch and dinner too!"

A tree druid rushed up to crush Grandfather Clock, but he held his staff aloft. The clock face at its peak spun faster and faster. The air around the druid vibrated, and the particles of its bark darkened and aged at hyper speed – until its very form dissolved into dust and collapsed back into the earth.

Aed and Chuffy battled back-to-back, the rabbit propped against the broad Ion. Aed's movements were like a dancer's, while Chuffy battered forth with his paws like it was his last supper.

While the heroes kept the monsters busy, Bernholt was dead set on Glenna. He was just about to reach the first layer of the villagers near the Big House when they all came back to life. They cried out in fear and terror, slowing Bernholt's advance.

"What's happening?! What has happened to our beautiful Sanctuary?!" This and other screams of terror overtook the village. All was chaos.

"There!" Bernholt yelled out as he pointed his sword toward Glenna. "There is your answer."

Glenna looked down at the ground. When she looked up, something was shimmering beneath her skin. "Bernholt... you look surprisingly well."

"You can thank the Gardener for that."

"I don't think I will." When Glenna now spoke, the teeth in her mouth seemed somehow different. Sharper. Her gray hair laid back closer against her scalp, almost cropped. Her skin pulled in about her face, growing tighter, smoother... but then the coloration altered.

From a distance, Graf found it hard to tell, but Amber gripped his hand tightly. "She's changing. I can smell it from here. *The true form of a Shoon.*"

Her legs extended up by at least two inches, becoming longer and more shapely. The age fell away from her as if she was under the effect of Grandfather Clock's staff. Thin, electric magic sparked around her body as she stepped forward toward Bernholt. Soon enough, Glenna's humble dress became silver and sleek. Her face grew pointed, and took on the features of a fox. Equally erotic and frightening, she radiated powerful magic that distorted reality around her.

"You've forced my hand, Bernholt. Let us bring these games of accusation to a close. We can settle this how you like it best – with blood."

Suddenly, propelled by unseen force, this new and improved Glenna shot across the two hundred yards separating her and Bernholt in a second flat. He raised his sword just in time to deflect her magic charge and dissipate the sparks in the air around the two of them. Glenna did not relent. She raised her hand and runes activated across her silver fur. When Bernholt attempted to strike, she threw forward her arm and caught the blade in her hand. The world seemed darkened except for the glow that surrounded Bernholt and Glenna's clash. A thousand-year grudge powered every move they made.

Graf understood how repressed rage could make one fight, but he couldn't comprehend what these two figures must feel toward one another. As Bernholt told him earlier, his imprisonment had left him with a lot of time to think. Graf wondered how much was devoted to the image of Glenna's face – her true face – hidden beneath the ruse.

And now here it was, fangs bared and all. She bent at the knees, and swiped Bernholt's legs out from under him. However, he caught himself before tumbling to the ground, and rolled out of the way just as Glenna shot a blast of energy into the dirt.

"Too slow, old woman." Bernholt responded by bringing up his greatsword with a mighty swing. It caught Glenna's chest. Flashes of runes lit up, protecting her from direct damage, but the force of it knocked her off her feet.

Uphill, the battle continued between Bernholt's heroes and Glenna's monsters. Coated in a thick layer of sweat, Burl was no longer bragging, caught between one of the flying beasts and a tree druid. Chuffy was in worse shape, as three tree druids combined their forms atop him, trapping him in a hellish thicket of sharp branches.

Grandfather Clock tried to assist, but then one of the demonic bats swooped down and snatched away his staff. "No!"

But it was too late. As soon as the staff left his possession, it cracked. The clock top fell to the ground and smashed to bits. Grandfather Clock fell to his knees... and he entered a cycle: aging up, then young again, over and over. The perpetual change paralyzed him. Tree Druids closed in. Aed gave up on hacking away at Chuffy's infernal prison and stepped in between Grandfather and the monsters. Yet even the heroic knight seemed broken by this fight. He wavered on his feet. He would not last much longer.

Graf said as much to Amber. "We have to help them."

Amber shook her head and more fireworks exploded between Bernholt and Glenna as they battled. "Graf... you won't reach them in time... but I could." Amber struggled to her feet, still caught halfway between beast and human. However, she shook herself awake, and her wolf-form hind legs grew strong once again. "Help Bernholt. Distract Glenna. He needs you." Amber leaned down and kissed Graf deeply.

"You won't make it, Amber..."

"We'll see about that." She winked, and before he could stop her, she bounded off to join the heroes of the Wanwood in their failing fight. She leapt from the ground and landed in the briar thicket that smothered Chuffy. She tore through it all until he was able to emerge and breathe free.

Inspired by Amber's heroism, Graf felt a renewal. He drew his blade and looked around at the villagers. "Do you see now what Glenna truly is? Her dark magic holds Sanctuary in its thrall. This place cannot be free as long as she rules it!"

But the villagers shifted, backed away from him, looked away. They were frightened. Yet this only made Graf angrier.

"We cannot allow Bernholt and these heroes to fall! Would you allow it? For them to die, fighting for your lives, while you do nothing?!"

He was met with silence... until a small voice spoke up. "No. No, we can't."

Graf searched through the crowd and smiled. "I see there are heroes amongst you after all!"

From the crowd, Small Fry emerged, with a miniature kitchen mallet in hand. "That's right. If Fry can do it, we all can! Can't we?" He tried to rally the crowd. Some of the larger residents grew restless, embarrassed, ashamed.

Finally, the purple fairy who had fallen in love with Buckley came forward. "I believe we can. We owe it to ourselves! Glenna has fooled us!"

More and more townspeople murmured in agreement. Some retreated into their homes and sheds, returning with items to be used as weapons. They distributed them amongst themselves as Graf, Fry, and the fairy rallied these ragtag troops.

All the while, Bernholt and Glenna fought to a stalemate. The aged Bernholt ached with every step he took, but Glenna seemed to possess infinite energy.

"You don't truly grasp my power, do you, Bernholt? Fight me until your last breath, but your sword shall never pierce me." Glenna grasped her hands together. The runic magic fed down her arms like glowing veins. An entropic gravity pulled Bernholt closer to her, his feet dug into the earth in a failing attempt to hold his ground. "It is your brother-in-arms who gives me this power. The hate that I have lit in his heart... undying. Eternal." Soon, Glenna's magic forced Bernholt's arms to his side, locked. His great sword fell from his hand and clattered to the ground. "Change... no one truly changes. They only hide from what they truly are... but you can't hide from me. Not anymore."

Life force drained from Bernholt's body, feeding into the runic lines that coated Glenna's form. She grew stronger with every passing second, the distance between her and her prey decreasing... the magic vibrations between them growing more and more chaotic...

A blue flash broke Glenna's concentration. She stumbled backward. Hanging in the air between her and Bernholt was Graf's blue-fire dagger. Caught in Glenna's web of magic energy, it hovered only inches from her face.

Graf rushed toward her, pulling the blade from the force field, and lunging again for her throat. Glenna knocked him back with a magic slap, laughing, though clearly shaken. "I'll get to you soon, Black Rose."

"And what about us?!" Glenna whirled to find Small Fry leading the charge of villagers toward her.

She raised her hand, creating an invisible wall between them. "Go back to your homes. This will all be over soon... nothing more than a disappearing dream in your minds..."

"I don't think so!" The purple fairy rose from the pack, hovering on thin wings – but her face was leaden with grim purpose. "Sanctuary rejects you, Glenna! *You traitorous Shoon!*" A chorus of confirmation followed from the other townspeople.

Using this moment, Graf again cut toward Glenna. She blocked him too, but now struggled beneath the weight of holding back Bernholt, the villagers, and Graf all together. "Fine," she spat out. "Try it! Try your best! I'll grind you all to dust! No, better yet... I'll break your bones, and chain you all beneath the Big House with that godforsaken bear! You'll all be kindling to my fire! You will all regret the day you turned your back on the Wanwood's true guardians! The Shoon will rise again–!"

A thin whistle cut through her speech. Manic, she whipped her head around, seeking the source. The villagers looked around, hearing it too. Graf just looked at Bernholt, still held in his magic bounds, and nodded. The ancient hero even cracked a grin. "Glenna," he spoke through gritted teeth, "why don't you try looking up?"

Glenna did, and her eyes widened. "What kind of black magic is that...?"

"Not magic," Graf said. "Just a space cowboy called Boomer."

***

"YEE-HAW!" Boomer gazed through the cracked glass of the escape pod bay and saw that target approaching. "Let's ride!" With his fist, he slammed down on the ejector.

With a sudden blast of g-force, Boomer's pod blasted free from the *Neon Cowboy* as the starship hurtled toward Sanctuary – or, more precisely, the Big House.

From the porthole in his escape pod, Boomer could make out the dark creatures that guarded it now. The heavier *Cowboy* fell faster than the pod, and soon blocked sight. Boomer crossed his fingers. "Let's hope my sharpshooter skills hold up when the bullet's a bit bigger."

The beasts in front of the Big House nervously shuffled as the *Cowboy* fell toward them, faster and faster, trailing jet fuel and flames. Boomer had lit a couple fuses before he bailed it, to make sure it'd be a fiery one.

On the ground, Graf waved to the villagers. "Get as far from the Big House as you can!" They had already begun to scatter.

Glenna's magic faltered as she watched this fate approach. Bernholt, released from that magic grasp, fell to the ground. Graf helped him stand. "Let's hope this works."

They wouldn't wait long to find out because just as Graf spoke those words, the *Neon Cowboy* slammed into the Big House. The explosion this kicked off instantly incinerated all of Glenna's hell beasts in the vicinity. Shards of wood and stone blasted into the sky like a geyser. It rained down, crashing into the closet village structures. Small Fry and the purple fairy guided the villagers to safety.

Boomer's escape pod zoomed through the huge cloud of debris, blocking his vision. He strapped in and prepared himself. With the house destroyed, the magic imprisoning Aldo was faltering. Stage one was a success, but stage two...

His entire body rocked as the pod crashed through the remnants of the Big House, through the weakened stone foundation beneath it, and skidded through the tunnels beneath. Finally, the pod came to a halt. Boomer opened his eyes. He was alive! "Yippie-ki-oh, you still got it, you clever son-of-a..."

Boomer unstrapped and kicked open the roof of the pod. He took with him a sealed container he'd found aboard the *Cowboy*. He shook his head, not wanting to think of his poor ship right now. He saw a piece of its burning wings nearby and averted his gaze. There'd be time to mourn later.

"Time for stage three..."

Boomer kept his hand on the lid of the container as he stalked through the dim, dank, dark heart of Sanctuary. That big blast must have given even the big guy a scare. Hopefully it didn't crush him...

But no, there he was. A growl shook the void. Boomer pulled a flare from his belt – another item rescued from the *Cowboy* – and tossed it ahead of him into the dark. It lit with a fizzy blast, and revealed Aldo, very much alive, in startling red light. And very pissed off.

The bear's eyes glowed in the infernal flame of the flare. He kicked his feet against the ground, preparing to charge. Yet still one great chain was bound about his neck.

"Easy there, bear boy. 'Member me? I didn't taste so good, did I? But thoughtful extraterrestrial that I am..." Boomer unscrewed the container's lid. It all depended on this moment. "I brought you something *real* tasty. From my favorite planet in the universe, a lil' blue place sometimes called Earth. There? They call this... *prime rib.*"

Boomer extracted a pristine slab of Texas beef from his container. A fog of dried ice emitted in its wake. He'd picked it up a few years back. "I was saving this thang for a special occasion... and I thought this might fit the bill."

Boomer could tell the beef was already working its magic, having been given a dry rub of magical spices supplied by Asa and made from the remaining petals of the Bellows. Aldo's preparations to charge slowed, and his eyes went wide and glassy. The aroma of the slab was enticing to Boomer enough – so he could imagine what it might mean to an Ion starved of satiation for millennia.

"*Yeah buddy.* It's that good. And more. I promise ya." Boomer waved it around, watching Aldo's eyes follow it. "But the thing is... this here beef is only for beings who don't submit to the dark will of witches. It's from the land of the free, and I fear it's only *for* the free too. So whatcha think?"

With a bit of dramatic flourish, Boomer wound back his arm, like a football player under Friday night lights. "Catch?" Boomer hurled the steak through a crack in the ceiling that leaked a thin beam of light. *Perfect throw.*

Aldo wasted no time. He bound forward, tugging the chain that affixed him to the wall. It caught against his neck. Boomer used this brief moment to make his way out of the tunnel, where he knew Glenna hid her secret entrance. The aroma of the meat fueled Aldo's rage against the last bits of the curse which bound him, and finally, Boomer heard the cracking of the metal as he took each shattered step up, two at a time. "That's right," he smiled. "That chain ain't nothing. And neither is that witch's magic. Not compared to USDA certified lean."

***

In the wake of the crash, even the battle at the outskirts of Sanctuary slowed. All waited as they heard a bellow and rumbling beneath the ground. It was as if the crash had unleashed something even darker than the eldritch beasts that ravaged under Glenna's command.

Graf saw it first – that glistening prime cut flying through the air. It was funny, his first thought was of his dogs, back home in Eastern Rising. *Oh boy, they would've gone wild for that...*

As if on cue, the earth erupted, as the Ion Aldo burst forth in pursuit. Bernholt gasped. Glenna fell to her knees in despair. "Impossible..."

Boomer ran through the clouds that still coated the remains of the Big House, whooping and hollering. Graf jumped up at the sight of his daredevil friend. Boomer ran right into him, tackling him in a hug. "That's what I'm talkin' 'bout!"

Aldo launched himself into the air and caught the beef in his razor-sharp teeth before he even hit the ground. Sanctuary shook with his landing.

Graf looked to Glenna. "You have no hold of him anymore." The sheen of her fur was already beginning to fade. Her beautiful, erotic features lost their luster. The runic energy that had surged through her before was simply gone. "And with it goes your advantage."

Tears streamed down her face. She snarled back at Graf, "You fool. I have no hold on him, yes. But now, *no one does*."

When Aldo finished his first meal as a free Ion, he roared to the sky and set his sights upon the village.

"Back up! Get back!" Small Fry commanded.

Graf looked to Bernholt. The triumph that had filled Bernholt's heart at seeing his old friend darkened. "Aldo... no..."

Aldo charged for the villagers. Glenna laughed again, low and wicked. "Now you all get what you deserve..."

Fear rushed through Graf, but he refused to give up so close to their goal. "Aldo! ALDO!" He ran toward the Ion, trying to intercept him.

"Graf, no!" Bernholt warned.

Aldo slowed and saw Graf waving. When he snarled, spit flew from his maw of a mouth. He turned toward the Black Rose of Eastern Rising and ran.

"Oh shit... oh shit, okay..." Graf stumbled backward, then kept moving. He looked around. No cover. No weapons big enough to fight an enraged Ion. But then he realized something...

Aldo is the weapon.

Graf brought his fingers to his lips and blew, the old whistle he'd used on even the most wild of dogs. High-pitched enough to be barely audible to man, but Aldo heard it clear enough. Graf rolled toward Glenna, and motioned his other hand as he sounded the whistle once more. Aldo took sight of Glenna, tricked into sensing her as the source.

Glenna cried out in terror. Aldo rampaged toward her, knocking through homes like they were driftwood at sea beneath a mighty ship. She tried to rally magic through herself, but she couldn't concentrate. The runic shield around her faltered, just as Aldo swiped his paw – it caught Glenna right across the chest. Blood rushed forth, and her scream pierced the sky.

Aldo opened his jaws and crunched down upon her arm. It shattered in his grasp. She managed to cast a minor spell that shot a spark into Aldo's eye, and she pulled her mauled arm free. "You listen to me! To me!" Glenna tried another charm, but the inky blackness that had once filled Aldo's eyes was replaced with bloodshot rage – free, yes, but also insane.

"Enough, Aldo! You've beaten her!" Bernholt hoisted himself up on his greatsword. With this small chance, Glenna rolled away from the beast. She fled toward the hills.

"Coward!" Graf called out her, but she did not slow. She raised her hands before her, and with the last burst of energy within her body, Glenna opened a portal. Trailing blood behind her, the greatly diminished and fallen leader of Sanctuary vanished in a flash of light.

The other eldritch beasts, now losing the fight to Amber and the other heroes, saw Glenna's retreat and turned tail themselves. Burl and Aed chased after them, calling out derisive names. The fluffy Chuffy grasped in his large arms a wailing infant.

Amber stumbled to his side and leaned against his formidable belly. She curiously stuck a finger toward the child. "Is that... Grandfather Clock?"

"It seems he'll have another go at it. Perhaps we call him Baby Clock..." Chuffy gazed mournfully down upon the maniac Aldo in the hollow. A single tear rolled forth from his eye.

"With this, the Shoons have truly triumphed against the Ions... we have lost our greatest hero to madness..."

Amber licked her wounds and kept a steady eye on Graf, still in the thick of it. "No," she said. "There is still one last battle to be fought." Chuffy looked to her, confused.

Aldo gave another great roar. Graf backed toward Bernholt. "What do we do?"

"You? You have done enough today, courageous Graf of the Eastern Rising. You get the villagers to safety. This... this is a fight I must do alone."

Graf sputtered in response, trying to find some clever retort, but Bernholt stepped away from him. He watched the ancient hero go and wondered how he had ever questioned the man's greatness. Glenna was wrong. A Black Rose could be redeemed. A Black Rose could find their purpose in the world.

With just such purpose, Bernholt readied his greatsword. Aldo spread his legs wide, gaining traction, and rose up on his hind legs. Bernholt held back tears as he spoke:

"Come, dear friend. Come and end this."

Chapter 25

Battle of the Black Rose

It happened as if in slow motion. As the other fighters recovered, and the villagers peeked out from their hiding spots. Graf stood back and watched, hating himself more with each passing second.

Bernholt and Aldo reunited as warriors do, locked in combat. Bernholt's greatsword caught between Aldo's sharp claws. Graf wondered if Aldo always did battle like this, with such animalistic fury, or if it was only due to the cursed state of mind inflicted upon him by generations of Glenna's torture.

Bernholt pushed forward, pressing closer to Aldo's twisted, consumed visage. "Aldo, look into my eyes. See who I am. *The man you made free.*"

Bernholt broke his sword away and feinted back, narrowly missing a swipe of Aldo's paw. Aldo stomped the ground in frustrated rage.

"That's it, old friend! Think. That great beating heart still belongs to you." Bernholt played defense, parrying more blows from the Ion. "This is not a battle for our lives. It is for our very souls!"

Aldo foamed at the mouth as he attacked. Something like words nearly leaked out. "Rrraargghhh! Hu... hunger... darkness... HUNGER!" Aldo fell onto all fours and lunged for Bernholt.

"No! Stand up, Aldo! Stand up! Like a true warrior! Remember, remember like I do. How you fought the Blaine! How you saved me..."

Aldo's teeth clamped down on Bernholt's sword, the only thing between him and certain death.

"Don't make me do this, Aldo... please," Bernholt begged. But Aldo would not relent. With an anguished yell, Bernholt twisted his wrist and brought his sword out – right through the side of Aldo's cheek. Dripping blood, Aldo reared back.

Graf couldn't help himself. "You must, Bernholt! You have the opening. Now!"

Bernholt didn't look at Graf, though he knew the young fighter was right. With a simple slash, he could spill Aldo's innards upon the grassy field of Sanctuary. Aldo's pain confused and disoriented him, but soon his unquenchable rage would reignite. "I know, Graf... but I can't."

Aldo caught his footing and brought down another strike. This one caught Bernholt across the shoulder, spilling his blood. Two shades now splashed across both former friends, mixing with the sweat, foam, and tears.

It was like no fight Graf had ever witnessed. The utter ferocity of Aldo's assault contrasted sharply with Bernholt's graceful but exhausted defense. Graf saw each opening that Bernholt exposed in Aldo, and watched each moment pass him by. In those spaces where Bernholt could have ended his friend, he instead chose to take a breath and ready himself for Aldo's next attack. Graf couldn't take it. He wanted to rush in, his own blade at the ready. He wanted to fill in those gaps, fix the flaws that Bernholt left so willingly on the table.

But then it flashed through his own mind... what if he were in Bernholt's position, and the attacker was Amber? What if Glenna had taken her prisoner, warped her mind as she did Aldo's? What if Graf was put in the position where he must kill the one he loved the most, or die trying. Graf knew what he would do. And he knew he would never accept someone else stepping in between.

"Enough, Aldo! You see me before you! See my blade! The one I swung as we took apart the Blaine, as we freed the

Wanwood from that horror. See my eyes, the ones into which you looked and gave mercy. I offer it to you now. I offer you another chance." In his desperate plea, though, Bernholt slipped up. Not in his own defense, but in his restraint. When Aldo's paw came down upon him, Bernholt raised an uppercut of his sword – and sliced two of Aldo's digits clean off. The blood rained down upon Bernholt. The pain was just as apparent in him as it was in Aldo.

He feels it, Graf thought. *That bond. I know it now. That precise pain unlike any other.*

"I'll cut my own off in turn, Aldo, if you just stand down!" Aldo came down upon Bernholt again. "STAND DOWN!" Aldo's claw pierced Bernholt's shoulder, but with his sword as leverage the ancient hero pushed back and cut it free from Aldo's paw. It remained lodged in Bernholt like a thorn.

Bernholt fell back, as did Aldo. Each licked their own wounds, although Bernholt did so only metaphorically.

"I won't kill you, Aldo," Bernholt spoke. Aldo growled in return. "I don't care what you do to me. You will not fall by my blade."

"Then..." It arose like volcanic rumbling. Distorted, animalistic, and strange. "Then..." Aldo growled. "You... die... by... my jaws." Aldo kicked back dirt as he readied for his final charge.

In response, Bernholt let the tip of his sword dip to the ground. It fell limply from his grasp. It clattered to the ground. "So be it, old friend."

Aldo's cry tore the fabric of reality. The many worlds that fed into the Wanwood must have heard some hint of it, mingled in the thunder of their skies, or so Graf thought. It shook his soul, made him stumble, made him silent in the face of inevitability.

Blood ran down Bernholt's arm. His blood, Aldo's. It twisted and intertwined with the aged ink upon his arm. It made his Black Rose red once more.

Aldo moved, closing the distance in three bounds. Bernholt closed his eyes right before the end. Graf wondered what he thought. A prayer? A wish? Or nothing at all. Maybe that. Maybe at this point, after so many long years, there was simply nothing left to say.

It sounded like it did in the dog pens, while Graf fed them scraps. Visceral, frenzied, frightening. Familiar.

Aldo grasped Bernholt between his jaws and broke the man down the middle. His body dropped to the dirt, mauled and twitching. His eyes remained open, but clouded now with the murky onset of whatever comes next. Aldo howled with victory, with sated rage, with dominant certainty. And then he looked down again at the corpse he made.

The triumph in him faded now too. He sank back upon his hind legs as he considered what remained of Bernholt. His friend's blood leaked from his mouth. Aldo raised his own mangled paw to brush it away, a faraway look in his eye. And then... he was no longer volcanic, no longer only an animal-filled with single-minded desire...

Aldo cried out again, a cry mournful, terrified, and as broken as Bernholt's body. Aldo, the real Aldo, he was still here. He was emerging. He was guilty.

With that, the rain began to fall.

The hollow of Sanctuary felt exactly like that – empty, devoid, soulless. The landscape was ruined. The flowers lay trampled, and fields scorched with the aftershocks of magic and soaked with the blood of demon and man alike.

Graf approached with deliberate slowness. Aldo was bent low over Bernholt's body, sobbing with full-bodied convulsions. Yet Graf still wondered if that other Aldo might emerge again, if this was but a reprieve from the violence.

No, Graf thought. *That look in his eyes... that's not the same beast that rampaged only minutes ago.* It was as if the sun had set and Aldo was reborn. Yet the cost was too high. Eyes full of tears, the Ion looked up and around at his surroundings.

"I... I don't understand." Gone was the fearsome monster. Gone even was the noble hero spoken of in legend. Here was just a sad, broken soul, finally emerging from Glenna's spell.

"Aldo... for hundreds of years you have been caught in the web of a monster. The Shoon Glenna. She tried to kill Bernholt, and she trapped your mind in an awful curse." Graf stopped a few feet from Aldo. He could smell the stink of death upon him. The years of desperation.

Slowly, Amber and the other heroes from the hill joined them and the villagers came out of hiding.

"She used the magic she drained from you to keep Sanctuary under her control. It was only due to Asa... and Bernholt... that this came to an end."

Aldo looked around at all the faces surrounding him. "Tell me... who are you?"

"I am Graf. Of the Eastern Rising."

Aldo's eyes fell upon Graf's tattoo. "You're a Black Rose..."

"Yes. Hundreds of years after Bernholt, but... yes, I was exiled and found myself here in the Wanwood." Amber came to his side, slowly returning to human form with Traveler's choker around her neck. "I met others who sought Sanctuary. But it turned out Sanctuary needed us... Bernholt needed us... you needed us."

Aldo raised his paws before him, horrified. "I have killed him... my greatest friend..."

The villagers murmured, some spat on the ground. Graf could tell the crowd might turn on Aldo at any moment. Truthfully, in his own heart, this pathetic wretch of an Ion also filled him with anger.

Chuffy sniffled, "...What has she done to you..."

Aldo's spirit broke all over again. He collapsed atop Bernholt's body, weeping. "No! Please, no... anything. I'll do anything. Please, Lord above, hear me... hear this prayer... Bernholt is the hero Wanwood deserves... He is the man who must guard Sanctuary... he saved this place, he saved my soul! Please, I pray... do not let his suffering be in vain..."

As if in response, the rain pitter-pattered to a halt. The clouds shifted above them. A faint ringing could be heard in the air...

"Well, well, well... ain't that a bite."

Graf and Amber looked at one another. They'd know that slang anywhere now. "*Asa.*"

The wind picked up – the North Wind. The smoke of the fire that still burned in the depths of the wrecked Big House cleared, and through this clearing stepped the Gardener. Behind him, more silhouettes took shape.

"Dry your eyes and mind that shiner taking shape, big guy," Asa quipped. "Your prayers do not go unanswered."

Next, through the clearing smoke, was the Traveler. Amber gasped at the sight of him. "Traveler!"

"Hey wolf, looking good. Graf, you too."

But Graf was speechless, because what stepped forth behind Asa and Traveler was simply unbelievable: One figure was born upon widespread white wings, a feminine figure coated in beatific, downy feathers, with ice-blue eyes.

Another was barely a figure at all, and more like a system of stars. Gleaming orbs like a thousand eyes circled and orbited a bright white center. Graf swore the eyes all moved in sync, sweeping across the denizens of Sanctuary. Yet he was not afraid... no one was. An utter calm had fallen across the world.

Next came a perfect physical specimen, coated in gold as if they were a walking statue, and another with a head like a many-faceted face of a diamond. Light bounced from it, coating the despair of Sanctuary in the colors of the rainbow. Another moved like waves, contained by some invisible field, with no other definable features than its reflective surface catching glint of the now-exposed moon above.

These... were the Helpers. The ones of which Traveler spoke. The weavers of Fate, and guardians of this and every other world. They were incredible.

Amber grasped at Graf and whispered, "Which one do you think it is... *the one Asa and Traveler spoke of?*"

As everyone took in this miraculous sight, as even Aldo sucked up his tears and calmed his soul, one would be excused for missing the man who walked behind all the others. The last to emerge through the smoke of the burning *Neon Cowboy*, and the least noticeable. Dressed plainly, he walked at a steady gait, letting the others take all the glory.

But it was this man that Asa turned to and spoke, with uncharacteristic surprise in his tone: "Boss? I... didn't expect to see you with us when I put out the call. But it's mighty fine to see ya. Whadda ya say? Want to take the lead?"

"Sure, Asa. We are all here to help." The Boss smiled, eyes downcast as if ever amused by Asa's nonchalance. "And I believe that Aldo is the one in need." The man walked to Aldo's side, brushing past Graf with a polite, "Excuse me."

Aldo looked up, lost like a lamb in the woods. "... I wasn't in control... no... no, I must take responsibility. I *lost* control. I lost myself. And Bernholt... he... he... I loved him, and yet, in his final moments he saw only a monster." Aldo was overcome again by emotion. The Boss reached out his hand and lightly touched the Ion's shoulder.

Graf saw them as the man's cloth sleeve pulled back: scars on the Boss' wrist and hand. Healed now, but they spoke of suffering long past.

"Aldo, you're mistaken," the Boss spoke in a gentle tone. "There is no greater love than to lay down one's life for one's friends. Bernholt did this for you. He loved you, Aldo, more

than you could ever know. Whether you were lost or found...
you were always in his heart until the very end."

Aldo reached down and grasped Bernholt's hand with his
remaining, good paw. "It wasn't enough. He gave it all, and it
wasn't enough."

"Would you do the same?" The Boss questioned.

"More. And everything else. I'd give it all for him."

"Then you understand why Bernholt did what he did. And
how he could forgive you."

Aldo squeezed his old friend's hand. Graf noticed a faint
glow arise from around Aldo's form. Aldo's voice took on a
greater conviction. "Together, Bernholt and I hoped Sanctuary
would be a place that set an example for the Wanwood."

"So let it be. Look around," the Boss told Aldo. "The
Wanwood watches. Every moment, every breath is another
chance to set an example."

"I... feel... something. Inside me..." Aldo whispered.

"Your prayer... your wish: to give Bernholt what he gave to
you."

"Yes," Aldo said, nodding. "Please."

The faint glow grew stronger now. It came off Aldo in
waves and traveled down his arm into the paw that grasped
Bernholt's hand. From that nexus, that point of connection, the
light continued to grow and grow. Graf and the others shielded
their eyes, but Aldo and the Boss stared down into it and soon
all was lost in the light.

***

When it faded, the sky was clear of clouds. Stars hung above in
the sky like it was a painted masterwork. The ruins of Sanctuary
were healed. The fallen homes and barns were rebuilt. The
Big House was gone, but in its place sat a wide stone circle,
a monument inlaid with gold and silver that traced the epic

history of Sanctuary in pictures. At its center were the figures of Bernholt and Aldo.

Yet where Bernholt and Aldo once battled, only one remained. The Boss stood above the body of Bernholt, and for the second time in as many days, the man once thought dead opened his eyes again.

He sat up, rubbing the center of his chest where Aldo's jaws had crushed him. Only the thin line of a scar remained. Graf noticed in his hair, a black streak cut across, like a flying V. It was just like the white V that once sat upon Aldo's chest.

Bernholt looked around, anxious compared to the docile denizens of Sanctuary, who still stood in a dreamy daze. "What... what has happened? Where is Aldo?"

The Boss crouched down. "Two friends have given their lives for one another. And the circle remains unbroken." The Boss touched the streak of black in Bernholt's hair. "Aldo is part of you, as you are part of him."

Asa and Traveler approached, helping Bernholt to his feet. "Atta boy, Bernholt. I'd say yer made in the shade," Asa laughed.

Bernholt flexed his joints. "But... Aldo's gone? All of him."

"No," Traveler said, shaking his head. "Never gone. Not all of him."

Suddenly, Bernholt tensed. He held up his hand, as it contorted, growing hairier and larger, before he shook it and it returned to human form. He looked up in amazement toward the Boss. "Am I..."

"You are Aldo, as he is you. Soon, you'll both learn to control it. To exist in this form. It turns out the true guardian of Sanctuary is not one alone, but both of you... *as one*."

Traveler held out a bracelet to Aldo/Bernholt, that looked a lot like the one Amber wore around her neck. "This might help, until you get the hang of it."

Bernholt took it and put it on.

"Wow..."

That voice... Graf looked to Boomer, who was fully alert. "What in tarnation... that sounded like..."

The crowd looked around, as Buckley himself wandered forth. "I sure am feeling peckish. What's been going on here?"

"Buckley! Good goddamn – excuse my French!" Boomer sprinted over to the tubby human and wrapped him up in a hug. "You're back from the dead!"

"Not only him, but all the victims Glenna fed to Aldo over the years. They deserve another chance too," the Boss spoke, pointing toward a large group of people stumbling forth from a glowing portal that sat above the Sanctuary monument. "His life force feeds them all."

The villagers ran to greet those once thought long lost. Many tears were shed. The purple fairy zipped over to Buckley and planted a huge kiss on his cheek.

Amber laughed, overjoyed, while Graf held back his own emotion at it all. The Boss caught his eye and gave him a wink. Then the Boss turned from Bernholt toward Asa. "A good day, no? I leave it to you and Traveler to continue winding the threads of fate today."

With that, the Boss and the other miraculous Helpers headed for the portal from which the resurrected had just stepped. The Boss let all the others pass through first and turned back one final time. "Let this be a lesson. Redemption is possible. Sacrifice is required. But love... love is worth it all." The Boss vanished through the portal, and it closed behind him.

Bernholt walked toward the villagers, including those returned from the dead. "People of Sanctuary. I... Bernholt... Aldo... the Black Rose redeemed... I apologize for the time you have spent in the shade. But now we all walk in the light."

Graf was snapped out of his daze as Asa slapped a hand down upon his shoulder. "All's well that ends well."

"Not so fast, Asa. You know a good hero's work is never done." Traveler approached, waving over Boomer and Buckley to join Graf and Amber. "The people of Sanctuary deserve some rest, but unfortunately…"

"What are you talking about? We've won!" Graf exclaimed.

"Traveler's a killjoy, but he ain't wrong. I'm afraid you four are getting a bit of the royal shaft here…"

Amber's mood soured. "Please don't tell me… *the witch.*"

Traveler nodded and smiled. "Amber's a smart cookie, Graf. A little hairy, but smart. I've always said it. Sanctuary may be won, but the cursed Shoon who nearly destroyed it is still on the loose."

"I saw her…" Boomer mused. "After my precious *Cowboy* crushed her home. When Aldo nearly chewed her up… she got away through some sorta new-fangled portal."

"She used the last of her magic to make haste to another realm," spoke a fresh voice. They all turned to see yet another miraculous Helper: spindly, with multiple arms sprouting from a central body like a spider; yet her flesh was made of flora, green and blooming with color. This thorny, arachnid rose of a creature's voice was melodic and smooth, yet she had a certain glint in her many eyes.

Traveler presented her with enthusiasm. "Everyone, meet Maxilla, the Veridian Weaver and one of our most trusted Helpers."

"She's just the ginchiest, trust me," Asa exclaimed. "Traveler and me, we made a personal recommendation to the Boss that Maxilla help you ragamuffins out in this next quest."

"Let me guess," Graf said. "We're supposed to chase her down. Because that's what our destiny dictates or some such?"

"Well," Traveler said. "You could probably stay for dinner tonight."

"Yes, please, dinner first…" Buckley whined.

"And then the good work begins with the rising sun," Amber moaned. "I'm not sure I love this whole questing thing too much, but it does keep the blood flowing."

Graf had to grin, and kissed Amber. "So, that's a yes, then?"

"Yeehaw!" Boomer whooped. "Where we off to?"

"Stranger worlds than the Wanwood, that's all I'll say..." Maxilla mused.

Graf checked his dagger, still securely latched to his belt. He looked around at all the happy villagers of Sanctuary. He saw Chuffy examining Bernholt's new streak of black, and Aed examining the unhappy Baby Clock wailing in his arms. He saw Burl and Small Fry pouring themselves some ale and commiserating about life at unusual sizes. He saw life, everywhere. Because of what they had done.

Heroes, Graf thought. *I suppose it's not so terrible...*

"All right, then," Graf spoke. "Tonight, we drink and be merry. Tomorrow..."

"We chase down that evil witch and let her know the Wanwood isn't done with her just yet," Amber said, clenched fist raised before her.

"Here, here," Buckley moaned weakly. "I guess I do owe something to the world after the Helpers saved me..."

"That's the spirit, Buckaroo! Keep it up, and maybe I'll teach ya how to fly a starship!" Boomer laughed.

Asa wrapped an arm around Graf. "Ah, fate. Ain't she just a bite?" And together, arm in arm, these friends and heroes all settled in for a night – if only one – of pure joy.

Epilogue

Do you hear that waterfall tinkling beneath the chintzy old tune? Open your eyes and spread your toes through the green shag at your feet. This isn't the Wanwood, no, not that glorious and strange world. This is just some hole-in-the-wall tiki bar, filled with fraudulent plants and ferns, and the glowering eyes of plastic Tiki heads pointed at all the downtrodden drinkers who've stopped in for a sip.

Why this dreary place, you may ask? Well listen closely to the crooner on the radio and identify: this is a place beyond time but certainly informed by one. Call it Earth, and more specifically America, circa the nineteen-fifties. And striding through the front door, with the light of a portal behind him, is a man in a red smoker's jacket, flaming cigar in hand.

"Ah, dear reader, I've been looking everywhere for ya," Asa the Gardener spouts as he puffs. The portal door seals shut behind him. "This is my favorite spot in the multiverse too."

"Keep it down!" Cast your eyes (imaginative, reading eyes that is) down the bar and find the only other patron in the joint: Traveler himself, the man who leaps between worlds. "What do you think you're doing?!" He seems a bit tipsy. Maybe that party in Sanctuary went on for more than just a night.

"Oh, calm down, you wet rag." Asa rolls his eyes and turns his attention back – to you, dear reader. "He's just upset that I'm breaking the so-called rules."

"They are rules for a reason! It's the source of drama, of excitement, hell, the laws of the universe depend on it! Just because you saved one pocket of it doesn't give you the right to go breaking the rules whenever you please..."

"Not whenever I please," Asa says. "Just now. You know, in the epilogue, chief. That's the part of the story when all bets are off."

Traveler downs his drink and taps the bar for another.

"Ya know there's no bartender, dreamboat," Asa laughs. He hops over the counter. "It's the kinda joint where you serve yourself."

"Whatever," Traveler says. "Just make it a double. I'm not ready for book two just yet..."

Asa whistles as he works, pulling together another concoction for his fellow Helper. "That's the spirit, let loose a little Traveler!"

"Just don't –" Traveler is interrupted by a mighty burp. He pounds his chest and coughs, getting it out of his system. "Just don't go breaking the fourth wall much longer."

"What's with the third degree about these fourth walls, eh?" Asa shakes and rattles the drink he's mixing up and serves it in a chilled glass with aplomb. "Reader, I gotta tell you. It gets exhausting sometimes, always pretending you're not there."

Traveler just sighs at Asa's continued transgressions and downs this latest serving. Asa holds out his hand. "What, no tip?" Traveler cracks a grin.

But then, dear reader, let your eyes fall where Asa's do – for on the far wall, very out of place in this décor, hangs a kitchen sink. "Hey," Asa mutters, "I don't remember that being there."

Traveler shrugs. "Ken threw everything else into the story. I figured, why break precedent?"

Asa guffaws. "Look who is playing fast and loose now! You dare speaketh our hallowed author's name?"

"Whatever, just wrap it up, Asa, they paid good money for this."

"Yeah, yeah," the Gardener says as he mixes himself a little something. "There's much more to come, don't worry. I know there was a lot going on here. Many worlds, beautiful women that liked to bite, witches and curses and giant bears, oh my... but there's a lot more where that came from. Ya see, Graf and his friends are about to pursue Glenna to another, even *more* terrifying world, where..."

"Hey!" Traveler shouts, drunkenness slurring his words a bit. "No spoilers!"

"Ah, quit frosting my cookies and zip it, will ya?" Asa shakes his head as Traveler's falls to the bar, passing out. *"Finally.* I made that last drink hit nice and hard. Anyway, as I was saying, the good Mr. Kenneth Kelly knew your head would be spinning at this point, so he thought a little *color commentary* might be necessary."

Imagine, dear reader, sitting at the bar yourself, as Traveler snores and Asa makes you something special. "Things will work out," speaks the Gardener. "For better or worse. But Ken, he's a nice guy, that one, he tells me there is one thing I can promise... this next one is going to be even more surprising than this journey was... Oh yes, friend. It's going to be a ball. See you soon..."

Just as your hand reaches out for the drink, you feel the pull, like magnetism. It draws you backward, away from the bar, away from the Gardener and the Traveler, and toward that blinding light beyond the front door. Asa raises his drink in your honor.

"Hope I didn't spoil too much, but know you can be sure of this – the fun's just beginning!" And there it goes, the tiki bar at the edge of the universe, going, going, gone... But it's all right, have no fear and hold no hard feelings. Next time, the drinks are on me.

Author Biography

Kenneth Kelly is a 32-year-old native of Plant City, FL. An avid reader of sci-fi/fantasy throughout his life, Kenneth draws much inspiration for his writing from his love for fantasy roleplaying games. Outside of writing, Kenneth is a 3rd grade ESE teacher and an avid martial artist, having a 3rd degree black belt in Taekwondo and recently discovered the art of Brazilian Jiu Jitsu. He still resides in Plant City, FL with his two dogs, Buffy and Kiki.

Previous Titles

Trespassing through Time
Virtue Inverted (Pakk book 1) – Co-written with Piers Anthony
Amazon Expedient (Pakk book 2) – Co-written with Piers Anthony
Magenta Salvation (Pakk book 3) – Co-written with Piers Anthony

Author's Note

Dear reader, thank you for taking the time to read this novel. It was a long way in coming and went through many changes before it became what it is now. The first idea for this novel began in 2018, while I was staring at the woods outside my classroom portable, waiting for my next class to arrive. I quickly jotted down my crude ideas into the journal I kept in my pocket, and nearly five years later, here we are! Writing this story helped me through some rough times in those years, and several times I nearly gave up. However, with the help of numerous friends and family, I saw this project through to the finish. If anyone would like to contact me with any questions regarding my writings, feel free to email me at trespassingthroughtime@gmail.com. I'd like to give a shout out to Jack Bentele, Josh Dibble, and Piers Anthony for helping me bounce ideas along the way and for proofreading at various stages.

Thank you,
Kenneth Kelly

FICTION

Put simply, we publish great stories. Whether it's literary or popular, a gentle tale or a pulsating thriller, the connecting theme in all Roundfire fiction titles is that once you pick them up you won't want to put them down.
If you have enjoyed this book, why not tell other readers by posting a review on your preferred book site.

Recent bestsellers from Roundfire are:

The Bookseller's Sonnets
Andi Rosenthal
The Bookseller's Sonnets intertwines three love stories
with a tale of religious identity and mystery spanning
five hundred years and three countries.
Paperback: 978-1-84694-342-3 ebook: 978-184694-626-4

Birds of the Nile
An Egyptian Adventure
N.E. David
Ex-diplomat Michael Blake wanted a quiet birding trip
up the Nile – he wasn't expecting a revolution.
Paperback: 978-1-78279-158-4 ebook: 978-1-78279-157-7

Blood Profit$
The Lithium Conspiracy
J. Victor Tomaszek, James N. Patrick, Sr.
The blood of the many for the profits of the few... *Blood Profit$*
will take you into the cigar-smoke-filled room where American
policy and laws are really made.
Paperback: 978-1-78279-483-7 ebook: 978-1-78279-277-2

The Burden
A Family Saga
N.E. David
Frank will do anything to keep his mother and father
apart. But he's carrying baggage – and it might
just weigh him down ...
Paperback: 978-1-78279-936-8 ebook: 978-1-78279-937-5

The Cause
Roderick Vincent
The second American Revolution will be a
fire lit from an internal spark.
Paperback: 978-1-78279-763-0 ebook: 978-1-78279-762-3

Don't Drink and Fly
The Story of Bernice O'Hanlon: Part One
Cathie Devitt
Bernice is a witch living in Glasgow. She loses her way
in her life and wanders off the beaten track looking for the
garden of enlightenment.
Paperback: 978-1-78279-016-7 ebook: 978-1-78279-015-0

Gag
Melissa Unger
One rainy afternoon in a Brooklyn diner, Peter Howland
punctures an egg with his fork. Repulsed, Peter pushes
the plate away and never eats again.
Paperback: 978-1-78279-564-3 ebook: 978-1-78279-563-6

The Master Yeshua
The Undiscovered Gospel of Joseph
Joyce Luck
Jesus is not who you think he is. The year is 75 CE. Joseph
ben Jude is frail and ailing, but he has a prophecy to fulfil ...
Paperback: 978-1-78279-974-0 ebook: 978-1-78279-975-7

On the Far Side, There's a Boy
Paula Coston

Martine Haslett, a thirty-something 1980s woman, plays hard on the fringes of the London drag club scene until one night which prompts her to sign up to a charity. She writes to a young Sri Lankan boy, with consequences far and long.
Paperback: 978-1-78279-574-2 ebook: 978-1-78279-573-5

Tuareg
Alberto Vazquez-Figueroa

With over 5 million copies sold worldwide, *Tuareg* is a classic adventure story from best-selling author Alberto Vazquez-Figueroa, about honour, revenge and a clash of cultures.
Paperback: 978-1-84694-192-4

Readers of ebooks can buy or view any of these bestsellers by clicking on the live link in the title. Most titles are published in paperback and as an ebook. Paperbacks are available in traditional bookshops. Both print and ebook formats are available online.

Find more titles and sign up to our readers' newsletter at
www.collectiveinkbooks.com/fiction